DOOMED
LEGACY

Also by Matt Coyle

Yesterday's Echo

Night Tremors

Dark Fissures

Blood Truth

Wrong Light

Lost Tomorrows

Blind Vigil

Last Redemption

DOOMED LEGACY

A RICK CAHILL NOVEL

MATT COYLE

OCEANVIEW (C) PUBLISHING
SARASOTA, FLORIDA

ISBN 978-1-60809-479-0

Published in the United States of America by Oceanview Publishing

Sarasota, Florida

www.oceanviewpub.com

10 9 8 7 6 5 4 3 2 1

PRINTED IN THE UNITED STATES OF AMERICA

For Juliet,

My beacon in the wilderness.

In Loving Memory of

Timothy Lane Coyle

and

Robert Eugene Wolfchief

ACKNOWLEDGMENTS

My sincerest thanks to the following people:

My agent, Kimberley Cameron, for her unrelenting advocacy and friendship.

Bob and Pat Gussin, Lisa Daily, Lee Randall, Kat Daue, and Faith Matson from Oceanview Publishing for all the hard work to get this book published and publicized.

Ken Wilson for continued marketing advice, Pam Stack for boots on the ground and digital marketing, and Jane Ubell-Meyer for off-the-page opportunities.

My family, Jan Wolfchief, Sue Coyle, Pam and Jorge Helmer, and Jennifer and Tom Cunningham, for their love and support and word-of-mouth marketing.

Nancy Denton for a vital copy edit and a lifetime supply of paper clips.

Kathy Krevat and Barrie Summy for the Thursday critiques.

Chuck Parme for information on defense contractors and an unnamed member of the Defense Counterintelligence and Security Agency for information on their background check procedures.

David Putnam for law enforcement information.

August Norman for information on fourteen-month-old babies.

Any errors regarding governmental background checks and law enforcement procedures are strictly the author's.

AUTHOR'S NOTE

Almost all of the events in my previous books took place around the time of each book's publication date. Because of events at the end of *Last Redemption*, the time frame for *Doomed Legacy* is set a few months in the future in May 2023.

DOOMED
LEGACY

CHAPTER ONE

THE NIGHTS WERE the hardest. I slipped quietly out of bed at 2:33 a.m. Leah stirred, but didn't wake. She almost never did when I made my nightly sojourn into our baby's nursery. I slept light and we had a baby monitor, but that was the last line of defense, not the first. At least, to me. Midnight, my black Lab, followed me from the foot of our bed across the hall into Krista's bedroom. He lay down next to her crib like he did every night I snuck into her room. I hovered above and watched Krista sleep. In the dark, I listened for her breaths and worried about her dreams with each shuddered movement.

I ran my private investigative business out of the upstairs office in my home. Leah watched Krista downstairs during the day. I knew she was safe then. Nights were different. I worried when she was alone in her crib. Intellectually, I knew she was safe, but my life experiences told me no one was ever completely safe.

Especially at night.

Fourteen months after Krista's birth, I still marveled that God graced me with a child. My heart ached with love for her. The deepest, freest love I'd ever felt. She was a little towheaded miracle who had her mother's blue eyes and too much of my stubborn disposition. I worried about that slice of me inside her. The trait that had driven me to discover buried truths, that had almost gotten me killed more than once and brought collateral damage to others.

Each of Krista's breaths brought me joy and relief. But I fretted about her future. Every night. And wondered how long I'd remain a part of it.

Chronic traumatic encephalopathy. CTE, the pro football disease. A definitive diagnosis could only be made during an autopsy, but my neurologist was pretty certain that my years of football, boxing, and violence had caught up to me in the form of CTE. And it was progressing. Slowly, but I felt it in ways that I hid from Leah. The headaches remained but hadn't increased in severity or frequency over the last year. The good news. The bad was more frightening than the headaches and the occasional search for once familiar words while speaking.

The last couple months a barely controllable, irrational rage infected my brain and sizzled along the nerve synapses throughout my body. Its trigger was often just the micro irritations of everyday life. A driver who cut me off in traffic. An argument with Leah over having to travel on a background check instead of performing it from behind my computer in my home office. Krista dumping her food onto the floor from her high chair. Things that settled spirits let go as quickly as they arose.

I did not have a settled spirit. Even years before the CTE diagnosis, my soul was scarred from the shrapnel my actions had wrought. But those actions, those decisions came after consideration. Thought. This was new. Unrecognizable and malevolent. A fury unconnected to thought. And its reins loosened from my grasp a little more with each smothered internal explosion.

Too often that rage was aimed at those I loved. So far, I'd been able to swallow the rage. Feel my skin burn hot and anger crackle inside me. When that happened, I'd pull over my car, or leave the room, or go into the gym in my garage and pound the heavy bag. Run from the trigger until the rage burned itself out. Sometimes it only took a minute, sometimes thirty.

And each new episode scared me more than the last.

I stood and watched Krista and worried about the evil in the world and how it might find her. The evil I'd fought, and sometimes become, for what I deemed the greater good. Living by my father's code. Crossing over the line into the darkness, then fighting my way back to the light.

I worried about the evil without. And the evil within me. A doomed legacy. Would there come a day when rage from the darkness consumed me after Krista tossed her food onto the floor one more time and I wouldn't be able to smother it?

I prayed that the God who gave me Krista would somehow intervene before that happened.

I watched Krista until my legs tired from standing stalk still for too long. I fought the urge to bend down and kiss her forehead. I'd done it a few times before and each time she woke up. Sometimes frightened. That drove a stake through my heart and shame down my spine.

Caution won out and I went back across the hall to Leah and our bed. But not before I split the curtains and scanned the street below Krista's second-story window. Clear.

Midnight stayed behind in Krista's bedroom, as he often did. He'd become Krista's protector the second we brought her home from the hospital and he sniffed in her scent for the first time. No jealousy from divided attention. The same bond that he'd shown me ever since I brought him home from Ramona as an eight-week-old pup twelve years ago. He followed Krista around the house and the backyard during her teetering jaunts. With each knock on the front door or unknown visitor to the house, Midnight angled himself in front of Krista, head pointed at the potential danger, hackles at full spike.

Tonight, he let go a contented sigh as I left the room.

The fuzzy red number on the clock next to my bed read 3:07 a.m. when I slipped back under the covers.

"Rick." Leah's soft voice floated over my shoulder. "You have to let her sleep through the night. She's fine."

"I didn't wake her." I kept my back to Leah, but I felt the rustle of sheets as she turned to look at me.

"But you have before." The whisp of a rebuke in her voice.

I wasn't the only one keeping secrets. Leah knew about my nights standing sentinel over Krista's crib. And she'd kept it to herself.

"Why didn't you tell me you knew I checked on her?"

"At first, I thought it was sweet. You being yourself. Protective." Space between each sentence, like she was choosing her words carefully.

"It's not sweet anymore?" I kept my back to her. A barrier from the true me.

Leah didn't say anything for at least ten seconds. Finally, "It's become an obsession. One night last week after you didn't come back to bed for an hour, I walked to Krista's door and watched you. Midnight wagged his tail when he saw me, but you didn't even notice. You were almost in a trance. I know that need to protect comes from your heart, but I think you need to give Krista some space when she's asleep. She probably senses your presence watching her as she sleeps. You need to let her wake up in the middle of the night and know she's okay being alone in the dark."

The dark is where evil hid.

"You think I'm stunting her growth?" An edge to my voice I hadn't expected. A smoldering ember tipped over inside me.

"Of course not." Her voice, blunt. Harder than the words. "Not on purpose."

My mind scuttled for a blanket, a water hose, a fire extinguisher. Anything to smother the flicker burning inside me. But it caught the edge of dangling resentment and whooshed a flame along my skin before I could tamp it down. Red. Rage. Violence.

I shot my arm to the nightstand next to me and grabbed my glasses. Instead of the lamp, which in my mind, I had already hurled across the room. If I stayed in the bedroom any longer, I feared that a broken lamp would only be the beginning of my fury. I snapped the sheets off myself and sprang out of bed, grabbed a pair of shorts off the back of an armchair against the wall and was out the door before Leah's voice caught up to me.

"Where are you going?" A hissed whisper.

I shuffled down the stairs without a word. The movement scrambled Midnight into protection mode and he bolted out of Krista's room and followed me downstairs.

A plaintive yowl from Krista. The commotion had awakened her. She was alone in the dark. Battling Leah's test of independence. My instinct was to go upstairs and comfort her. The rage boiling inside me overrode instinct. I yanked on my shorts and jammed my feet into the cross-training shoes next to my recliner in the living room and bolted for the front door. Midnight close to my side, his ears perked in alert.

"Rick!" Leah's voice over Krista's wails.

"Stay!" I snapped at Midnight, stopping him dead in the foyer.

I whipped open the door, went through it, and slammed it shut all in one movement. My car sat in the driveway, but I'd left my keys inside. My hands clenched into fists, my face on fire. I bolted into a sprint. Down the street to the intersection. Shorts and shoes and rage. I turned left up the hill on Moraga Avenue. Arms, legs, and lungs pumping, still in a full sprint a hundred yards away from my house.

My arthritic knee throbbed and my lungs burned, but I continued to climb. After another hundred yards, lactic acid and lung capacity did what my will could not. With each gasp of breath and faltering stride, the rage ebbed from my body. And my mind.

I continued the push up the hill, straining against my physical limits. And the limits of my mortality. The cool night chilled the sweat pouring off my body. An inhuman stink emanated from my sweat glands. Feral. Savage. I finally broke down into a lopsided jog, my left knee swelling with each step. Moraga plateaued and I kept going. I didn't stop until I hit Clairemont Town Square.

If I ran back home, it would take me about fifteen minutes and add an extra half hour of ice to my knee. And Leah would undoubtedly still be awake. A discussion I wasn't ready to have. I didn't have a good explanation for my actions. And I wasn't ready to tell her the bad one, yet. The real one.

Before Krista was born, I vowed to myself that I'd never lie to Leah again. I'd hidden the presumed CTE diagnosis from her back then until the day I got out of jail. I'd been truthful with her ever since. Until the last couple of months when the red rage surfaced from years of accumulated concussive head injuries. And from the depths of my soul.

I'd told only my neurologist, who prescribed antidepressants. Selective serotonin uptake inhibitors. SSRIs. But the side effects had been more dangerous than the rage. To me. Lethargy or the other end of the scale, severe anxiety and agitation interspersed with suicidal urges. No more red rage but intense mood swings that were damaging my marriage. I quit the drugs cold. No more suicidal thoughts. But the rage returned. More intense than before.

Not telling Leah about the new violent progression of my disease was a lie of omission. The CTE affected her, too. Especially if I wouldn't be around to help raise Krista into her teens. Or, if I *was* going to be around and be a burden due to my mental deterioration. Or, worst of all, if I was going to be a threat to Krista and her. A ticking time bomb of rage I couldn't tamp down or run away from that could go off with the slightest provocation.

CHAPTER TWO

THE LIGHTS TO the house were off when I returned home a little after 4:00 a.m. Hopefully, Leah went back to bed. Midnight was waiting for me in the foyer when I opened the door. Leah stood ten feet behind him in the living room. Arms folded across her chest. The silhouette of a bathrobe around her body. Too dark to see her facial expression, but the body language said enough.

"I'm sorry." I was.

"I'm taking Krista up to Santa Barbara this morning after breakfast." Leah, arms still folded.

She took Krista to Santa Barbara, her hometown, about every five or six weeks. Her family was there as well as her design business, for which she'd brought in a partner after Krista was born here in San Diego. She was planning to open an office in her new adopted hometown once Krista turned two and a half or three.

I went with her and Krista to visit her family when my private investigative business would allow. Even though they weren't my biggest fans. Or fans at all. The family and I had a truce in regard to Krista, the namesake of Leah's murdered sister and my onetime partner on the Santa Barbara Police Force.

We were planning on all going up as a family the next week. Although, per my usual, I'd only stay a couple days then take the train home to San Diego alone. An unwritten rule of the truce I had with Leah's family.

"I thought we weren't going until next week."

"No, Krista and I are driving up this morning." Cold. The truth that the words didn't spell out clearly. I wasn't invited.

Midnight nuzzled his head under my right hand. Twelve years together had attuned him to my moods. He felt the tension in the room.

"I can meet you there on Saturday." I heard the plea in my own voice.

"It's better that you don't come up this time." Leah walked toward the staircase. I met her at the landing. Midnight at my hip the whole way.

"I'm sorry I took off. That was wrong." I gently put my hand on her forearm. "You were right about me watching Krista when she sleeps. I have to scale that back."

"So now you want to talk about it?" She put her hands on her hips. "You've been disappearing in a huff any time I want to talk for weeks and now *you* want to talk about it? At four in the morning? Do you want to talk about this now, too?"

Leah walked over to the foyer and turned on the light. She opened the hall closet and raised her hand up to the top shelf. And pulled down a gun. My Colt Python.

I didn't say anything.

"You told me you weren't going to do this anymore." Leah held the gun to her side, her index finger flat against the frame. She knew how to handle guns. She came from a cop family. "I understand you wanting to protect your family. But you can't keep hiding loaded guns all over the house. You have a gun safe for that."

"None of them are anywhere where Krista can reach them." I kept my voice low. "And the safe is upstairs. I might not have time to get up there and unlock it if someone breaches the house when I'm downstairs."

"*Breaches the house?* Our home isn't a war zone. You have us living in an armed camp." Blond eyebrows squinting down above Leah's blue eyes. None of the warmth in them that used to caress my soul when she looked at me. "This is not healthy, Rick. We have an alarm on the house and Midnight to warn us if someone tries to break in. And keeping the guns out of Krista's reach is not the point. Guns hidden in every room is paranoid. It makes me wonder about the mental health of the man I sleep next to every night. The father of my child."

The remark wounded me viscerally. A cut that slashed closer to the bone than she could have realized.

She brushed by me still holding my Colt Python down to her side and went upstairs. I let her go, to sleep alone for the rest of the night. So she wouldn't have to worry about the mental health of the man lying next to her.

I already worried about that on my own twenty-four hours a day.

*   *   *

Leah put on a happy face for Krista as she carried her out to the car later that morning. I put their suitcases in the back of Leah's Ford Escape. The only conversation at breakfast had been directed at Krista by Leah and me. Separately.

"Daddy has a lot of work to do, but we'll see him soon," Leah sing-songed to Krista as she put her in her car seat in the back of the SUV. Krista didn't understand all the words or their meaning, but we'd done this routine enough for her to probably understand that Daddy usually came with her and Mommy when he put suitcases in the back of the car.

Leah left the back seat door open for me to say goodbye to Krista and then got into the driver's seat. I bent down and looked my daughter in the eyes. The same blue eyes of her mother. Her wispy blond hair freshly combed by Leah. She looked more like her mother every day.

"I love you, Krista Cahill." A smile I didn't have to fake broke across my face. Krista smiled back and pumped her pudgy little arms in front of her.

"Dada."

My chest filled up and warmth spread across my body. It happened every time Krista smiled at me or said my name. I kissed her on the forehead. "Be a good girl for Mommy."

I closed the door and stood next to the driver's window, which was rolled up. Leah started the car, rolled the window down, and looked at me. Cold, hollow eyes again.

"Give me a call when you get to your parents' house, okay?" Our usual procedure when one of us had to travel without the other.

"I'll text." She rolled the window back up. No opportunity for negotiation. I had a weak hand anyway.

Leah backed out of the driveway and drove off. Krista's little face disappearing as I walked down the sidewalk waving. Leah made the right-hand turn onto Moraga Avenue and they were gone.

Despair sucked all the hope out of my body so quickly that I could almost hear a whoosh. I always felt lonely when Leah and Krista left or when I went out of town on business. But Leah and I had never parted on such bad terms before. This felt different. Open-ended. Broken.

CHAPTER THREE

My PHONE RANG at 11:03 a.m. as I sat in front of my computer in my office. Too early for Leah. She'd left about 9:20 a.m. It would take her close to four hours to reach Santa Barbara. More if she had to make multiple stops for Krista. Besides, I was getting a text from her, not a phone call.

I checked my cell phone's screen and didn't recognize the number. It had an 858-area code, so it was local. I answered.

"Rick, it's Sara Bhandari." A hollow echo like she was calling from an employee bathroom.

"Hi. I didn't recognize the number. Are you in the office?"

Bhandari was my contact in the human resources department for Fulcrum Security, a defense contractor that built radar and sonar systems for the Navy as well as the cruise ship and luxury yacht industry. The civilian side gave me steady business running background checks on prospective employees and Fulcrum was my biggest recurring account.

"Yes, but I'm on my cell phone." She spoke quickly and didn't have the usual cheer I remembered. We did most of our communication via email, but talked on the phone at least a couple times a month. "Is there any way you could meet me for lunch today?"

"Is this about work?" Sara and I had never met in person during the two years that I'd done background checks for Fulcrum Security. We'd developed a work friendship, but nothing beyond that. And she knew I was married.

"Yes."

"Pick a spot in Escondido that you like and I can meet you up there at 12:30 p.m." Fulcrum Security's offices were in Escondido, an inland city in the northern sector of San Diego County. I had other background checks I needed to finish for other clients, but I couldn't say no to my biggest client.

"No, not up here." Rapid fire again. "Do you know the Hamburger Factory in Old Poway Park?"

"No, but I can find it." The city of Poway was about fifteen miles south of Escondido. I guess Sara wanted some distance from the office or maybe she only worked half a day and would be on her way home. Wherever that was.

"Okay, I'll see you there at twelve thirty. Thanks." The last word came out on a burst of air.

* * *

Poway is a wealthy enclave surrounded by steep, rocky rolling hills. The great Tony Gwynn, baseball Hall of Famer and Mr. Padre, raised his family there before he sadly died of cancer in 2014.

The Hamburger Factory was a bit off the beaten track in Old Poway Park. A surprising choice for Sara Bhandari if she had to get back up to Escondido for work after lunch. I would have chosen a restaurant closer to Interstate 15, the main north/south highway in inland San Diego County.

Old Poway Park looked to have been cut from the Old West, circa 1870. A scaled-down train complete with open-air wooden passenger cars ran through and around the property, which included a heritage museum, a historical house, and the Hamburger Factory.

The restaurant had wood beams and pillars and carried on the railroad and Old West motif with a barred window ticket booth, railroad crossing signs and pictures, paintings of trains, and a framed photo of John Wayne in a cowboy hat. A family-friendly, homey vibe that, now having seen it, I planned to take my tiny family to once Krista was old enough to chomp bits of a burger on her own. And once I could make my family whole again.

I told the bright-eyed hostess that I was meeting someone, and she led me over to a table where a thin woman in her mid to late thirties with perfect posture sat facing the entrance.

"Sara?"

"Rick, nice to finally meet you in person." She smiled and held out a hand, which I shook, then sat down.

She flipped her straight black hair over her shoulder. She was dark complected and looked to be of Indian heritage. Her eyes showed tension. On the phone, Sara usually had a dry, snarky sense of humor, which explained our friendship. I sensed none of that now.

"Business or food first?" I asked and eyed one of the two menus on the table.

"Let's order first. I have to go back to work."

That answered the question about whether she was done for the day.

A couple minutes later, a waitress took our orders. Sara ordered a chef's salad and I chose a Kobe beef burger. The waitress left us alone. And in silence. Sara wasn't ready to look me in the eyes, but I had work still to do at home.

"Long way to drive just to order a chef's salad," I said. "I wouldn't have minded meeting you in Escondido."

"I wanted to get away." She gave me the same nervous smile she had when I sat down.

"I'm glad we got to finally meet in person, but we could have done that anywhere." I smiled but my eyes searched hers. "You chose this place to be sure you wouldn't run into anyone from work, right?"

"Yes." A head nod, but nothing else.

"Why? Is someone giving you a hard time at Fulcrum?"

She was in HR. Harassment complaints at work were the kind of things she probably handled regularly. If the harassment was aimed at her, she must have had someone she could report it to in her own department.

"No, but something strange is going on at work." She spoke quietly and looked around the quarter-full restaurant, presumably scanning for familiar Fulcrum Security faces.

"Like what?"

"Upper management hired some people without getting proper background checks."

"Are you the only person who sends out for background reports?" She was the only person I'd ever been in contact with during the time I'd been running checks for them.

"No. They hired someone new in the department a few months ago and she has also been securing background information on potential employees."

"Then wouldn't it make sense that she got the background checks on the new employees? I'm sure I'm not the only private investigator Fulcrum Security uses." I tried to hide the exasperation growing inside me. My interaction with Leah this morning had already left me in a bad mood.

Sara unfolded her arms and leaned forward. "It would, but she didn't get any for three new hires a couple months ago."

"Are you sure they weren't hired for the defense contracting side and vetted by DCSA?" The Defense Counterintelligence and Security Agency was the arm of the U.S. government that was responsible for vetting and giving security clearances to all defense contractor employees who worked on any classified projects contracted by the Department of Defense. I handled the civilian side.

"I've worked for the company for seven years. I think I know who is hired for which division and what the process is." Sara's face clenched. "Dylan handles the paperwork on hires for the civilian division, just like I do. There's a whole other team in the department that handles hires for the defense contractor division."

The name Dylan sounded familiar. I'd done a background check on a Dylan Helmer for Fulcrum a few months ago. The reason I remembered the name was because Dylan Helmer was a woman and I always associated the name Dylan with men. I also remembered that her father had been a cop and been killed on the job. I was a cop who'd been kicked off the force, but always a brother in blue to those who gave their everything protecting the public.

"I didn't mean that as an insult. I'm just trying to get all the facts." Lunch with Sara Bhandari was a nice capper to the morning I had with Leah. "Is Dylan the Dylan Helmer who I ran a check on for you a few months ago?"

"Yes."

"Why did you check on her work?" My recollection was that Helmer had a stellar work and personal history. Nothing stuck out.

"She was out sick Monday and I took a call at her desk from a prospective employee who wanted to know the status of his potential employment. I got into Dylan's files and found his paperwork, which wasn't completed yet. I checked some other files and found the discrepancies."

Natural curiosity or a deep dive to get ammunition for office politics? I didn't know Sara Bhandari well enough to make that determination. I hardly knew her at all.

"Wouldn't whoever has the final say in the hiring notice there were no background checks?"

"Yes." Her eyebrows rose and she nodded her head. "The production manager for the civilian side. I asked him about it and he told me he was sure that he'd seen a background check report for all the new hires."

"Well, did you ask Dylan about it?" I was thinking up early exit excuses in my head. For some odd reason, Sara Bhandari thought I was the right person to reach out to regarding office incompetence or irregularities. I used to be the person you'd call when you wanted someone followed or disrupted.

"Yes. I asked her about it Tuesday when she came back to work, and she produced the background check paperwork for the three new hires." Sara's eyes were big again.

"Problem solved." I scooched back my chair and took out my wallet right as the waitress arrived with our lunches. "I really need to get some work completed for a new client by the end of the day. Let me pay for lunch. Sorry." I turned to the waitress and handed her a credit card. "Could you box that up for me and run this against the check? Thanks."

The waitress set Sara's salad down and went back into the kitchen with my burger. Sara squinted down one eye and glared at me.

"You could have just told me you had a lot on your plate when I called." She folded her arms and tilted her head to the left. "I would have waited until I got home from work and called you then."

"You're right, I should have mentioned it. I didn't realize the drive out here would take as long as it did." I gave her a sheepish grin. "But honestly, this sounds like something that you should talk to your boss about or some higher up in the company."

"You didn't let me finish." She unfolded her arms. "There was something I wanted to ask you about before I talked to the CEO of the company."

"What did you want to ask me?" Which she could have done on the phone an hour and a half and twenty miles ago.

"Are you familiar with a San Diego detective agency called Leveraged Investigations?"

"No." I knew most of the other investigative agencies in San Diego. I'd bumped up against a few in my years as a P. I. I competed with a couple of the big ones for background check work, but I'd never heard of Leveraged Investigations. "Why?"

The waitress returned with my boxed burger, the check, and my credit card. I signed my copy of the check, left a guilt-induced extra-large tip, and grunted a thanks.

"I want you to check them out. See what you can find out about them."

"Why?" An odd request.

"That's the agency who did the background checks on the three employees that magically appeared in Dylan's files the day she got back to work. We used to only have you and one other agency get us background information, Brady Investigations. We just started using Leveraged Investigations a couple months ago. I used them once and their work was inferior. Something is off about them. I can't put my finger on exactly what, but I got a bad feeling about them."

Brady was a large agency that had offices all over Southern California and my biggest competitor. Leveraged Investigations drew a blank.

"Why the change?"

"My boss said that Buddy recommended Leveraged Investigations."

"Who's Buddy?"

"Buddy Gatsen. He's the production manager."

"This really sounds like an internal work problem, but I'll look into Leveraged Investigations and follow up with you on what I find."

"Please send it to this address." She handed me a slip of paper with an email address on it. "That's my personal Gmail account."

More cloak and dagger for a sweater and butter knife problem.

"Will do." I grabbed the boxed burger and stood up. "Sorry about having to leave early."

Sara threw up a hand and looked down at the table. A sign of dismissal or exasperation. I took it as both and left.

CHAPTER FOUR

I WARMED THE burger in a fry pan and the bun and fries in the oven when I got home. Feeling guilty for leaving Sara Bhandari to eat alone at the Hamburger Factory, but most of my guilt was directed elsewhere. I checked the time on my phone. One thirty-five. Leah should have already gotten to her parents' house in Santa Barbara. No text yet.

I called her. Straight to voicemail. So, that's how it was going to be. I sent her a text asking if she'd made it up okay. A reply came thirty seconds later.

We're here. Everythings fine.

Nothing else. No *I'll call you tonight* or *Krista already misses you.* I was still doing time for my behavior before dawn this morning. I couldn't blame her, so I didn't. My behavior was my responsibility. The red rage was out of my control, but how I handled the afterwards wasn't.

Alone at home with the consequences of my inability to deal with my disease.

I thought of Krista's little face in the car window disappearing this morning as Leah drove off. My heart ached. Palpable pain in my chest. This little human who was a part of me. Who two years ago didn't exist, and who I had no conception could ever exist, had forever changed my life. I now had more of a reason to live than I'd ever had and less control of the ability to stay alive than ever before.

I'd been in many life and death situations over the years. Even when things were most dire, I always could take action to try to stay alive. Now I couldn't do anything. My enemy was as intractable as time.

I sat down with the burger at the butcher block island and stared at Krista's high chair next to the table in the dining area. Empty. No gurgles or giggles coming from it today. Or for at least the next week.

The burger and fries were sustenance, nothing more. I put them into my mouth through rote movement. Survival instincts, embedded in all living beings' DNA. If there was any flavor at all in the food, my brain wasn't in a position to register it. Midnight wagged his tail and looked up at me from his spot on the kitchen floor. Still a true believer. In me.

I went upstairs to my office with Midnight in tow. I sat at my desk and he lay down under it.

Sara Bhandari. Dylan Helmer. Leveraged Investigations.

Office politics.

Spending time checking up on Leveraged Investigations wouldn't make me any money. Straight pro bono. Which I did from time to time. Usually for a friend in need.

Today, I hadn't acted much like a friend.

There was still time to remedy that. I googled Leveraged Investigations on my computer. It was located in the First Allied Plaza building on West Broadway in downtown San Diego. The eighth largest city in America's version of a skyscraper. The high rent district for office space downtown. An odd place for ninety-nine point nine-nine percent of the private investigative agencies in San Diego to be located. Most P.I. agencies I knew chose cheaper strip mall locations or operated out of P.O. boxes and home offices like me. Hell, even Brady Investigations was in a single-story building next to a pizza joint in Pacific Beach.

I read the cascading services offered, which were boilerplate P.I. practices: background checks, business surveillance, missing persons, workers comp, and corporate, financial, infidelity, criminal, and child custody investigations. There was a link at the bottom of the services page titled: personal services. I clicked on it and a page came up that read: Details available upon request. I'd never seen that on any other P.I website, but I figured it was something meant to appeal to wealthy clientele. A clever hook that when spelled out probably just constituted common P.I. practices that were implicit when signing a contract. Or, they could be code for intimidation and harassment of those targeted in an investigation.

I'd harassed people on cases before, but never at the request of my clients. I'd instigated the harassment on my own when I'd gotten so deep into cases that finding the truth blinded me to everything else. A danger and an obsession that I no longer employed now that I was a family man.

Something else about Leveraged Investigations struck me as odd. The agency had been in business for five years, but didn't have a single Google review. No reviews listed at all. Why?

I'd been a P.I. ten years and had thirty-seven reviews on search engines when looking up Cahill Investigations. Brady Investigations had been around seventeen years and had over a hundred. Leveraged should have had at least nine or ten. Apparently, their customers weren't into writing reviews.

Maybe their clients didn't want to be publicly identified with a private investigative agency. When it came to investigations, private had more than one meaning.

There was no one mentioned as the founder of the agency or any names listed at all, which wasn't unusual. My last name on the agency was as personalized as I got on my website.

Commercial leases are not public records, and I had no luck online trying to find out who signed the lease on Leveraged Investigations' office space.

The agency was a private company so I had no way of checking up on their finances, either. Beyond Leveraged Investigations' address and years in business, I had a big goose egg on the company for Sara Bhandari.

Even with the little oddities I found, there didn't seem to be anything nefarious about the agency. I didn't think I needed to show up at their office and check them out in person. They were just another P.I. firm that apparently catered to the wealthy elite. My report to Sara would only be a couple paragraphs long. She was getting her pro bono money's worth.

There was one other avenue of potential information to tap, but I wasn't sure I wanted to. Moira MacFarlane. My best friend and occasional partner and someone who'd been a P.I. in San Diego for almost twenty years. She knew more about me than anyone alive. Things I'd never told Leah. Things that might change her opinion of me or solidify the opinion she had of late that culminated in her taking Krista to Santa Barbara this morning.

Moira was family before I met Leah, and family still. Part big sister, part judgmental father. Today, I was worried about the judgmental half. But I'd told Sara Bhandari that I'd see what I could find out about Leveraged Investigations, and part of finding out meant talking to Moira.

I pulled my phone out of my jeans pocket and tapped her number.

"How's my goddaughter?" Moira's greeting ever since Leah gave birth to Krista fourteen months ago. Her staccato voice ping-ponged around my office through my iPhone's speaker setting.

"She's fine." A guess since I couldn't see her and wasn't sure when I would again.

"Well, *you* don't sound fine. What did you do now?"

The judgmental side even before I gave her anything to judge me on.

"I didn't do anything." I cringed at the defensive tone in my own voice. "I called because I need your help."

"You make that sound like it's a rarity."

At least I'd moved her past the interrogation phase.

"Ever hear of a P.I. shop called Leveraged Investigations?"

"Yes. They're in the First Allied Building downtown. Why?"

"My contact at Fulcrum Security asked me to check up on them."

"Same question. Why?"

"I'll keep that between the client and me." My clients' business was just that, their business. No one else's. Even for something as vanilla and off the record as Sara Bhandari's request. Moira and any legitimate P.I. were the same way. "Pretty mundane reason. What do you know about them aside from where their office is?"

"Understood." Not offended. We'd been in the opposite position a few times over the years. "I've only come across them once on a case when I was working a domestic about a year ago. The usual. Wife of a wealthy couple thought her husband had a woman on the side. He did. Three of them. Anyway, one day while I was discreetly filming him on my phone in the lobby of the Manchester Grand Hyatt with girl on the side number three, a man stood in front of me to block my view. He called me by name and said that my client, using her name, no longer needed my services. Then he pulled out a phone, punched a number, and handed it to me. I recognized the phone number as my client's. She thanked me and said that she just sent me a check with an extra week's pay. I asked her if someone was pressuring her to fire me and she said no and hung up."

"How do you know the guy with the phone worked for Leveraged Investigations?"

"Because I followed him to the First Allied Building when he left the hotel."

"Why?" But I was pretty sure I already knew the answer. Because I knew Moira.

"I wasn't going to let somebody bigfoot me off a case and intimidate my client without finding out who he was."

Yep. That was the Moira I knew. And trusted with my life.

"Okay. You got him to the building. How can you be sure he worked for Leveraged Investigations?"

"I checked the businesses listed in the lobby and figured he had to work for the one investigative agency there. So, I changed into my backup surveillance outfit from the trunk of my car and put on my Padres hat with the blond wig in it and waited in the hallway outside their office pretending I was on the phone. It paid off because the guy came out of the Leveraged Investigations office at 5:30 p.m."

"Did you get his name?"

"No, but I did get a picture of him. I didn't dig any deeper after I called my client. I asked her what was going on and if she needed my help. She'd already paid me for the extra week and I didn't like the way everything had ended. She said everything was fine and played it off like she and her husband had come to an understanding, but I could tell she was rattled."

"Now I get the leveraged part about their name." Intimidation was definitely an option for the personal services they offered. "The husband must have gotten a whiff from his wife that she'd hired a P.I. or that someone was watching him and he hired his own to snoop around and intimidate her."

"Yeah, that's the way I saw it. But there were a couple things that kind of baffled me." Moira's normal machine gun voice slowed to normal human speed. "The wife was a tough, intelligent businesswoman who had run her own real estate office before she met the creep she married. She didn't seem like she'd be easily intimidated. In fact, her husband hiring someone to intimidate her would be a benefit in divorce proceedings. I told her that even though she was smart enough to know it herself. She said no one had threatened her and that I should mind my own business and hung up."

"Maybe it was true love and the husband came to his senses." I played devil's advocate even as I didn't believe my own words.

"Yeah, right."

"What was the other thing? You said a couple things baffled you."

"The other one is more about pride than anything else." As close to sheepish as she could sound. "You know I'm pretty good about being aware of my surroundings, right?"

"Yeah." She was. Almost had a cop's sixth sense to her. Like me.

"I don't know if the guy from Leveraged Investigations just got lucky that day in the lobby or had been following me for a while, but I had no sense that I was being watched."

"He knew where you were going to be all the time. Tailing the creep. That made it easier. He didn't have to follow you. He only had to know where the creep was going to be and when. He could set up early and wait for you to show following the husband. Or, like you say, he might have started that day at the Grand Hyatt and staked out the lobby and you stuck out just enough for him to spot you as a tail."

"Maybe. Still, it was a little unsettling. It was kind of a reality check. Made me realize that I'd gotten a little lax." She blew out a breath. "Anyway, do you want the picture of the guy? I'm pretty sure it's still in my phone."

"Sure." For due diligence's sake. Except for the part about Moira concerned about not knowing she'd been followed, the story wasn't too nefarious or that unusual. Powerful men, and women, had used unscrupulous private eyes to intimidate people, even spouses, since Edgar Allen Poe created Auguste Dupin. Still, it sounded like Leveraged Investigations wasn't as shiny clean as their address would imply.

I got off the phone with Moira and wrote up what little I knew about the agency, including a very brief summary of what Moira told me, and sent it to Sara Bhandari. A few minutes later my phone pinged with a text from Moira. The photo of the guy from Leveraged Investigations. He looked to be average height and weight. Dressed in khakis and a blazer. Short brown hair, matched by brown eyes. Nothing special. The kind of guy who could get lost in a crowd. A beneficial attribute for a P.I. on surveillance.

I closed the picture and closed my side work for Sara Bhandari.

CHAPTER FIVE

I WOKE UP from a fretful sleep at 2:25 a.m. My sheets sticky with sweat. Midnight's face emerged from the darkness next to me at the side of the bed. My dreams had been violent enough to wake Midnight up from his spot at the foot of the bed. But luckily, the dreams were unrecoverable.

I got out of bed by rote and walked across the hall to Krista's nursery. Midnight followed behind me. His routine, too. I knew Krista wasn't there but checked her crib anyway. I picked up her little pink blanket and held it against my face. Her baby smell clung to it and I breathed it in. First soothing, then upsetting. Her essence still here, tangible, but she was two hundred miles away.

I put the blanket back in the crib and returned to my bedroom. Tonight, Midnight followed me back inside.

* * *

I called Leah multiple times over the weekend and she responded with terse texts, only giving me updates on Krista but nothing else. I stopped apologizing on the voicemails I left her after the second day. Monday, she agreed to a Skype call. Between Krista and me. Leah held the phone in front of Krista's face. That and making the call was the extent of her participation.

Krista sat on the floor in a little cornflower blue onesie that matched her eyes. She bobbed up and down, pumping her chubby little arms. A wet smile showing half a dozen teeth.

"Dada!" Her chirpy voice filled my soul like no other sound ever had. Or ever would again.

"Hi, Krista Kumquat!" A lilt in my voice straight from my heart that I had no power to control. "I miss you, little girl, but I'll see you soon."

"Dada!" She tapped her tiny index finger against the screen of Leah's phone. I did the same to mine.

Leah's voice from off-screen. "Say goodbye to Daddy."

I swallowed the urge to ask for more time. Pride and not wanting to cause a furor in front of Krista kept me silent. I had no control over time in my life anymore.

"Ba, Dada!" She waved her little hand.

"I love you, Krista Kumquat." My voice caught in my throat. I waved and blinked away the tears collecting in my eyes. "Tell Mommy that Daddy loves her."

The call ended with a Skype metallic pop.

* * *

Later that afternoon I received a call from a former employer of one of the potential employees for Fulcrum Security that I'd run a background check on a couple weeks ago. A mom-and-pop sporting goods store owner that the candidate had worked for as a teen over fifteen years ago. The store had been out of business for six years. I'd gotten employer references from his last two jobs, as well as character references from friends and former roommates, which had all been positive. I'd sent the report in and noted that I hadn't been able to contact the sporting goods store owner at the time.

I hadn't found anything negative on the person and figured he'd either been hired or was at the top of the potential employee list by now. The information the former sporting goods store owner gave me might make Fulcrum rethink the candidate's position. The owner had caught the teenager stealing a baseball glove. The kid claimed he was only going to borrow it for a tryout for the high school baseball team. The owner accepted the apology and cut him some slack. Until the same style glove and a baseball bat disappeared after one of the kid's shifts a month later. The owner fired him after six months of employment, which the Fulcrum Security candidate stretched out to a year on his job application, the end of which coincided with his leaving for college.

I sent an email with the updated information to Sara at Fulcrum at three thirty that afternoon. She didn't reply that day or on Tuesday morning. I sent another email at 1:00 p.m. Nothing. It was unusual for her not to respond to an email from me. Particularly when I followed up. In fact, I don't think I'd ever had to follow up before.

I wondered if my lack of enthusiasm for Sara's office politics problem had ended my relationship with her and, thus, Fulcrum. A financial hit that would be hard to make up. I had a family to take care of and a mortgage to pay. Even if my family was having an extended stay in Santa Barbara. Leah didn't plan on working full-time again for at least another year. And she'd be searching out a new client base in San Diego when she did. It would take years for her to get near the income she made in Santa Barbara. If she ever could.

I grabbed my cell phone off my desk and called Sara's number at Fulcrum. Her voicemail was full. I'd never encountered that with her before. She'd always returned my calls promptly and seemed too efficient to let her voicemail fill up.

A faint ping echoed along my spine. The kind I used to get when I was a cop and sensed something was wrong. Danger. The sensation I got as a P.I. when I worked cases out in the world instead of behind a computer at my desk. A feeling I hadn't felt in a year and a half. The sensation was odd, yet familiar. And one I couldn't let lie.

I called Sara's personal phone number. The call went straight to voicemail. I left a message for her to call me right away. I said it was urgent. I didn't know if it was or not. Just that the ping along my spine vibrated louder and louder with each minute I didn't hear from her.

I waited an hour without a response then called Fulcrum Security's main number. A recording answered instead of a human being. I listened and punched in numbers corresponding to Dylan Helmer's extension. She was the one person that worked in Sara's department whose name I knew.

"Dylan Helmer, how can I help you?" Pleasant. Professional. Matched the information I'd turned up when I ran a background check on her a few months ago. I wouldn't have predicted the issues Sara had with her.

I'd never met or spoken with Dylan before. I very rarely interviewed the subject of a background check personally. Only if a client wanted me to. I interviewed almost everyone else in their life I could find, though.

"Dylan, this is Rick Cahill. I work with Sara Bhandari on background checks for Fulcrum." I gave her my business-friendly voice. Pleasant, but resolute. "Is she in today?"

"No, I'm sorry, she's not. Can I help you?" She sounded like she really wanted to.

"How long has she been out?"

"Is there something I can help you with?" Still polite.

"No, but thanks for asking." I stayed friendly, but still resolute. "Was she out of the office yesterday, too? I've left her a few messages and she hasn't responded."

"I'm sorry, sir, but I'm not allowed to give out employees' personal information."

A legitimate rule that I'd advise any business to adopt if I was offering security advice. But it might also be a tell.

"She's been out the last two days, hasn't she?" More a jab than a question. "Did she call in sick? Has anyone spoken to her?"

"As I explained, I can't discuss other employees."

"Just one last thing. Please have Sara contact me if she comes back to work this week."

"Very well." Dial tone.

The ping echoed louder.

CHAPTER SIX

AN HOUR LATER I pulled up in front of Sara Bhandari's house. She lived in the community of Sabre Springs, about fifteen miles south of Escondido and twenty miles north of downtown San Diego. I found her information on a pay website I used when searching the internet for clients. Something I did every day and got paid for. This was pro bono. For me.

Sabre Springs was best known for the tragic kidnaping and murder of seven-year-old Danielle van Dam by neighbor David Westerfield twenty years ago. I remembered watching bits and pieces of the trial between shifts during my first few months as a rookie cop on the Santa Barbara Police Department. I'd never heard or thought of Sabre Springs since. For me, it would always be connected to the evil and depravity in some men's souls and the destruction of innocence.

I sat in my black Honda Accord parked along the curb in front of Sara Bhandari's beige-colored stucco house. I bought the Accord back when surveilling targets was one of the most often used services of my P.I. work. Honda Accords were ubiquitous in Southern California and blended into the background. Once the most popular car in California, the Accord lost its ranking and was now hovering around the top five. The Tesla Model 3 was now the most popular car in the state, but the government wasn't giving rebates to people buying Accords.

I hadn't been on surveillance in almost two years. I even deleted it from my business website as one of the services I provided. At Leah's request. Surveillance, in itself, wasn't the danger that Leah worried about. What it could lead to was. It put me out in the world, in uncertainty. A place where I'd once thrived, but where I'd also been injured and almost died. More than once. Leah understood my compulsion and the damage it could do. So, she preferred me to be cocooned behind a keyboard in my office, upstairs in the home we shared while she took care of our child below.

A decision that becoming a husband and a father had compelled me to make. Now, with Krista and Leah in my life, the trade-off more than balanced out.

I pulled out my phone and called Sara Bhandari's personal cell phone number one more time. If she was home and answered, I didn't want her to know I'd tracked down where she lived. An intrusion that could be taken wrong and cost me Fulcrum Security's business. If I even still had it.

The call went directly to voicemail. Again. That ping along my spine vibrated deeper. All the way into my gut. Unwanted intrusion or not, I had to take action. Sara Bhandari had become my responsibility when I agreed to check up on Leveraged Investigations for her. Pro bono or not, she was a client. And she was no longer just a disembodied voice over the phone or a faceless emailing work contact. We'd met. She'd asked for my help. I gave it to her. But I could have handled it better. Been more understanding of her concerns.

And I could have stayed for lunch.

I got out of my car and knocked on the front door. A desperate yowling from inside the home startled me. A cat, seemingly in pain. Nothing else from inside. Just the cat's desperate cry for help.

I knocked again and the cries shrieked higher. More desperate. Heart wrenching. I called Sara's name and pounded harder on the door. Scratching on the other side now joined the yowls. Feverish. The cat was frantic to get out. And scared that I'd leave it inside.

Had Sara gone somewhere and forgotten about her cat? Either on her own volition or someone else's? This wasn't a vibe or a gut feeling anymore. Something was wrong. Sara Bhandari might be lying injured or worse inside her house.

I had to find out.

I tried the door handle. Locked. The cat continued to screech and claw at the door. I stepped off the porch and looked at the front of the house. The drapes were closed in the front window. I walked around to the east side where there was a wooden fence with a gate. I pulled the string on the latch and the gate opened.

Decision time. To trespass or not. A thought that wouldn't have entered my mind eighteen months ago. I would have gone into the backyard without a second thought. Or a first one. Moving forward. Always moving forward. Led by my sense of right and wrong. I broke the law often back then. In pursuit of the truth. My truth. Before I was married and had a child. Now such decisions had consequences for people beyond just me.

But Sara Bhandari was my responsibility.

I went through the gate.

I followed the concrete walkway in the narrow side yard up to a door to the garage. It had a window in its upper third. Enough daylight shone through the window to reveal a car parked inside.

Shit. If Sara Bhandari left her house, she didn't use her own car. But the car meant she was most likely home. Not answering her phone or knocks on the front door. A hole opened up inside my stomach.

Fifteen feet along the wall was another window. Curtains were drawn across it, but not all the way. I peeked through the opening. And saw it. A bare foot lying on the end of a bed and three or four inches of a bare ankle. Sole facing upward, like the person was lying on her stomach. Cylindrical indentations bit into the ankle, like it had been recently bound.

I tapped on the window. No movement. I tapped again.

"Sara! Sara!" Nothing.

I sped around to the back of the house. A sliding glass door led out to a patio. I grabbed the metal handle on the door and pulled. The door opened. A calico cat dashed out between my legs. Along with it came a breeze of chilled air. I dashed inside the house. A familiar smell hit me in the face. A rank, sickly sweet odor that clung to the icy air.

Death.

I went down a short hallway and turned left into the first bedroom. And found Sara Bhandari. Naked. Propped up on all fours by pillows and bedding. Death and gravity pulled her head low, her black hair covering her face, but I could see fabric sticking out of her mouth. Women's panties. Cylindrical gouges around her neck. Blood dried black stained the sheet against her chest. A metal dowel from a toilet paper holder protruded from her rectum. A postmortem insult. Taking her life wasn't enough. The killer had to take her dignity, too.

I gagged and hovered over the death bed. There was nothing I could do now. Too late by days.

I silently said a prayer for Sara Bhandari's soul.

I shoved my hands in my pockets to keep myself from removing the object violating her body. The final insult. But I understood the need to keep the crime scene as pristine as possible. If a scene of such vulgar violence could be considered pristine. There were clues hidden in the destruction of Sara that might help reveal her killer's identity to the police. Her despoiler.

I retreated from the death house the way I came in and closed the sliding glass door. The pinging echoing throughout my body stopped. The world stilled and went silent. Another person who'd entered my orbit was now dead. A friend? Business contact? Acquaintance? The only label I had now was deceased.

The world started up again. Birds chirped from a tree in a neighbor's yard. The mechanical hum from Sara Bhandari's air-conditioning unit. The buzz of a car driving down the street out front.

Life went on for the rest of the world.

But Sabre Springs was as I remembered it. A town shrouded in death.

CHAPTER SEVEN

I WAS HOLDING the calico cat on Sara Bhandari's front porch when a San Diego Police Department patrol car pulled up in front of her home ten minutes later. The cat was thin, bordering on emaciated. It had been skittish at first, but drank water from the hose that I cupped in the palm of my hand. The cat went through a dozen refills before it finally stopped. I wished I'd had a sandwich or some beef jerky in my car. But the cat let me hold it. Nestled into my arms, I could feel the rapid palpitations of its racing heart against my chest.

After probably days of being locked inside with the dead body of its owner, the cat's fur had the stench of death woven into it. I held it anyway. I might have to burn the shirt I was wearing, but the cat now had nowhere else to go.

The cop car was an L vehicle, a one-officer patrol unit. The officer's name tag read Mateo. Early thirties, warm copper complexion, close-cropped black hair, command presence present. I told him everything that had happened since I arrived at Sara Bhandari's house, right up to my phone call to 911. Exactly how I remembered it. The truth and nothing but the truth. Divergent from my pre-family practice when dealing with law enforcement. Back then I usually withheld just enough information to give my client or myself cover. But now my *client* was dead inside her home.

Officer Mateo sat me down on the curb in front of his patrol car and called for backup on the shoulder mic connected to the radio on his duty belt. I still held the cat. Mateo was being cautious. If he left me alone and went inside and found a dead body, I, a possible suspect, might flee. Even though I called the police to report the dead body, he'd wait until backup arrived before he went inside the house and found Sara Bhandari's desecrated body.

Five minutes later a patrol vehicle with two officers in it rolled up. The driver was female and had a sergeant's chevron on her sleeve. Forties, tall, dirty blond hair in a tight bun and aviator glasses. Name tag read Lentz. Her partner was a young female. Also white. Hair brown, up in a bun like the sergeant's. Her name tag said Davis. On the short side for a cop. By her age, twenty-two, twenty-three, I put her as a boot. A rookie.

Sergeant Lentz conferred with Officer Mateo, then told him to stay with me and commanded Officer Davis to go with her into the backyard.

Mateo didn't say anything. I stayed seated on the curb, still holding the calico cat.

"You got any food in the car, Officer Mateo?" I asked. "I'm guessing this cat hasn't eaten in a few days. It lapped up a bunch of water out of the hose when I corralled it after it ran out of the house."

Mateo looked at me, at the cat, then turned and opened the passenger door of his cruiser. He reached in and came out with a Jack in the Box paper bag.

He must have been in the middle of a code 7 when he got the call. Radio code for stopping for a meal.

Mateo pulled out a hamburger from the bag, ripped off a small portion of the meat, and set in on the grass next to me between the curb and the sidewalk. The cat leapt from my arms and pounced on the scrap of meat before I could even set it down.

It inhaled the food like a hungry Labrador Retriever. Without chewing it. Mateo ripped off another piece and dropped it onto the grass. The cat jumped on it as soon as it hit the ground. Mateo had gone through almost half of a patty by the time Sergeant Lentz and Officer Davis returned.

Davis's skin was gray-green. Her brown eyes lost in a zombie trance. My guess, her first dead body. She wasn't a rookie anymore. Her life had changed forever.

"Officer Davis, get the tape out of the trunk and secure the scene." Lentz, precision and certainty in her voice. "Officer Mateo, you keep the log. No one enters the scene without signing in."

"D.B., Sarge?" Mateo asked, using the police acronym for dead body. Guess he didn't take my word for it.

Sergeant Lentz nodded almost imperceptibly.

"Mr. Cahill, I'd like you to stick around and speak to a detective. Is that okay with you?" It didn't sound like a question, but I would have waited to talk to a homicide detective anyway.

"Sure." I stood up holding the calico cat again. It had retreated back into my arms after scarfing down the burger bits.

Sergeant Lentz walked back to her car. A smattering of neighbors had collected outside their homes to look at the police tape and squad cars outside of Sara Bhandari's house.

Officer Davis finished stringing the yellow *POLICE LINE DO NOT CROSS* tape around Sara Bhandari's house, using the backyard fence, hers and Officer Mateo's patrol cars, and the corner of the next-door neighbor's hedge as anchors. She stood outside the tape, ready to fend off any looky-loo who got too close.

Officer Mateo was inside the tape on the front lawn, black sign-in binder in hand. I stood just outside the tape on the curb next to Mateo's patrol car, still holding Sara Bhandari's cat. Sergeant Lentz returned from her vehicle, where she probably used the privacy of the car radio to call in a code 187. Homicide.

"Sergeant Lentz?" I called out to her before she went under the tape. "What about the cat?" I raised my arms, lightly holding the calico.

"Officer Davis." Lentz to the boot. "Call animal control and get them here to secure the animal."

The cat clung to my side, its newfound protector.

"Sergeant, can we ask one of the neighbors here if they'll look after it until we can find out if there's a next of kin who can take it?"

"That's what Animal Control is for, Mr. Cahill."

"I know, but the cat has been through a horrible experience and now you want it to be taken away by strangers to a cage in some unfamiliar building? Maybe someone here knows the cat and will look after it."

"What I want doesn't matter. We have procedures to follow. Animal Control will handle it."

I had my own wants and my own procedures.

I turned toward a young couple next door standing on the porch of a yellow house. The woman's arms were clamped against her chest. Round eyes full of worry. The man held her close with one arm around her shoulders.

"Can anyone here look after the cat for a few days?" I asked.

"Is Sara . . . is Sara dead?" the woman asked, her voice cracking.

I'd let Sergeant Lentz handle that one.

"I don't know." I started walking toward the couple. "But can you take care of her cat for a few—"

"This is a police investigation." Lentz, moving toward me. "The public will be informed about the specifics at the appropriate time. And the cat will be given good care by Animal Control."

"I'll take care of Trico." The woman on the porch broke from her husband's hold and hurried over to me.

I handed her the cat, with Lentz's footsteps close behind me. Tears broke free from the woman's eyes and ran down her cheeks. She cradled the cat and nuzzled it with her nose.

"Ma'am?" Lentz.

"I take care of Trico whenever Sara goes out of town. He'll be happier with me than Animal Control." The woman spun and hurried back to her husband who met her halfway between their house and me.

Lentz let the woman go and turned toward me. She was only a couple inches shorter than me and looked like she spent her free time competing in CrossFit events.

"Mr. Cahill?" Command control with her spine up. "Perhaps it would be better if you waited in the back of my patrol unit until the detectives arrived."

"Whatever you say, Sergeant." I followed her to her patrol car, where she opened the driver's-side passenger door. I got in and she left the door open, which I thought was a nice gesture considering I'd just defied her command. She could have closed the door and charged me with criminal trespass to punish me for my insolence. It most likely wouldn't stick, but would be a time-consuming hassle.

Sergeant Lentz followed the book instead of her emotions. My kind of cop. Most of the time.

CHAPTER EIGHT

TEN MINUTES LATER a dark blue slick-top Ford Taurus pulled up and parked in front of the squad car I sat in. A San Diego Police Department—SDPD—detective car. A man with a high forehead and short gray hair in tight curls stepped out of the car. Blue blazer, tan slacks. He looked to be in his early sixties, but I knew he was close to ten years younger. Life as a cop ages you. Even after you've made detective.

Homicide Detective Brian Skupin walked over to Sergeant Lentz in front of the squad car. I watched them through the windshield and the cage wire between me and the front seat. I heard the murmur of a conversation but couldn't make out the words from inside the car.

I got out and Detective Skupin walked over to me. Cop eyes and a head shake.

"Jesus, Cahill." He stopped in front of me and put his hands on his hips. "You turn up around more dead bodies than a vulture in the desert. And another chance to get your name in the paper."

We had a history. Skupin had always been fair to me, but was by no means a fan. Not that I had any of those in law enforcement.

I didn't have a witty rejoinder to his remark, and if I did, he wouldn't want to hear it.

"Detective."

Another slick top pulled up and a detective got out and walked toward Skupin. Male Latino, at least ten years Skupin's junior.

"Wait here, Cahill." Skupin met the man over by Sergeant Lentz just outside the police tape. More conversation I couldn't make out and a couple head nods in my direction.

The circle broke up and Skupin walked back toward me while Sergeant Lentz and the other detective went under the tape and walked over to sign in with Officer Mateo.

Unlike what you see on TV shows and in the movies, police don't allow a parade of people to trounce all over a murder crime scene. Reporting officers, coroner and assistants, crime scene investigators, homicide detectives. That's about it. No lieutenant, captain, or newspaper reporter smoking a cigarette staring at the body. And everyone has to sign the crime scene log when they enter and exit the scene.

Most homicide teams split up duties at a crime scene. One stays outside the tape to interview witnesses and the other examines the crime scene without touching anything and staying out of the crime scene investigators' way.

Skupin arrived back where I stood at the same time a white coroner's van pulled up. He frowned and surveyed the growing crowd of neighbors edging toward the crime scene tape. By this time, three more patrol cars had arrived and a total of six officers stood outside the tape directing people to stay twenty feet back.

"Let's talk in my car, Cahill." Skupin led me over to his Taurus and opened the back passenger-side door. I climbed in and he went around the front of the car and got into the driver's seat. The windows were rolled up and there was enough of a temperature in the air to make it uncomfortable inside. He turned on the ignition and the air-conditioning started up.

He looked at me through the rearview mirror.

"Some environmental activist in the crowd is probably going to call the department and complain that I'm needlessly polluting the air." Skupin turned and looked at me over the front seat. "So, what brought you to Sara Bhandari's house today?"

"I do background checks for her company, Fulcrum Security. They make radar and sonar equipment for the Department of Defense and the cruise ship industry. I do the checks for the cruise ship side. Sara is, or was, my contact person. The one who sent me the background check requests."

"You make a habit of going to business contacts' homes?"

"No." I told him about my meeting with Sara in Poway last Thursday and her concern about the missing, then found, background checks, my report to her about Leveraged Investigations, my subsequent unreturned emails and phone calls, and the conversation I had with Dylan Helmer that afternoon. He took notes on a little notepad throughout my summary.

"You have a thing for this woman, Cahill?" Skupin raised his eyebrows and his voice pitched higher. Like it was just between us.

"A few things have changed since we last talked, Detective." That last talk took place at San Diego Police Department headquarters in downtown San Diego and was about someone invading my home. And the violence that ensued. I raised my hand and tapped the silver band on my left-hand ring finger. "I'm married now. And I have a daughter."

"That doesn't exactly answer my question." More just between the two of us voice and a head tilt. "You seemed to have taken a deep interest in Miss Bhandari."

"You're right, I did take an interest in Sara." I folded my arms. Defensive body language, but it had been a reflexive action and if I unfolded them now, it would signal awareness of my physical response and possibly indicate deception. "All my clients are my responsibility. I was worried about her when I found out that she hadn't been to work this week and didn't call in sick."

"How many times have you been to Miss Bhandari's house?"

"Today was the first time."

"But you knew where she lived?" An accusation as much as a question.

"I found her address online. The kind of thing I do every day in my business."

"And what made you trespass and illegally enter her home?"

Trespass. That term again. Meant to unsettle me. Mildly effective.

"I was concerned about Sara." I unfolded my arms. Enough time had passed. "Her cat was yowling and frantically scratching at the front door from inside after I knocked. So, I looked for a way to call into the house for Sara and to let the cat out. I looked through her bedroom window and saw her foot and ankle. And furrows around her ankle like she'd been tied up."

"I guess you're used to peeping through people's windows with your job."

I absorbed the dig. Those kinds of barbs didn't even leave a mark anymore.

"How soon until you get off me and start looking for the real killer?"

"Your DNA is already in CODIS." The Combined DNA Index System. The FBI's DNA database used by law enforcement agencies all over the world. My DNA went into it when I was arrested for my wife's murder eighteen years ago. Way back when I was a cop in Santa Barbara. "I'll let you know if it shows up in places it shouldn't."

"I didn't do this, Skupin, you know that."

"How long have you known Miss Bhandari?"

"About two years, but we met in person for the first time last Thursday at that lunch in Poway."

"So, none of her neighbors will remember seeing you or your car around here until today." More fishing. Another empty hook. The police hadn't even canvassed the neighborhood by the time he arrived and talked to Sergeant Lentz.

"Nope."

"Thanks for your cooperation, Rick." He finally called me by my first name. We were buddies now. "I have your contact information on file if we need to talk again. You can head on home."

"I'll help any way I can, Detective." I put my hand on the door handle but didn't open it yet. "I can send you what I found out about Leveraged Investigations, if you like."

"Who?"

"The private investigative agency I told you about that Sara had me look into." I fought back the frustration again. "The one that supposedly ran the background checks on the three hires that Sara couldn't find the files for then suddenly turned up the next day."

"Sure. Send it." His tone told me what I sent would get a perfunctory look from an underling, at best. He opened his door and started to get out of the car.

"Are you going to check them out?" I stayed seated. "They take the leveraged part of their name seriously."

Skupin resettled into the front seat and turned his head toward me. "If we need any further help looking into some P.I. agency, you'll be the first person we contact. Time to go, Rick."

"Dig deep, Skupin. Something here doesn't fit."

Skupin scowled at me and let go an angry breath. "Go home, Cahill."

CHAPTER NINE

My phone rang at 7:55 the next morning. I was sitting on the deck in the backyard eating a couple of one-eyed sandwiches that I'd cooked for breakfast. Usually my favorite time of the day. On most mornings, I'd have Krista sitting on my lap nibbling at the bits of egg yolk I fed her with her Munchkin teething spoon. She liked the baby blue koala spoon the best.

Today the food was sustenance, nothing else. Midnight lay on my bare feet under the picnic table. He'd spent each day since the morning Leah left with Krista following me around the house, tail low, even on the rare wag when I cooed to him. He missed Krista, too.

I stabbed at the phone on the first ring, hoping Leah had finally forgiven me enough to settle back into our old routine of early morning phone calls when we were apart. I checked the screen. Moira. Shit.

"Did you read today's paper yet?" Her greeting when I answered the phone.

"Not yet." I typically only read the sports page and ignored the rest of the news. My usual practice ever since my wife was murdered and I became Santa Barbara Police Department's number one suspect. I got tired of seeing my name on the front page of the *Santa Barbara Free Press*, week after week.

My name turned up in the *San Diego Union-Tribune* a few times over the years since I moved back to my hometown, but never on the front page. I read a few of the articles. I'd gone from ex-cop who might have gotten away with murdering his wife to local P.I. who helped solve a couple murders, including his wife's cold case. The publicity had been good for business at the time, but I never sought it out. Despite what Detective Skupin thought.

Today, I ignored the entire paper for another reason. I didn't want to be reminded of what I saw in Sara Bhandari's bedroom yesterday. Even if it was already stuck in my mind on a replay loop. A horrific scene played over and over.

"A woman who worked for your big account, Fulcrum Security, was raped and murdered." Moira wasn't a gossip. There was no excitement in her voice. But she was curious, like any good private investigator, and we looked out for each other. "Her name was Sara Bhandari. Did you know her?"

"Yeah. I did." Not very well, but I still carried the weight of what happened to her. Even knowing there was probably nothing I could have done to change the outcome. The way I handled her request for help still gnawed at me. Downplaying her concern and leaving her to eat lunch alone. But it was too late to do anything about it now. "She was my contact at FS."

"Oh, wow. I'm sorry." Genuine care in Moira's voice. Care. Something we didn't show to each other very often, but knew was there. Buried under a prickly friendship, but born from moments of extreme stress and danger. There was no one I trusted more to have my back when it mattered most than Moira. I knew she felt the same way. "Did you know her very well?"

"Not really. We worked together for a couple years, mostly through emails and occasional phone calls. We met in person for the first time last Thursday." I could have left it there. Or left it well before I even got there, but I hadn't talked to anyone but the police about Sara Bhandari's death. Leah was still replying to me with cool, terse texts. Discussing my feelings, my guilt, wasn't the kind of thing I wanted to volunteer tapping out impersonally on a phone screen. "I was the one who discovered her body at her house yesterday."

"What?"

"She was the client I was checking out Leverage Investigations for." No need to keep that confidential now. My client was dead. I told Moira about the missing, then found, background check files and that they'd been done by Leveraged Investigations. And about sending Sara the information Moira'd given me about the agency and not receiving a response and her not showing up for work this week. "Did the paper give a TOD?"

Time of death. Something that isn't nearly as precise as most TV cop shows and movies make it out to be. There were a lot of variables that could affect an accurate determination. Exposure to the elements, animal predation, temperature and environment inside a building. There was a blast of chilled air that came out of Sara Bhandari's house when I opened the sliding glass door. The air conditioner was on and seemed to be running at full bore.

Unlike most people's perceptions of the weather in San Diego, it can get hot. And it can get very hot in May. But it hadn't gotten hot yet this May. Running the air conditioner at max output didn't correlate to the weather we'd been having. But it did correlate to someone who was trying to slow a dead body's decomposition and hinder the ability of the coroner to determine the time of death.

Sara's killer wasn't a beginner. She probably wasn't his first. Something that hadn't struck me until now. I was rusty at being out in the field and investigating anything other than prospective employees lying on their resumes and what their former employers thought of them.

"No. They just said the body had been discovered yesterday and that the police believed it had been there for over twenty-four hours."

The paper didn't say that the body had been discovered by me. Good. I knew the police would never give the media that kind of information, but a cop beat reporter with a police scanner could have heard the call and gotten to Sara's house in time to see me talking to the police. If the reporter had been around for a while, they might recognize me from my multiple fifteen minutes of fame. And occasional infamy.

"I'm sure the coroner has the TOD nailed down better than that," I said. "They want to leave it vague so that when they get a suspect in the box, they can force him to spread out his alibi over a number of days. Plus, make it easier to eliminate fake confessors if they get any."

"Does the timing of the murder being so close to your meeting with Sara Bhandari bother you?" I could almost hear the synapses firing in her brain.

"It bothers the crap out of me." I decided I needed to read the article in the paper to get a better feel for where the police were on the case and what they might be holding back. I owed Sara that much. "But her death seems unconnected. Random evil. Or, maybe not random. The killer may have been stalking her, and turning up the air-conditioning makes me think he's killed before or is a very fast learner. But regarding Sara's murder, I think the timing is coincidental."

"You're probably right." She tried to sound convinced.

But her question and the tone of her voice brought back that ping along my spine. Moira wasn't a conspiracy theorist. Far from it. When we worked together, she spent much of the time trying to reel me back in from whatever ledge my gut had taken me. I was right a lot of the time, but not always. She was the reasoned one. I was the reactionary.

"What's on your mind?" I asked.

"Nothing that I can validate."

"How about unvalidated?"

Silence. I waited. There was something she wanted to get off her chest. I just had to wait and let the building pressure of silence do its job.

"When you asked me about Leveraged Investigations the other day, it brought back the feeling I had when I encountered their P.I. on that case I told you about." She left it there.

"And?"

"The guy who told me that my client didn't need my services anymore gave me the creeps." Slightly hesitant, like she didn't want to admit someone had the power to make her feel uneasy.

"Anything in particular?" I pulled up the photo of the P.I. from Leveraged Investigations on my phone that Moira sent me a few days ago. My take on him hadn't changed since my first look. Average everything, innocuous, easy to blend in. Creepy didn't come to mind.

"It was his eyes. Dead. And they looked right through me like I was inanimate." I could almost feel a shiver in Moira's voice over the phone. She didn't spook easily, but the Leveraged Investigations guy had gotten to her.

I looked at the picture again. Specifically, his eyes. They did look lifeless in the two-dimensional photo, but not menacing. Just dull. But I trusted Moira's instincts. And I trusted that sixth sense for danger that our ancestors handed down to us, but modern human beings too often ignored. It had saved my life more than once. And it had spooked Moira, one of the toughest people I knew.

"I sent Detective Skupin the same report about Leveraged Investigations I sent Sara based on what you told me. He didn't seem interested, which makes me think that he's zeroed in on a theory already and it doesn't involve Sara's job." I closed the picture of Leveraged Investigations P.I. Dead Eyes. "I'm not as tuned into the local news as you. Have you seen anything about a recent series of rape/murders?"

"Nothing too recent, but I think there have been two or three rapes over the past few months. However, none of the victims were killed. Maybe the police think this is the same guy and that he's graduated to murder."

"Murder and worse." I told her about the toilet paper dowel. Maybe I should have kept it to myself. For Sara Bhandari's benefit. And Moira's, too. A visual best left unexposed. But Moira had cop friends. The vicious detail could prove important in finding the evil that perpetrated it.

"What a sick son of a bitch. Sorry about all of this, Rick." The care poked through again. "Hey, when are you and Leah going to invite me for dinner again or ask me to babysit? I miss that little nugget that was somehow coproduced by your loins."

I didn't have an answer to her question. I didn't have an answer to my own.

"Soon." I hoped.

CHAPTER TEN

I GRABBED MY plate and went inside the house to the kitchen with Midnight at my hip. I rinsed the plate and utensils and put them in the dishwasher, then sat down on one of the wooden stools at the butcher block island. Midnight rested his head on my leg. I scratched him then shuffled through the morning newspaper I'd left on the island and found the local section.

The whole section was only six pages. I was old enough to remember newspapers before people got their news on the internet where it's neatly curated to fit one's particular worldview. Newspapers were inches thick before Breitbart, the *Huffington Post*, and Twitter. Now a morning paper had barely enough pulp to set kindling on fire on a weekend camping trip.

Nothing about Sara Bhandari's murder on the front page of the local section. I found the article on the second page in the Local Reports under Crime & Public Safety. It was short and to the point and contained little more than what Moira had already given me. Only two new pieces of information. The first, that Sara had been strangled to death. The ligature marks around her neck. And she had an unnamed sister who lived in San Diego.

I wondered if the sister wanted Sara's cat. By thinking about the cat's psyche and handing it over to the neighbor, I may have made it difficult for the sister to get custody, if she wanted it. Animal Control would have probably worked with the police to track down Sara's next of kin. Now the sister would have to be contacted by the neighbor and they might not even know each other. Maybe Sergeant Lentz had been right. I should have let Animal Control take care of the cat.

I now felt responsible for connecting Sara's sister to the next-door neighbor. Or maybe I was trying to assuage my guilt for how I handled Sara's request. It didn't matter how I wanted to position it; I had a task to perform. I went upstairs to my office, pulled up a pay people search website on my computer, and looked up Sara Bhandari for the second time in two days. There were four women's names listed as relatives, but not their actual relationship to Sara. I didn't want to disturb all of them needlessly in what had to be a horrible time of grief.

I needed help.

I looked up the article on Sign On San Diego, the *Union-Tribune's* website. As a subscriber, I also had access to the digital edition of the paper.

I checked the byline at the bottom of the article to see who wrote it. Max Andrus. The name sounded familiar. He might have been the reporter who wrote an article about what happened in Santa Barbara when I solved my wife's cold case murder a couple years ago. And what happened to me there. He'd been fair in the article. Maybe even a bit too fair, considering I didn't return his phone calls. Leah prodded me to call him, but I wouldn't budge.

Although bits and pieces of my life had been spread throughout newspapers over the years, I wanted to keep my private life just that, private. Leah thought it would be cathartic for me to talk to the reporter. Probably because I didn't talk to her about it, even though we'd gone through most of it together and she'd been a big part of what happened in Santa Barbara. Her story was more heroic than mine, but

I was a known entity, had been severely injured, and was a redemption story. In the public's mind, at least. A redemption story. The only thing Americans loved as much as a hero's fall was his Phoenix rise.

I'd been in newspapers enough over the past two decades to be considered a hero. Mostly in the tragic sense.

Max Andrus's email address at the paper was listed below his byline. I sent him an email requesting that he call me, but didn't say why. Hopefully, my name was enough for him to return the call. I listed my business number, not my personal one. Even though they connected to the same cell phone, I kept the numbers separated with different ring tones. Chimes for personal calls. A bong for work. I liked to be able to know whether each name that popped up on the screen on an incoming call was business or personal and which to let go to voicemail. Ninety-five percent of the calls were for my private investigations business, not my private life. That was fine by me.

I spent most of the afternoon on office paperwork, including sending out second expense invoice notices to a couple of delinquent clients. With the possible loss of Fulcrum Security as a client, I had to really stay on top of cash flow.

My phone bonged at 2:15 p.m. Blocked number.

"Cahill Investigations."

"Rick, this is Max Andrus with the *San Diego Union-Tribune*." Young-sounding soprano voice. "You sent me an email asking me to call you."

"Yeah, thanks for calling." My business voice. "I read your article about the murder of Sara Bhandari—"

"Did you know her?" He jumped in at the slightest pause between my words. He was smart and looking for information on follow-up articles he probably planned to write. That might benefit me.

"You willing to go off the record for the next few minutes, Max?"

"Yes." No hesitation. Eager, but could I trust him? He'd been fair when he'd written the article about me a couple years ago. Hopefully, he still was.

"I didn't know her on a social level, but her company hired me to run background checks on potential employees and she was my contact."

"Isn't Fulcrum Security a defense contractor?" Andrus had done his homework.

"Yes, it is." I knew where he was going. "But they also have clients in the cruise ship and luxury yacht industry. That's the side that hired me. The Defense Counter Intelligence and Security Agency with the federal government does background checks for the employees doing defense contractor work."

"Ah, I see. Thanks." He sounded happy to get a bit of information that might help him somewhere down the road. "So, why exactly did you want me to call you?"

"I need a favor. You mentioned in the article that Sara is survived by a sister who lives in San Diego. Can you get me in touch with her?"

"Why?" I could almost hear his antenna spring up.

I didn't think I could get around telling him that I found Sara's body without him helping me contact her sister about the cat.

"Sara had a cat that, right now, is being taken care of by her next-door neighbor. I want her sister to know where the cat is in case she wants it for herself."

"I thought you didn't know Sara Bhandari socially."

"I didn't. We only met once."

"Then how do you know that the neighbor has the cat?"

"You're just going to have to trust me on that."

"You found the body, didn't you?" Electricity in his voice. A reporter on the chase. Max Andrus was smart and eager. That used to get you far. I wasn't sure it still did. I hoped so.

"I might be able to help you with background on your next article about the murder, Max, but you have to swear to me on your mother's soul that I'm off the record and you won't report what I tell you until you get everything confirmed by a second source."

I chose his mother because he sounded young enough that he might not yet be married or have children. The odds of him loving his mother were better. And I wanted him to know how serious I was about staying anonymous.

If Andrus identified me in the paper, or gave enough information for Detective Skupin to figure out that I was his source, Skupin would be up my ass about interfering with a police investigation. He could make my life difficult when it was already difficult enough. Although we'd developed a decent relationship after our first contentious encounter four years ago, he still thought I was a publicity-seeking show-off. He was wrong, but I couldn't deny that some of the pub I got in the news helped my business over the years. But some of it had hurt, too.

"Deal!"

"On your mother's soul."

"I swear on my mother's soul."

I now felt creepy about making him say it. It sounded worse coming out of his mouth than mine. Still, creepy shame or not, I didn't feel comfortable telling Andrus about my involvement over the phone. He could be taping the call. And he might hate his mother.

"Meet me at Muldoon's Steak House in La Jolla at five thirty tonight. Tell the hostess you're there to see me. She'll show you the way."

CHAPTER ELEVEN

No HOSTESS AT Muldoon's tonight. Turk Muldoon greeted me at the hostess station at the end of the hallway of his family's namesake restaurant at 5:15 p.m. Greeted may have been too generous.

"Look what the cat dragged in. And gnawed on." Barrel-chested voice. He flashed a freckle-faced grin below pale blue eyes that hadn't changed in the almost thirty-years I'd known him. "You here for business or pleasure? Haven't seen you for either in quite a while."

Turk had, at various times, been my mentor, best friend, boss, and business partner. Now we were friends again after a rough patch that stretched over five or six years. He let me use a booth in his restaurant to meet clients when it wasn't busy. Saved me a bundle on office rent. I never met clients at home. Or let them know where I lived. Especially now with my daughter living there.

"Business." Sort of. "Is booth four open?"

"Of course. Your office awaits you." He lifted the wooden cane he needed to walk because of the bullet he took the night he saved my life and pointed it into the dining room.

"Thanks, Turk." I'd never be able to repay him for the physically independent life he sacrificed for me and he wouldn't want me to. Although, I did my best to help him out of a jam during the worst time of his life a couple years ago. We regained some of the closeness we'd lost at that point. I was thankful for that.

"Limp you up a beer while you wait for your client?" Forgiving as he was, he never tired of sticking the needle in by joking about his diminished physical status.

"Sure. Watch your step," I needled back and walked through the carpeted dining room with mosaic wooden tables and captain's chairs and went up the two-step platform to booth number four. There were a handful of customers seated at tables. The restaurant had only been open for a couple minutes and the dinner rush didn't hit until around 7:00 p.m. At least it hadn't when I managed it ten years ago.

Turk was right about me not coming into Muldoon's for a while. I rarely met new clients face-to-face anymore. Ninety percent of my business was with existing customers or word-of-mouth referrals to new clients from those same customers.

I was nursing a Ballast Point IPA ten minutes later when Turk's six-foot-three, two-hundred-fifty-pound presence loomed over the booth. Next to him stood a short, roundish man with brown hair in a modern pompadour, a close-trimmed beard, and black horn-rimmed glasses.

"I give you Rick Cahill," Turk bellowed then left.

"Have a seat, Max." I raised an open hand toward the Naugahyde-covered bench on the other side of the booth.

"Thanks." The soprano voice I'd heard over the phone. He wore blue jeans and an untucked gray shirt under a blue polyester windbreaker. He pulled out a small notepad and pen from the windbreaker pocket after he sat down.

"You want something to drink?" I asked.

"No thanks. Mr. Muldoon already asked me." There was a lilt to his voice that made me wonder if he sang choir at a church or lead for a garage pop band. It matched his youthful appearance. He looked to be in his early thirties. "I'll buy yours, though."

"You remember our deal, right?" I pushed my beer aside and leaned onto the table, stone-faced.

He quickly nodded, eyes round behind his glasses.

"I see you brought a notepad to take notes." My voice matched my expression. Hard and immovable. "You don't have anything else on you like a tape recorder or the recording function running on your phone in your pocket, do you?"

"No. A deal's a deal." His voice spined up a bit. "I gave you my word."

The "word" of most the media I'd encountered was as solid as room-temperature mercury, but there was an earnestness to Andrus that made me believe him. Or at least want to.

"I discovered Sara Bhandari's body."

"How?" No change of expression. He wasn't surprised.

I told him about going over to Sara's house and finding her body. I left out the horrific details of what I found in her bedroom. If he wanted those, he'd have to get them from the police.

"What are you going to do with the information I gave you?" I asked.

"I'm going to try to corroborate it and then, possibly, use it in a follow-up story. Nothing you told me is significant enough to write a new piece about. Except maybe the bit about the cat as a human-interest story after the fact."

"Have you talked to Sara's family yet?"

"Just her father and her sister," he said, his eyes still trying to figure me out.

"Which sister?"

"Shreya Gargano. She's Sara's older sister. She was pretty shaken up."

"Does she live in San Diego?" If not, I wondered how interested she'd be about picking up Sara's cat.

"Yes."

"Do you think it would be okay for me to contact her about the cat?" I didn't want to intrude on Shreya Gargano's grief. I knew what that was like firsthand. From the police and the press. I'd be a third intrusion. But, unlike *my* situation with my late wife, none of the intruders would be accusing her of murder.

"That's your call."

The circumstances surrounding Sara Bhandari's death and Detective Skupin's disinterest in the information I had about the last few days of her life still bothered me. The chance to test the theory Moira and I attributed to Skupin that she may have been murdered by a serial rapist sat right across from me.

"Do you know of a serial rapist currently preying on women in San Diego?" I asked.

"Why do you ask that?" His gaze held steady on me.

This was my chance to follow my gut on Sara's murder or set it aside for good.

"I have information about some things happening at Fulcrum Security that Sara thought were peculiar, but the police don't seem interested. I think they're connecting her death to a series of rapes that were committed over the past few months."

"Three rapes in six months, plus Sara Bhandari's," Andrus said.

Turk suddenly walked past our booth and sat an older couple in the one behind us, then glanced in as he passed on his way back to the hostess station. I peeked my head up over the top of the booth and looked down at the dining room. Tables were starting to fill up with customers.

My deal with him was I could use the booth until he needed it for paying customers, unless I was eating dinner with a client. I wasn't hungry and didn't want to pay for Andrus' meal if I couldn't expense it. Which, I couldn't. I was my own client. I'd either have to move our discussion into the bar or end it soon.

"Do you know that the police have linked all of them, including Sara's, firsthand or are you speculating? Is there DNA?"

Andrus studied me. Finally, "What can you tell me about the irregularities Sara Bhandari found at her work?"

"Quid pro quo?" I asked.

"Call it what you like." Andrus folded his arms and leaned back in the booth. His first feeling of advantage.

"Sara thought someone in Human Resources hadn't run background checks on three recent hires. She searched for the files when the person responsible was out sick but couldn't find the background reports. She checked with the production manager who was responsible for the hires and he assured her that the background checks had been done. The next day, the person who had been out sick returned and produced the reports."

Andrus started taking notes again.

"Couldn't you have corroborated that you'd done the background checks through your own records?" he asked. Smart.

"I didn't do those checks. They used a new agency for them. Leveraged Investigations."

"Why did she tell you about this? I thought you two weren't very close." He angled his head to the left, side-glancing me. A show of suspicion.

"Because she trusted me." I looked Andrus dead in the eyes. "I take trust very seriously. Sara asked me to investigate Leveraged Investigations after the other employee produced the background checks for the new hires."

"When was this?" More earnest.

"Last Thursday. She called me that morning and asked to meet for lunch. I said I could meet her up in Escondido, where Fulcrum Security is located, but she wanted to meet in Poway instead."

Andrus rubbed his chin hair. "Do you think she wanted to meet in Poway so there was no chance that someone from work could see her talking to you?"

"Yup." My cadence picked up. Andrus was on the same page. "I asked her why she didn't tell someone higher up in HR about the situation instead of the cloak and dagger with me. She told me she didn't want to get this other person in trouble if there was nothing to it."

"Did you investigate"—he looked down at his notepad—"Leveraged Investigations?"

"Yes."

"What did you find out?"

"Not a whole lot. They've been in business for five years and have an office in the First Allied Plaza building on West Broadway." I told him what Moira told me about Leverage forcing her off a case.

"Is that unusual in your line of work?" He did a good job of not making my line of work sound like peeping through people's bedroom windows.

"If you mean hiring a P.I. to intimidate a wife to stop having her husband followed, it's not unheard of, but it is rare."

"I've been inside First Allied Plaza. The lease for office space is probably as high as any in downtown. Is that normal for a private investigative agency to have an office in a building like that, too?"

I looked at Andrus, then from side to side to side around the booth. "This is my office. Even Brady Investigations' office, which is the biggest outfit in San Diego, isn't in a downtown skyscraper. They're next to a pizza joint in Pacific Beach. So yeah, having an office in First Allied Plaza is unusual."

"Did you give all of the information about Leveraged Investigations to Ms. Bhandari?"

"Yes. I emailed it to her, but she never got back to me. A few days later she was raped and murdered."

Andrus looked up from the notes he'd been scribbling. "Do you think this office intrigue stuff could have something to do with her murder?"

"You tell me. Do the police think all these rapes have been committed by the same suspect, including Sara Bhandari's?"

"Yes, but there's no DNA. The rapist uses a condom."

"But no one else was murdered, right?"

"Right. They think the rapist has now escalated to serial killer."

"Have any of these details been reported in the newspaper?" Maybe I should start reading the front and local pages before I flip to the sports page.

"A few." Andrus chose then to look down at his notes again. He must have had a source inside SDPD who would shut off the spigot if Andrus went public with everything he knew.

"What's the suspect's MO?"

"We agreed that I'd give you her sister's name. I'll even give you her phone number." Andrus wrote something on his notepad, ripped off the page, and handed it to me. "Here it is."

The piece of paper had the name Shreya Gargano on it and a phone number.

He scooted to the edge of the booth.

"Hold on." I stopped him before he got out. "I told you everything I know about the last few days of Sara Bhandari's life and that I found her body. I need to know more about the person who supposedly killed her."

"Why is this so important to you? You told me you hardly knew Sara Bhandari."

I looked at him, surprised by his words. Surprised that my need was so obvious. I thought of the people I'd tried, but failed, to help over the years. I thought of Krista and Leah in Santa Barbara and the empty house waiting for me at home. I thought of Colleen, my dead first wife.

"Because she was my responsibility." My voice cracked and liquid filled around the edges of my eyes. The emotion snuck up on me, much like the rage that came from out of the dark. The flip side of the anger. I steadied my composure. "And I have to make sure she gets justice. If that's the police arresting the serial rapist who graduated to murderer, so be it. But if it turns out that the police have tunneled in on one theory and Sara's death is just a box to check in that column and her real murderer remains unknown, then I have to expose him and bring him to justice. Or help the police do it. Or help you do it."

Andrus now looked perplexed.

"What you've told me so far seems coincidental. The rapist is a stalker. He plots the crimes out. He could have been stalking Ms. Bhandari for weeks and last weekend happened to be the time he decided to attack her?"

"I'm not saying it's someone else. I just want to know all I can about the serial rapist and Sara's murder." I leaned forward and pressed against the table. "So, part of his MO is to stalk. How do the police know that?"

"They don't know for sure, but two of the women who were raped said they had the feeling they were being followed. Each within a week of being attacked."

"What else? What were the living arrangements of the women? Were they raped at home? How did the rapist subdue them?"

"They were all raped in their homes. All lived alone in freestanding houses and each had sliding glass doors that opened into their backyards. The police think the suspect entered through the sliding glass doors before each victim arrived home from a night on the town.

Either by jiggling a locked door open or getting in through one that was already unlocked."

Locked sliding glass doors were notoriously easy to breach. I'd done it myself more than once.

"So, the suspect, seemingly knowing that the women were out on the town, also led the police to conclude that he must have stalked them." The disease hadn't yet robbed me of the ability to put clues together and run scenarios. "He knew they were out, so he went to each woman's house under the cover of the night and snuck inside and waited."

"Right."

"How did he subdue the women?"

"He came up behind them and got them in a headlock, then showed them a big knife and told them to do as he said and he'd let them live."

"So what is the signature?"

"They were all gagged with their own underwear and tied facedown on their beds and anally penetrated with the dowel that held the toilet paper in their bathrooms." Andrus swallowed air. "Is that how you found Sara Bhandari."

"Yes." My voice a croak. The memory flashed across my mind. Again. I fought back the anger and sadness. "But now he's escalated to murder."

"That must have been horrible to see." Andrus looked at me, his complexion paler than when he first sat down in the booth.

I didn't say anything and Andrus went on.

"The rapist cut the third victim's breast. So the police think that's when he started to escalate more violently. Was Ms. Bhandari's breast slit?"

The blood on Sara's bedsheets. "Yeah."

"Geeze." Andrus slowly shook his head. "The only thing different about her rape, aside from the rapist murdering her, is that her cellphone geo-tracked home all night so she probably was, too."

"So they've nailed down the TOD? When was it?"

"Saturday night between nine and eleven."

"What time were the other women raped?"

"Hmm." Andrus rolled his eyes up to the left, searching for the information in his memory. "I think they were all raped between two and four a.m."

I sat silent for a minute and thought about everything Max Andrus just told me. According to him, the police hadn't released any information about the rapist's MO and his depraved signature. Tying women to their beds and using a knife wasn't unusual for a serial rapist, but I'd never heard of a sick SOB using a toilet paper dowel the way he did to the women. There was no way a copycat rapist could come up with that on his own. If Sara wasn't raped and murdered by the serial offender, the person who committed the crime must have had inside information.

But everything Andrus told me made me think that Sara had been the rapist's latest victim and his first murder. And that there was nothing I could have done to save her. Sadness for Sara's life cut short sank in as the shadow of guilt disappeared.

The police were on the right track. Now I just had to stay out of their way.

And I had to make sure that Sara's cat ended up in a happy home.

CHAPTER TWELVE

I sat in my car at the dead end of Marine Street in La Jolla, about a mile from Muldoon's, and looked out over the beach that carried its name. The sun was a minute or two from setting and I waited for a chance to see the elusive green flash as the sun disappeared below the water. The phenomenon occurs when the sun slowly slips below the horizon and water vapor in the atmosphere absorbs the sun's orange and yellow colors leaving the green light's steeper wavelength as the last visible color.

I'd only taken the time to try to see the natural wonder a dozen or so times in my life. And been disappointed all but once. But that once had been worth the misses. Tonight, I could use a little of God's and natures's beauty when I contacted the grieving. An infinitely more common occurrence on earth.

Shreya Gargano answered her phone on the fifth ring. Her voice was much lower than Sara's had been. It had a trained quality to it and sounded older than I expected. But maybe that was just the grief.

"Shreya, my name is Rick Cahill. I ran background checks for Fulcrum Security over the past year and Sara was my contact with the company."

"Background checks?"

"Yes. I'm a private investigator and Fulcrum contracts me to run background checks on prospective employees for their cruise line and luxury yacht business."

"Okay." Weary. Probably tired of calls of condolence or wondering why some P.I. who worked with her murdered sister would choose now to invade her grief.

The last edge of the sun slipped below the horizon and a flash of green sparked, then disappeared with it. The green flash. An unnatural natural collision of science and nature that produced a brief moment of unearthly beauty. I wanted Krista to see it when she was old enough to marvel at it.

"The reason I'm calling is that I wanted you to know that Sara's next-door neighbor in the yellow house is taking care of her cat right now."

Silence.

"In case you want to pick the cat up." I stumbled down the dead end my call had created. Maybe I should have just forgotten about the cat and let everyone fend for themselves. If they even wanted to.

"Were you and Sara dating?" A little life in her voice.

"No. We only knew each other through work. We met for the first time for lunch last week."

"Then why do you know where her cat is?" Back to wary.

I should have let Animal Control take the cat. The dead end had turned into a sinkhole that I probably should have considered might occur before I made the call. Too late now.

"I . . . I was the person who called the police. I was worried about Sara because I'd left her some messages that she didn't return and she missed a couple days of work without calling in sick. So I went to her house to see if she was okay."

"I thought you only knew my sister through work." The word sister came out protective. And angry. "Why were you so worried about her and how did you know where she lived?"

"She was concerned about some things at work and asked me to check on something for her. I didn't find anything too out of the ordinary and sent her a report the next day. But when she didn't return my messages, I got a little worried. And I didn't know where she lived, but I'm a private investigator so I know how to find out where people live. Hell, anybody can do it now on the internet."

"What was she worried about at work?" The anger shifted to concern.

I told her about the missing, then found, background check files for the new employees and Leveraged Investigations. There was no client/P.I. privilege now and the issues at Sara's work didn't seem to have anything to do with her death. Still, agitation that Shreya Gargano didn't need as she mourned her sister.

"Do you think any of these discrepancies at the office could have something to do with Sara's murder?"

"No." Not after what I learned from Max Andrus about the serial rapist and the way Sara died. "What have the police told you about . . . about Sara's murder?"

"Not very much." The anger resurfaced. "Just that they think whoever killed Sara probably raped three other women in San Diego."

At least SDPD gave Sara's family something. And it matched the theory they were running with. Hopefully that was enough for the family for now without having to explain how they got there.

"That's my understanding, too." Time to close the call down without further damage. "I know Detective Skupin to be a dogged professional. He'll do all he can to find Sara's killer. She was a wonderful person and a pleasure to work with."

I meant it, but bordered on cliché. The best I could do for someone I communicated with almost every week, but barely knew.

"You never explained how you know where Trico is."

"Trico?"

"Sara's cat."

Shit. Time to rip the Band-Aid off.

"When I knocked on Sara's door, the cat started desperately yowling and scratching on the door. I went around the back and found that the sliding glass door was unlocked. When I opened it, the cat came running out."

"Did you go inside the house?" Her voice pitched high with anxiety. Asking questions because she needed to know what happened to her sister, but afraid to hear the answers.

"Yes."

"So, you found Sar . . . you found her body?" The words heavy with emotion.

Sara Bhandari's body, grotesquely posed in death, flashed through my brain. I'd opened this Pandora's box when I made the phone call. Now I had to empty its contents.

"Yes."

"Oh." Hoarse. She went silent

"I'm really sorry for your loss. And for intruding on your grief." The shock and pain of losing a loved one to violence was hard enough to deal with without having to talk about it with strangers.

"You're not intruding, but thank you." Her voice quivered and she took another deep breath. "I'm sorry I was little rough on you when you first called. You made sure Trico was safe when most people wouldn't even have thought about that and then you even called to let me know where he was. I'm so glad you did. My daughters love Trico and they'll want to take care of him. We'll give him a loving home and he'll be a sweet reminder of Sara. She loved that cat. Thanks again, Rick."

"Well, I'm glad he'll have a good home." I didn't know what else to say. "If you ever need my help in dealing with the police or anything else, give me a call. You have my number on your phone now. Call anytime."

We hung up and I looked out at the ocean. The horizon kept pulling the night down over it. Darker and darker.

*   *   *

Midnight greeted me at the front door when I got home. He wagged his tail, but I could see the longing in those expressive Labrador eyes. We'd spent twelve years together. I felt sure I could read him almost as well as he read me. He felt the same hole in his belly that I did in mine.

It used to just be the two of us. Midnight and me. I was his pack and he was mine. But I had a family now and his pack had grown. He missed them like I did. Especially the newest member. The little one who was close to the ground, on his level, and who hugged him around the neck and sometimes slept with her tiny head resting on his chest.

We both needed to make our pack whole again. Soon.

CHAPTER THIRTEEN

SHREYA GARGANO CALLED me on my way to a biotech company in Mira Mesa at 1:40 p.m. the next day. With Fulcrum Security possibly out of the rotation for background check work, I needed new clients. San Diego was a hotbed for biotech and many of the companies were located in Mira Mesa. The community was about twenty miles north of downtown San Diego and seven or eight miles from the coast. Most companies looking to hire independent contractors doing the work I did handled interviews over the phone or via email. However, the head of HR at Restorigen, a company that focused on restorative therapeutics, wanted to meet me in person. I was fine with that. Gave me a chance to get out of my house. And maybe, for an hour or two, get away from my thoughts.

I answered Shreya Gargano's call via my Honda Accord's Bluetooth.

"I picked up Trico from Sara's next-door neighbor this morning." Weariness in her voice. "Thanks again for making sure he was taken care of. The family is very nice and were happy that we're giving Trico a good home. My girls are giving him lots of love."

"That's good to hear." I exited Highway 52 onto 805 North and wondered if the cat's new residence was the real reason for the call.

"I went into Sara's house while I was over there . . ."

The police must have released the scene, but there would still be the residue of Sara's death there. Blood on the mattress from the monster mutilating her breast. Death is messy and acrid. The police don't clean up crime scenes after they investigate them. That's left to the survivors. Hiring crime scene cleaners to scour and disinfect and rid a living space of the leftover particulates of death, if not the memory.

I hoped Shreya didn't go into her sister's bedroom.

I didn't say anything. I didn't have an out for her. There was no out. She finally continued, "Her phone and laptop computer are missing."

"The police may have taken them as evidence. I'm afraid you may not get them back until after a trial." Which, even if they already had the suspect in custody, would probably be over a year away. Maybe even two, three, or four years away, depending upon how long the defendant was able to delay hearings and the trial. But again, I kept the realities of the justice system to myself. Shreya had already had an awful morning.

"But they don't have them. I called Detective Skupin from Sara's house and asked him about them. He checked to see if they'd been collected for evidence like you said. They weren't. The murderer must have taken them."

"Did Skupin say anything else? Was he surprised that they weren't there?"

"I don't think so. He sounded the same way he sounded when I talked to him yesterday."

Max Andrus didn't mention if the suspect who raped the other women had stolen anything from their homes. Maybe he did and the police had kept it under wraps. There was a possibility that Sara had left her phone and laptop at work, but I doubted it. It could also be an example of Skupin's shifting MO theory: the suspect was now killing *and* robbing the victims. Whatever the case, I felt an obligation to look into it.

"Was there anything else missing that you know of?" I asked.

"I don't think so." Shreya went quiet for a second. "That's the exact question that Detective Skupin should have asked me when I told him about the missing phone and computer."

I couldn't argue with her on that, but I didn't want her to lose confidence that her sister's killer would be caught.

"The police will be thorough and work through all the angles and find the son of a bitch who killed Sara. Detective Skupin knows a lot more about the crime than we do."

"I'm sure he does, but I think he's happy with what he knows and doesn't care about what he doesn't know. But you have questions about what you don't know. That's why I want to hire you."

"Hire me to do what?" I hadn't expected that response. I exited the highway onto Mira Mesa Boulevard. My search for a new client was here, in Mira Mesa, not with a grieving family looking for answers to questions that might never be answered or might be best left unanswered.

"Investigate Sara's murder." It sounded like a command. "Look into the things the police are ignoring. I did some investigating on my own after we talked yesterday. I know you've solved some big cases before. And I know you solved your own wife's murder after the Santa Barbara Police Department couldn't do it for fifteen years. You're not just some fly-by-night private eye. You've got a good reputation."

My reputation varied drastically depending upon who you asked about it. Shreya must have found the article Max Andrus wrote about what happened in Santa Barbara four years ago. The article went into the good reputation file.

"Whatever reputation I may have, an investigation of your sister's murder will be best handled by the police. I've already looked into it a little bit on my own and I think the police are on the right track."

I could use the money with suddenly uncertain times in front of me, but if I took the case, I'd have to tell Shreya everything I knew.

That was only professional and fair, but it would be extremely unfair, too. Everything I knew meant I'd have to tell her what was done to Sara. Horrific images of her sister that would be forever etched into Shreya's mind. That was my job, to find the truth and tell it to her, but would the extra money for work that might have nothing to do with finding Sara's killer be worth it?

"They may or may not be on the right track, but I don't think they're ever going to look at other tracks." A slow burn was building in her voice. Someone had coldly and viciously killed Shreya Gargano's sister and she was battling the dark pit of grief while being shut out from what was being done to find Sara's killer. "You told me yesterday to call you if I needed help dealing with the police or anything else. Well, I need help with both. Are you a man of your word, Mr. Cahill?"

"Yes." I was, for better or worse, a man of my word. And a man of my convictions. And all that that entailed. "I'll find out what I can. If anything I find can help the police, I'll make sure they get a look at it. And you don't have to pay me. This is for Sara."

"No. I'm going to pay you and sign a contract. That way I'll have a document to hold you to your word."

Shreya may have read some news stories and done her homework on me, but she didn't know me at all.

CHAPTER FOURTEEN

RESTORIGEN WAS A modern two-story building located in a small business park off Mira Mesa Boulevard. The business park consisted of three identical buildings with a vertical span of dark windows that made them look like the face plate of a Cylon from *Battlestar Galactica*. The head of HR for Restorigen didn't look a thing like Tricia Helfer, the actress who played Six, the Cylon in human form.

Linda Claireborn had dark brown hair with frosted tips and was somewhere in her fifties. She wore a smart business suit and was very much all about business sitting across from me in a small unadorned conference room.

I was pretty sure Linda Claireborn didn't like me from the start. Or before the start. I'd spent most of my adult life with the majority of the people I met not liking me from the start. Or before the start. It came with being portrayed by the press and a network true crime show as the guy who got away with murdering his wife. That had mostly changed over the past few years. It had even swung back in the opposite direction after Max Andrus's article about me in the *Union-Tribune* four years ago and some other favorable press.

But Linda Claireborn wasn't having any of it. Made me wonder why she even gave me the face-to-face interview. Her jaw was clenched as tightly as her arms across her chest. I couldn't see her legs under the oak table, but I guessed they were pretzeled tightly together, too. She opened a leather portfolio in front of her that contained the resume I'd emailed her after we spoke on the phone yesterday afternoon. She'd been quite pleasant on the phone. Something had changed.

"Well, Mr. Cahill." Subzero icy. She closed the portfolio. "I've looked at your resume and checked some of your references and we're going to pass on contracting you for background checks."

Short and to the point. I liked that in a prospective client. Less so in a no longer prospective client.

"What changed?" My voice was even, no rancor. I was simply collecting the facts.

"I don't understand what you mean." Her voice deliberately patronizing. Her demeanor now short and avoiding the point.

"We had a pleasant conversation on the phone yesterday afternoon and you invited me to come here for a face-to-face interview." I eased my chair back from the table and folded my right leg over my left at the ankle. "I sent you my resume, which is fairly impressive, and recommendations from happy clients. I'm here less than twenty-four hours later and you've already changed your mind and made a decision without interviewing me. I repeat, what changed?"

"Not all your clients are as happy as you think they are." A crooked "aha" smile.

I'd had a few unhappy clients over my ten years as a private investigator. But the vast majority of the people who were unhappy were the ones who were the targets of my investigations, not the ones who paid me to investigate them. And the few unhappy ones that I knew of had problems with paying me what they agreed to on the contract they signed.

"Maybe you could enlighten me." I knew she desperately wanted to. Why else keep the appointment after she learned something that, in her mind, disqualified me for the job?

"Madolyn Cummings is a friend of mine." Smug.

"I don't know who that is." The name was vaguely familiar, but I couldn't place it.

"She's the Vice President of Human Resources at Fulcrum Security."

Now I remembered. We'd exchanged emails when I solicited Fulcrum for the background check gig two years ago. Before she turned me over to Sara Bhandari.

"I never spoke directly with her. All of my communication was with Sara Bhandari who found my work to be excellent and more comprehensive than was even asked." I kept my voice calm. A reasonable person who you could depend on. "And I turned every report in early. Every single one. What is Ms. Cummings' complaint?"

"That's a lie. Your work was unsatisfactory and you had an inappropriate relationship with Ms. Bhandari and now she's dead."

"What?" My head jerked like I'd been slapped in the face and I bolted upright in my chair. "That's bullshit. What did Cummings say that I did?"

"You know what you did." Arms folded. Morally superior

"Pretend I don't." I managed to tamp down my anger. For the moment.

"You sent highly inappropriate emails to Ms. Bhandari. And don't try to deny it, because I have a copy of a disgusting one." She turned and walked to the door.

"Show me." My face, a blast furnace. I sped to the door and put my hand against it before Claireborn could open it.

"Let go of the door, Mr. Cahill." Her voice pitched high and fear flashed in her eyes.

I could feel my own eyes plastered wide open.

"Show me the fucking emails." The conference room turned red. My lips receded, exposing snarled teeth. Rage.

Claireborn fumbled through her portfolio, hands shaking. She pulled out a sealed manilla envelope and the binder dropped to the carpeted floor.

"Here." Her voice fluttered as she held out the envelope.

I snatched it from her hand, whipped open the door, and bolted down the hallway toward the foyer and the front door. I couldn't risk staying in the building in case my rage erupted out of control.

"Whoa." A twentysomething dude with a long squared-off black beard in khaki shorts, Hawaiian shirt, and Birkenstocks pressed himself against the wall as I strode by. A second later, "Linda, are you all right?"

"Yes." Anger in her voice behind me. "Just make sure he exits the building."

"Wha?" Square Beard. Then footsteps behind me.

Claireborn didn't have to worry. I banged open the glass door and was into the parking lot before Square Beard could catch up to me.

I jumped into my car, skin still burning, and opened the manilla envelope. My breath hyperventilated out of my mouth. There were nine or ten letter-size sheets of paper in the envelope. I pulled them out and looked at the top sheet of paper. It was a printed email. I tried to focus my eyes to be able to read the page. I fought to control my breathing and zeroed in on the email. It was dated last Tuesday and appeared to be the last background check report I sent to Sara about a couple of potential employees. The email was much as I remembered it. I gave a brief summary of what Sara would find in the report, like I did every time I sent in completed background checks. Sometimes I'd directed her to pay specific attention to a particular section of the accompanying report. That wasn't the case this time, as I recollected both applicants had spotless employment and personal histories.

There was nothing remotely inappropriate about the email. The boil along my skin reduced down to a simmer and my breathing normalized.

The next few pages were the body of the background check report of the first applicant. Then, the report on the next applicant filled out five out of the last six pages. I flipped over the last report page to the final piece of paper that had been in the manilla envelope that I'd snatched from Linda Claireborn's hand.

A color-printed image of an erect penis stared up at me. It didn't look familiar.

I blinked a couple times. Stunned. A dick pic. Something I'd never taken in my life, much less emailed to someone. I was content with what I had down there, but not proud enough to show anyone but my wife. And certainly not in a photograph. Much less to a woman who directed enough work my way so I could feed my family.

But someone had tried to make it look like I sent a pornographic selfie to Sara Bhandari. A few days before she was murdered.

CHAPTER FIFTEEN

MIDNIGHT GREETED ME at the door, but I brushed past him and ran upstairs to my office. He lumbered after me. I pulled up my work emails to Sara Bhandari and checked the attachments on that last background check email I sent to her. Two attachments. I opened them both, even though I knew exactly what was in them. The two background check reports were there. Nothing else.

I was relieved. Not because I thought I might have taken a picture of my penis, sent it to Sara Bhandari, and then completely forgotten about it. My disease was progressing and accentuating the worst part of my personality, my temper, but it hadn't changed who I was at the core. I knew I'd never take or send that type of picture. I was relieved because whoever had somehow attached the dick pic to the email I sent after the fact hadn't been able to do it through my computer. But it had gotten there somehow, and the head of HR at Fulcrum Security, or someone else, must have found it when they went through Sara's company emails, presumably to check for pending work that needed to be completed.

Whoever attached the picture to the email must have done it after Sara was dead. If she'd seen it, she would have confronted me about it. And she certainly wouldn't ask me to lunch two days after she supposedly received it. Why had someone gone to the trouble to try to discredit me after Sara was murdered? Was it related to her murder? The murder the police were seemingly convinced was committed by a serial rapist who'd assaulted three other women? Their evidence, or what I knew about it, was hard to refute. The MO and, more importantly, the signature of the rapist was the same at Sara Bhandari's murder scene.

But there were a couple differences that I needed to investigate. For Shreya Gargano. And for myself.

I had to talk to Max Andrus again. Detective Skupin would be better, but there was no way he'd tell me what I needed to know. Andrus, who seemed to have an inside source close to the Sara Bhandari murder investigation, might know enough and might even tell me.

I checked my emails before I called Andrus. Two of the three queries I sent to companies about background check work replied while I was away from my house. Both were negative replies, but said they'd keep me in consideration in the future. Those were the kind of letters I usually received when a company replied to a job query. Either those or ones with personal notes.

The other rejection I received was terse and personal in its blunt impersonal tone. There was no thanks for contacting us. Just, we don't need your help. The message between the brief lines was—we don't want your help now and never will so don't contact us again.

They'd checked my references on my resume, Fulcrum Security being at the top of the list. Calls or emails for references to Fulcrum must have been routed up the chain to Madolyn Cummings. And nothing good would come from that. A woman I'd never met who thought I was a pervert who sent dick pics on business emails. She'd be only too happy to send out the kind of negative references that so few heads of HR ever gave me on prospective employees I investigated for Fulcrum Security.

The kind of irony I could do without.

Especially now. I needed to take Fulcrum Security off my resume. And I needed a lawyer. I intended to sue whoever attached the dick pic to the email. But before I hired a lawyer, I needed to find out who we were going to sue. There was one other thing I needed to do, even before that.

I pulled out my phone and called Fulcrum Security and told the receptionist that Rick Cahill was calling for Madolyn Cummings. After a two-minute wait, as expected, I was connected to Cummings. I figured she couldn't pass on the opportunity to tell me what she thought of me. Someone she'd never met.

"Did you call to threaten me, too, Mr. Cahill?" Confident voice.

"I don't know what you're talking about." Not exactly, but I had a pretty good idea.

"Linda Claireborn at Restorigen Solutions called me after you nearly assaulted her at her office."

Another victim from my implosion of rage. I didn't assault Linda Claireborn, but what would I have done if she hadn't given me the envelope? Three months ago, the answer would have been: nothing. Today, I wasn't sure. I needed to stop asking myself questions that I didn't know, or wouldn't like, the answers to.

"I didn't send the attachment with the picture to Sara. Somebody attached it to the email I sent after the fact." I stayed calm, rather than giving her confirmation to what she already thought of me. "The picture is not of me and it didn't come from my computer. I'm going to find out who sent it and sue them for all their worth. In the meantime, I'd appreciate it if you stop telling companies that contact you for references that I sent that kind of filth to your employee. If you continue, you'll get a call from my lawyer. And any help in finding those responsible would be very much appreciated."

"You have a lot more to worry about than prospective clients." A sick joy in her voice. I waited for the dagger. "I've already contacted the police about the photograph."

Cummings hung up before I could tell her that she'd be hearing from my lawyer. After I hired one. I could have also told her that sending unsolicited dick pics, unfortunately, wasn't against the law in California. But I doubted that declaration would have boosted my claim of innocence. And, legal or not, I didn't want the police, or anyone else, thinking I was capable of such a despicable act. Worst-case scenario, it might make Detective Skupin think that I had some kind of obsession with Sara Bhandari or a creepy relationship and start digging into me if the serial rapist direction dead-ended. Best case was that Skupin would just think I was a creep and completely blackball me with any information about the case. So not much would change.

CHAPTER SIXTEEN

SHREYA GARGANO WANTED to meet in person to hire me. Her house at six p.m. I didn't want to miss an opportunity to have a Skype call with Krista. Leah had texted me that maybe it could happen tonight. Krista was usually in her crib for the night by seven o'clock.

I texted Leah. Calling would have been a self-inflicted wound.

Me: *What time can I Skype with Krista tonight?*

A response came back four or five minutes later.

Leah: *Not going to be able to tonight. Have a business dinner.*

Me: *Can you have your mom set one up?*

Leah: *She's not set up on Skype. I'll try to do one tomorrow.*

I didn't bother replying. My relationship with my wife wasn't going to be fixed until I fixed it and that would only happen when she was ready to let me try.

Not yet.

I called Max Andrus for the third time that day. He hadn't returned my earlier calls even though I left messages asking him to.

Voicemail again. This time I changed up the message.

"Max, Rick Cahill. Again. I've got new information about Sara Bhandari's murder. I'll give you until five o'clock to call me back and then I'm calling the *Times of San Diego*."

The *Times* was a much smaller newspaper than the *Union-Tribune*, but I knew they had a crime beat because I'd ignored inquiries from their crime reporter a few times over the years.

Two minutes later, my phone rang.

Max Andrus.

"Sorry I didn't get back to you earlier. It's been a busy day." He didn't sound sorry, but that was okay. We'd both lied. But I'd gotten the desired result. We were talking. "What is the new information about Sara Bhandari's murder?"

"Did the rapist steal anything from his victims' homes?" I asked.

"I don't think so, but I thought you called me because you had new information." Irritation lowered his normal soprano voice. "Not the other way around."

"Sara Bhandari's cell phone and computer are missing from her house."

"The police probably took them as evidence." Now a sizzle of exasperation. "They'll check voicemails, texts, email contacts. This is standard stuff, Cahill. I thought you'd know that being a former police officer."

"You're right, but the police don't have them."

"How do you know?"

"Sara's sister, Shreya Gargano, went by the house today and couldn't find them. She talked to Detective Skupin and he told her they hadn't been taken into evidence." My voice calm, reasonable. "So, if it's the same suspect, he altered his M.O. three different ways in Sara's attack. He attacked her much earlier than he did with the others, he escalated to murder, and he stole the victim's laptop and phone."

"You're right. Those are all slight variations from his earlier rapes." Andrus now sounded professionally engaged. "But the police figured that he would escalate to murder eventually, so that's not surprising. And there's still the signature. That stayed the same and is very specific to this perpetrator. It would be an impossible coincidence for two un-connected rapists to have that sick and particular signature."

"I agree with that. If it's not the same guy, it would have to be some-one with inside police information who committed a copycat rape but went all the way to murder. Are you sure that nothing was stolen from the other victims?"

"I'm almost positive, but I can check with my source to be sure."

"Your source sounds like he or she is pretty close to the investiga-tion." I tried to sound impressed. "A detective?"

I knew there was no way Andrus's source was Detective Skupin. He was less a fan of the press than I was. But he wasn't the only detective working the case. San Diego PD detectives worked in teams. Plus, with the theory that Sara's murder had been committed by a serial rapist preying on women for months, there would probably be even more detectives working this case than usual. And all the ancillary personnel around it. Uniformed cops canvassing the neighborhoods around the crime scenes, crime scene techs, police brass.

"Nice try." A dismissive blast of air. "But I have a couple questions for you, Cahill."

"What happened to *Rick*?" I asked.

"We're not friends. You wouldn't give me the time of day when I tried to interview you about solving your wife's murder a couple years ago. Now you want to pretend to be my friend so you can use me for information."

"Don't act like you're above the fray." No anger, just matter-of-fact. "We're both using each other. Information is our business and neither one of us is precious about how we get it."

"Whatever." His millennial came out for the first time since we met. "Anyway, why are you so interested in this case? Is it still the white knight syndrome, or is there some other reason? Most people would move on with their lives and try to forget about someone that they knew only tangentially through work who got murdered."

"I told you last night. Once Sara hired me, she became my responsibility. I just want to make sure the police get the right guy, and they seem too tunneled in on one theory. But beyond that, the family hired me to look into Sara's death."

I normally wouldn't tell anyone, much less a newspaper reporter, who I was working for and what the case was. But I figured I could leverage the possibility of getting Andrus an interview with Shreya Gargano into him telling me everything he knew about Sara's murder.

"Oh." He strung the word out into an accusation. "That answers the next question I was going to ask."

"How's that?" I didn't think I was going to like his answer.

"I was going to ask you why you thought that someone else could have murdered Sara Bhandari." He left it there like I was supposed to read his mind.

"And?" I hit the "d" hard.

"Well, if the police are right about the murderer being the serial rapist, then there's no reason for your side investigation. On the other hand, as long as Sara's family thinks the killer might be someone else, they'll still need you to investigate."

"You don't know me, Andrus." I could take an insult. I'd had a lot of practice. My voice remained calm, but the remark stung on a day when my reputation had already been sullied by a dick pic frame job. "I want to find the truth for Sara Bhandari. That's all that matters. Check with your source at SDPD. When you confirm that nothing was stolen from the other victims and that Sara's phone and computer are missing, give me a call."

I hung up and felt heat radiate across my face. Not the fire that came from red rage, but run-of-the-mill, controllable anger. Like most people dealt with.

CHAPTER SEVENTEEN

SHREYA GARGANO LIVED in Rancho Santa Fe. Known for its horse properties, Rancho Santa Fe was one of the wealthiest enclaves in San Diego County. In the whole country. The Gargano home was built on a bluff above a valley with green rolling hills for neighbors. No housing tracts in sight. No horses either. Just a view that stretched for miles. The home was an expansive two-story estate made of peach-colored concrete and stone masonry.

I parked on the circular brick paver driveway and admired the view. A massive oak front door to the mansion with a large wrought-iron adorned window opened when I got out of my car. I held a leather portfolio containing the contract for Shreya Gargano to look over and sign. A tall woman stood at the door in an elegant gold and blue flowing dress. She was somewhere in her forties. I couldn't figure out which end. Dark smooth skin with brown eyes that seemed to sparkle in the porch light and silky black hair to her shoulders. Stunning.

"Mr. Cahill?" The precise cultured voice I'd heard on the phone.

"Shreya? Please call me Rick."

We shook hands. Her grip was firm. I walked inside to a large foyer that opened up into a living room with a view of the pristinely landscaped backyard and the valley below. To the right a sweeping staircase with carpeted steps and a polished wood and wrought-iron banister led upstairs. The entire interior of the house had an elegant colonial vibe.

A girl with light brown naturally curly hair stood in the living room holding a calico cat. The girl was thirteen or fourteen and looked like her mom, but had a lighter complexion. The cat looked familiar.

"Thanks for saving Trico," the girl said and stroked the cat's head. The cat purred. I'd done the right thing.

"You're welcome. He's a lucky cat to have a family that will take such good care of him."

A little face popped up from behind a chair next to a window in the back of the living room. She looked a lot like the girl's sister but was only five or six. She smiled. I smiled back.

"This is Lakshmi." Shreya opened a hand toward the girl holding the cat, then nodded at the one playing peekaboo behind the chair. "And this is Anushka. Girls, say hello to Mr. Cahill."

"Hello." In unison.

Their greeting touched me deeply in a way I didn't expect. It reminded me of the bits and pieces of Krista's life that I was missing in just a week without seeing her. I hoped that she would be as sweet and well behaved as Shreya Gargano's daughters when she reached their ages. And I hoped to still be cognitive enough and have enough self-control to be able to help shape her to get there.

"Nice to meet you." I looked at Lakshmi, then Anushka and smiled at each of them.

"Let's talk in my office." Shreya led me through the living room, past a large cook's kitchen with gleaming stainless-steel appliances, and down a hall into a large room that had an oval office curve in the back of it. Five vertical windows with the same view as the living room filled out the curve. Two glass doors sat on either side of the bank of windows.

The windows and architecture of the office were grand, but weren't the most impressive things about the office. The bookshelf behind the mahogany desk that held at least a dozen gold statuettes of a winged woman holding a slatted globe was. Emmys. I did a quick count. Fourteen.

"My earlier life." Shreya caught me staring. "Please, have a seat."

I sat in front of the desk in an armed chair covered in a white textile with little blue roses. Shreya sat behind the desk in a white leather executive chair. Below the three shelves of Emmys on the bookcase were pictures of Shreya and her family. There was one of a teenager holding a little girl's hand. The girl was only about three years old and the teenager was probably seventeen or eighteen and looked like a younger version of Shreya. That probably made the little girl too young to be Sara.

I looked at Shreya and tried to solve the Emmy mystery.

I wasn't completely up on contemporary television, but I think I'd be aware of an actress who'd won fourteen Emmys. Unless they were for soap operas. Then I thought about the syrupy smooth command of Shreya's voice and it hit me.

"Television news?' I asked.

"Yes." She slipped on a brief smile. "I was a reporter and then anchor for KTLA 5 in Los Angeles for thirteen years."

That explained why I'd never heard of her. I didn't watch local news, much less L.A. telecasts,

"More Emmys than years of service. Amazing."

"Thanks." No more smile. "That was a long time ago. Seems like a different lifetime ago. I got married and then we decided to have children. I quit because I wanted to be a stay-at-home mom."

"You've done well. Your daughters are adorable." I noticed Shreya had a large diamond ring on her wedding finger. Still married. There were a couple family photographs of Shreya, her daughters, and, presumably, her husband on the walls. He was fit, but looked to be a good ten years older than Shreya. "What does your husband do?"

"He's a sports agent. He's out of town right now trying to woo a prospective new client. He didn't want to leave my daughters and me after everything that happened with Sara, but I made him." She linked her hands together on the desk. "Let's talk about Sara's murder and what you've learned so far."

She looked suddenly older after saying her sister's name. I guessed her true age put her in her early fifties. Probably fourteen to fifteen years older than Sara and not the nine or ten that I first thought. I realized then that the little girl holding teenager Shreya's hand in the picture was Sara.

Professional responsibility required me to get the business end taken care of first. I pulled the contract out of the portfolio and slid it across the desk to Shreya.

"Why don't you take a look at the contract first?"

Shreya read the contract, a boilerplate that covered almost all contingencies. She looked up after she was done.

"This is only for a week. What if it takes longer?"

"Then we'll go forward on a per diem. I didn't want to lock you into anything that might be longer than needed."

She slid the contract back at me along with a Mont Blanc ballpoint pen.

"Let's make it two weeks. If it takes longer than that, we can write up another two-week contract and another for as long as it takes." Conclusive, like I didn't have an option. I was fine not having one in this situation. I needed the money. "I don't want to have to worry about you taking another case before we find out the truth about who killed Sara. You can write in the changes and initial them. It's fine with me. I'll make you a copy."

I made the changes, initialed and signed the contract. The first time I'd ever held a Mont Blanc pen. It felt substantial, but the black ink it left on the document looked the same as the ink in the half dozen Pilot G-2 pens sitting in a mug on the desk in my office at home.

Shreya looked at me expectantly, but I wasn't ready to give her the contract back yet.

"There's something I want you to know before you hire me." I looked her straight in the eye. "Something odd happened to me this afternoon that you should know about before you decide whether or not to hire me."

I told her about meeting with the head of HR from Restorigen. And the dick pic. She listened patiently and didn't change her expression when I got to the nasty part.

"Is it possible for someone to be able to add the picture to your email in Sara's inbox?" Her voice gave away nothing.

"It has to be." I set the contract down on the desk and leaned forward. "I didn't send it so someone must have attached it. After the fact."

"Why do you think someone did that?"

"I don't know. The only thing I can think of is that someone wanted to ruin my reputation. Whoever it was had to have access to Sara's email account. Someone at Fulcrum Security."

"Do you think it could have anything to do with Sara's murder?" Shreya's voice was under control. The consummate news professional. She seemed to be able to compartmentalize her grief over the death of her sister from the resolve to stay focused on trying to find who killed her.

"I doubt it, but I certainly can't rule it out. The police are probably right in their theory that a serial rapist killed Sara and whoever attached the dick pic to my email is just someone who has a grudge against me. Something completely separate."

Although the timing seemed more than coincidental. But finding out who exploded a stink bomb on my reputation was at the bottom of my priority list in relation to investigating Sara's murder.

"Attaching a disgusting image to an email and making it look like you sent it and then waiting around for someone to find it as they go through Sara's emails for work purposes is diabolical. Do you have enemies like that?" Her voice pitched above buttery news anchor professional into shocked onlooker.

I'd had enemies that were worse. But most of them were dead. Some by my hand.

"I've had a few, but the only person I dealt with at Fulcrum was your sister."

"This is all very strange. Anyway, as unsettling as the picture is, I don't believe that you had anything to do with it." She wiggled her fingers again. "I'm ready to sign the contract."

I slid the contract and the Mont Blanc pen across the table to her. I wondered if I'd ever have a Mont Blanc pen in my hand again. Shreya made a copy of the document on a Canon copier on her desk and gave it to me.

"So, that's half up front and the other half at the end of the week, correct?" She pulled out a checkbook from the middle drawer of the desk.

"The other half at the end of the second week."

"Well." She squinted at me and pursed her lips. "I'm going to write one check for the two weeks now. Makes it easier. Okay?"

"Okay." I suddenly felt guilty that my financial windfall came at the expense of Sara Bhandari's life. The best thing I could do to remedy that was make sure the police arrested her killer.

Shreya wrote on the check, then ripped it from her checkbook. She set it on the table in front of her instead of immediately giving it to me.

"Now, tell me what you've learned about Sara's death." She rested her elbows on the table and laced her fingers together.

I told her everything I knew so far, except for the ghastly specifics about the killer's signature and the condition of Sara's body when I found it.

"Why are the police so sure that Sara was killed by this serial rapist? He's never killed anyone before, correct? Why would he start now? And aren't there some differences in Sara's situation than with the other women who were raped?"

As I feared when I agreed to work Sara's case for Shreya, I wouldn't be able to shield her about the horrific details about her sister's death if she wanted to know the whole truth.

"Are you sure you need to hear this?" The words hard and blunt. No compassion in my voice or in the expression on my face. I didn't want to give Shreya the impression that I could hold her hand and walk her delicately through the specifics of her sister's death. There was no easy way. Horrible images would be seared into her memory forever.

Shreya didn't say anything at first. She swiveled in her chair and looked at the photos below the Emmys on the bookshelf to her right. I guessed she was looking at the one of her and Sara holding hands when Sara was a toddler. She must have been deciding if she could bear to let new terrible images intrude on the warm memories she had of her sister. The silence in the room pounded in my ears.

Finally, after what seemed like two or three minutes, but was probably only thirty or forty seconds, she turned back to face me. And her decision.

"I need to know the truth." Her jaw tight.

A compulsion that had caused me great injury over the last ten years. Physical and emotional. And injury to people I cared about.

"As you may know from your years in the news industry, many violent serial offenders repeat physical acts—called signatures—while committing crimes." I paused to try to find the least painful path to explain what happened to Sara.

Shreya filled the brief silence. "I thought that was considered an M.O.—modus operandi."

"It's a little different. An M.O. is the methodology a criminal uses to commit a crime. Breaks into a victim's home by popping a sliding glass door off its track. Subdues his victim by holding a knife to her neck. Things like that." I could no longer avoid the black hole of depravity the killer wreaked upon Sara. "A signature is something the criminal does during the crime to serve his emotional and psychological needs. Like the kind of injuries the criminal inflicts upon his victims."

Another silent pause. I wasn't going to explain further unless Shreya asked. She studied me for a few seconds, then finally spoke.

"What kind of things did this monster do to Sara?" She set her jaw so tight it could have crushed diamonds.

I waited a couple seconds, then ripped off the Band-Aid.

"He used the rod from the toilet paper holder to anally rape his victims." I kept talking to try to shuffle past the image I'd just tattooed into Shreya's brain. "Although I'm sure this son of a bitch isn't the only offender to do this, it's unique enough that it would be very unusual for two unconnected rapists in the same geographical area to have this same signature at the same time. And the killer also . . . he also cut Sara's breast. Something he'd done to his most recent victim before Sara."

Shreya's expression didn't change, but she blinked a couple times. Her jaw remained clinched until she spoke again.

"What about a copycat? That's not that unusual, right."

"No, it's not, but none of the specifics about the rapes have ever been reported in the press."

"Well, you have access to this information. Somebody at the San Diego Police Department must be talking. Is that where you got all this?"

"No." Like a good reporter, I didn't give up my sources. Even when my source *was* a reporter. But this was Shreya Gargano's sister and I'd just told her things about the last minutes of her sister's life that she'd never be able to forget. She'd get everything I knew. "A reporter at the *San Diego Union-Tribune* has an inside source at SDPD."

"Is the reporter Max Andrus, who wrote the article on Sara's murder?"

"Yes. Of course, we have to keep that under wraps if we hope to get more information." I could name names, but she couldn't.

"I spent twenty-one years in the news business, Rick. Starting out as a stringer in Sparks, Nevada. I know how to keep a source confidential."

"No offense meant." I raised open hands to chest level. "I'm just being cautious. I'm going to do everything I can to find Sara's killer. That includes protecting sources. One other thing. How would you feel about giving Andrus an exclusive interview at some point? It could help keep the information flowing."

"If that's what it takes." She grabbed the check, rose up out of her chair, and reached across the table. I met her in the middle and put the check in my pocket.

"Thanks."

"Thank you for helping my family." She settled back into her chair. "And by the way, the check is for $7,000. I expect you to work weekends whenever possible. But I understand that family sometimes takes precedence. Family is everything."

Her eyes moistened and she blinked three or four times.

"I'll be working the case seven days a week." I agreed with her on family. I just wasn't sure when I'd see mine again.

CHAPTER EIGHTEEN

I CALLED LEAH from my car on the way home. No answer. I didn't leave a message. The phone call was enough. She told me she had a business dinner tonight. It was only 6:50 p.m. She was probably still at dinner or on her way to it. There wasn't going to be a Skype call tonight. Another day without seeing or talking to my daughter. Precious time lost now that my life was on a clock that ticked faster and faster every single day.

*   *   *

I grabbed some Chinese takeout on the way home and had just stuck my chopsticks into cashew chicken when my phone rang. I dropped the chopsticks and reached for the phone on the butcher block island. Maybe Leah had taken me out of the deep freeze and returned my call.

Shit.

Max Andrus.

I took the call.

"Rick, Max Andrus." I didn't respond so he continued. "You were right about Sara Bhandari's missing computer and cell phone. And that she was the only victim who had something stolen."

"What does your guy or gal at the department think about that? A sudden change in M.O., or possibly another suspect?" I took a bite of the chicken. Already starting to cool. Damn.

"I never said I had a contact inside the police department." Defensive.

"I thought we moved past the part where you think I'm stupid." I put down the chopsticks. I wasn't hungry anymore. "But I'll play along for the sake of brevity. What did your source on high conclude regarding the different M.O.?"

"My source only provides information, not conclusions." Andrus' snippy millennial came out again. That was okay. My Generation X cynicism was already in play. Or maybe it was just my own cynicism. Wasn't fair to blame my personality on an entire generation.

"Well, what do you think then? Are the M.O. differences and the murder enough for you to think that Sara's killer could be someone other than the serial rapist?"

"I think it's the Coastal Rapist's evolution."

"The Coastal Rapist? SDPD has given the suspect a nickname?" I asked.

"You can read about it in the *UT* on Saturday. That's when the dam's going to break."

"What do you mean?"

"I've got a front-page story on the rapes and Sara Bhandari's murder. Twenty-five column inches." Pride in his voice. I couldn't blame him. Everyone wanted to be good at their jobs and get the recognition they thought they deserved. "SDPD is going to have a press conference about the crimes at noon on Saturday and lay out the Coastal Rapist theory."

"Is SDPD aware that you're beating them to the punch with your news story?"

"Yes. I could have run it tomorrow, but they asked for an extra day so they could put everything together for the Saturday news conference." More pride.

"So you went to them and said, 'I'm running this story, be prepared'?"

"Something like that." He hung up on that note.

Andrus had a cozier relationship with the police than any newsperson I'd ever heard of.

I called Shreya Gargano and told her about the police news conference coming up on Saturday and about Andrus' article dropping that morning.

"SDPD is certain enough about their contention that the rapes and Sara's murder were done by the same person that they're going public. I can rip up the check you gave me this evening if you want to mail me one for one day's work." I wanted to be fair, but I couldn't be so magnanimous that I didn't take any money for the work I'd already done. Not anymore. The financial realities of feeding a family took precedence over principle.

"What do you think?" Laid back onto me.

"The news conference and SDPD, more or less, okaying Andrus's article strengthens my opinion that the police probably are correct in their serial rapist theory."

"*Probably* correct." She hit probably hard.

"Nothing is a hundred percent without a confession from the killer and corroborating evidence like DNA, which I'm pretty sure they don't have."

"Precisely. I'll expect daily reports on how your investigation is going. They can be brief, but I expect to see them every day. You can email them to me and call or just email them."

The contract that Shreya signed stated that I'd send reports at the end of each week. The only time I'd ever given daily reports was when the mob conscripted me to work a case for them. That didn't turn out well for anyone. Still, I understood Shreya's need to know everything as it happened. And her need to feel some control over something when her life had been turned completely upside down.

"Will do. Here's a piece of information that I'll email you as soon as we hang up: Andrus confirmed that Sara's stolen electronics were the only things missing from any of the rape victims."

"And there's also the different time of death, right?"

"Right, but I don't think that's as significant as the stolen phone and computer. The earlier time could be because Sara didn't go out like the other victims. So, he went against his M.O. and broke in while she was home."

I felt a little uneasy discussing the murder of Sara Bhandari with her sister like it was some puzzle to put together on a kitchen table. But Shreya continued to demonstrate her ability to compartmentalize and work through the information without getting emotional. That took a lot of strength and a tremendous amount of energy.

"I guess that's plausible." She didn't sound convinced. Maybe she didn't want to be convinced. Maybe she didn't want her sister's death to have been just another statistic of a serial rapist turned killer. I understood. Leah had felt the same way when her sister was killed in a hit-and-run car "accident." Shreya probably thought Sara's life was significant and that her death should be, too. "Thanks, Rick. For taking the case and for being honest with me. You're probably right that the police are on the right track, but I need to be sure. I'll talk to you soon."

"Whatever happens, I'll find the truth."

Even as I said the words, I realized the significance they could have on me and my family. The need to find the truth. The quest that I'd set aside for the sake of my family. Maybe, subconsciously, that was why I was willing to give Shreya an out from the quest now that the police were going to go public. If she took it, I wouldn't have to try to balance my compulsion to find the truth against the safety of my family. But Shreya wanted to press on. And, I realized now, so did I.

Maybe this quest was a desperate substitute for having my family at home. Whole. Maybe, like Shreya Gargano, I needed to feel in control of something while my life spun out from under me. I now had a de-lineated mission. Find out who killed Sara Bhandari and make sure they were brought to justice. Something, seemingly, impossible without carrying a badge, but I now had a mandate and I could control how I went about attempting to achieve it.

But before I jumped in, I had to make sure the path was righteous.

"One last thing." I stopped Shreya from signing off. "Has anyone in your family picked up any belongings that Sara might have left at Fulcrum Security? We have to make sure her laptop and phone were actually stolen."

"Funny that you should mention that. They called my mom today and asked her where she'd like them to ship Sara's things. Momma asked me to handle it. I called them back and talked to someone and gave them my address. They said they'd mail everything tomorrow. I didn't ask what they had. I probably should have."

"What are you doing tomorrow?" I asked.

"Making arrangements for Sara's burial and memorial service and dealing with her estate. Such as it is."

"How would you like to take a break from that for a couple hours and drive up to Fulcrum Security with me and pick up Sara's belongings? We can get there early before the mail goes out."

"Why?"

"It will give me a valid reason to get inside the office and look around. And talk to Dylan Helmer, the employee who had the missing files."

"Sure."

"They open at eight. I'll pick you up at seven forty-five. It could get ugly. You know I'm not very popular there right now."

"I'll have your back."

CHAPTER NINETEEN

I PICKED SHREYA up at her estate in Rancho Santa Fe the next morning. We went over the game plan on the drive north to Escondido. That only took a few minutes and she was quiet the rest of the way. Alone in her thoughts.

Fulcrum Security was at the end of a cul-de-sac in an industrial area. We arrived at eight fifteen. Time for the human resources department to be settled in at work, but before the mail would go out. Fulcrum's warehouse was smaller than I expected. Not small, probably fifteen thousand square feet, but I'd expected something bigger. Even though I knew Fulcrum just built radar and sonar for ships and didn't actually install them. The units themselves must have been a lot smaller than I thought they'd be. Despite living in San Diego for most of my life, I knew nothing nautical.

We went inside the building, which was concrete and built more for function than style. The entrance had a cement floor, and a receptionist area sat in the middle of a large lobby. Behind it to the left were two heavy metal doors that had a keycard reader next to them. The factory for radar and sonar systems production. A metal staircase off to the right led up a second story on that side of the building. My guess was this is where the sales, customer service, human resources offices were.

A young woman with shoulder-length blond hair in a pink blouse and rectangle glasses on a round face sat next to a private security guard in an olive-green uniform. Her name tag read, "Janice."

The security guard wasn't wearing a name tag. He had dark close-cropped hair and looked like a retired NFL linebacker. Muscular, but jowly. I wasn't surprised the security guard was there. I'd been inside golf manufacturers' warehouses that had security guards and they were only protecting company secrets, not Department of Defense systems.

The guard raised his head from a bank of monitors and looked at Shreya, then eyeballed me hard. I was used to stern looks from men in uniforms. I'd been getting them for most of the last fifteen years. Before that, I gave out some of my own as a patrolman in Santa Barbara.

The world turns. You find a way to turn with it or spin off into the dark.

We walked up to the counter and Shreya took the lead as planned.

"Hi, I'm Shreya Bhandari." She used her maiden name, which was what she used as a newscaster, but also made her connection to Sara evident. "Sara Bhandari was my sister and I'm here to pick up her belongings."

"Oh." Janice blinked a few times with her mouth open. "I'm so sorry for your loss. Sara was always very nice to me."

"Thank you." Shreya smiled reassuringly to the woman. "Now how do we go about picking up Sara's things?"

"Of course. Please have a seat and I'll get someone to come talk to you." Janice waved her hand toward a couple of hardbacked office chairs and a vinyl sofa with an industrial steel frame against the wall. We each chose a hardbacked chair. They were hard bottomed, too.

"Ms. Cummings, Sara Bhandari's sister is here to pick up Sara's things," Janice said into a phone handset. Old school at Fulcrum Security. "Okay. Thank you." She hung up the phone and looked at Shreya and me. "Someone will be down to see you in a minute."

"Thank you," we said in unison.

I hoped Madolyn Cummings wouldn't be the person to greet us, but we were ready for that possibility if needed. We'd probably run across her even if she didn't come downstairs because we wanted to get a look at Sara's workspace.

A few minutes later, a woman in her mid-thirties came downstairs. Tall, willowy, with long strawberry blond hair. Dylan Helmer. At least she looked a lot like the photo I remembered I had for Helmer when I ran a background check on her for Fulcrum a few months ago. She'd had stellar references, no run-ins with the law, at least none that made paper, and had a four-year degree from some well-established university. Couldn't remember which. I was happy to be able to pull up that many memories. The disease hadn't beaten me, yet.

"Ms. Bhandari." Helmer spoke when she hit the landing. She wore a blue blouse that matched her eyes and gray slacks. Her expression was calibrated just right to convey condolence and warmth. Maybe it was sincere. "I'm Dylan Helmer. I worked with Sara and liked her very much. I'm so sorry for your loss."

"Thank you. That's very kind. Nice to meet you." Shreya stuck out her hand and they shook. "This is Rick, my associate. He's here to help with the belongings and to make sure we get everything."

That was one way of putting it.

Helmer smiled at me and I nodded. She didn't appear to recognize me, which made sense. We'd never met. Very few of my background checks for clients required me meeting the prospective employees. Helmer might have recognized my full name if Shreya had given it and that I was the Rick who called her on Tuesday.

"We have everything boxed up in the mail room, which is in the warehouse. I can go get it for you." Pleasant.

"That would be great. Thanks." Shreya flashed her newscaster, point-of-the-triangle-in-the-news-team-promos smile. Dylan smiled back. "But we'd also like to go through her workstation to make sure nothing's left behind."

"We got everything." Dylan nodded rapidly and blinked. "I made sure of that."

"I'm sure you did, but I promised my mother that I'd personally check everything. She's very protective of family keepsakes."

Shreya recited my script like a pro. The newsreader in her? She didn't seem to have any problem conveying my fake news. She lied with ease. Like me. All for the greater good.

"Well, I'll have to check with my supervisor." Helmer rubbed her hands together and looked uncomfortable. "I'll get the boxes first and then I'll talk to Madolyn, okay?"

Madolyn. Cummings. Shit.

"Sure." Shreya.

"Steven, could you buzz me in?" Helmer looked at the security guard, who nodded, then she walked to the metal doors in the back of the lobby.

The guard must have pushed a button under the counter because the door clicked and Helmer opened it and went into the warehouse. A couple minutes later she came out pushing a hand truck with two medium-sized moving boxes on it. She stopped in front of us. Shreya took off the top of the first box, ran her hand along a white cashmere sweater. I caught a glimpse of a strip of blue material next to it.

"These are her belongings." She put the lid back on the box. "I gave her that sweater."

"I'll put these in the car," I said and picked up the boxes. Both fairly light, the bottom heavier than the top. I took them out to my car and put them in the trunk.

Dylan Helmer was gone when I went back inside the building. Shreya stood at the reception counter.

"She had to talk to her boss," Shreya said to me.

Janice smiled and the guard deadpan-stared at me. Normality.

A couple minutes later, Dylan Helmer returned down the stairs, smiling.

"I'll be happy to show you Sara's workstation, but first we have to get you visitor passes."

"Can I see your driver's licenses, please?" Steven, the security guard, spoke as soon as Helmer stopped speaking.

I pulled out my wallet and flipped open the clear compartment holding my CDL and showed it to Steven while Shreya fished through her black quilted leather handbag with vertically interlocking gold YSL letters.

"Could you please remove it from your wallet?" Steven.

I did as Steven asked and handed him my license. He took it and propelled his roller chair with his feet to a printer to his left at the back of the reception enclosure. He made a copy of my license, then brought it back to me. He did the same with Shreya's after she handed it to him. Finally, he had us sign our names on a visitor log attached to a clipboard and handed us visitor badges attached to lanyards. Shreya and I hung the lanyards around our necks and followed a smiling Dylan Helmer up the stairs to the second floor.

There were windows to a large office area with a row of four pairs of back-to-back gray three-walled office cubicles in the middle of the room at the top of the stairs. There were also four or five cubicles against the far wall and enclosed offices on either end of the room. All the cubicles were full with people on phones and tapping on computer keyboards. A gentle hum like a beehive emanated through the walls. My guess was the sales department, along with customer service. A nameplate on the wall next to the door confirmed my suspicion as we passed.

Next up was a much smaller office with two back-to-back pairs of cubicles in the middle of the room. Two women sat with their backs to the window in cubicles on their phones. There was an office to the side. Accounting.

Next, an office with the blinds drawn in front of the window. The nameplate read: Production. I guess it made sense for a company that derived over half its income from Department of Defense contracts to not want prying eyes to see too much. Company secrets. There was probably also a production office down on the warehouse floor, closer to the action.

There were two offices left, a small one set up like the accounting office and the last one that looked to be larger and, no doubt, had a corner window behind the closed door and blinds. The CEO, Trent Boswell's office. Dylan led us into the smaller room.

A woman's head prairie-dogged up above one of the cubbyholes when we entered the office. Only her hair and eyes showed. Crow's feet framed brown eyes below bottle brown hair. The head disappeared after a quick scan of us visitors.

There was an enclosed office with a window in the far corner of the room. The blinds were up and a dark-haired woman in her forties sat behind a desk talking to a man standing opposite her. He was balding and schlubby. A white dress shirt with tails hung untucked over his cushiony back end. They both stopped talking and turned and stared at us. The man had a black mustache with specks of gray that dragged down the corners of his mouth. They looked away and the man put his hands on the desk and leaned forward.

Dylan led us over to the four cubicles in the middle of the room. One of the two facing us was empty, and the other one had a nameplate adhered to the side of it that had Dylan's name on it.

"This was Sara's cubicle," she said in front of the vacant workspace.

The top of the desk had nothing on it and looked like it had been wiped clean. Shreya opened the long middle drawer. Nothing, not even a leftover paper clip. She opened the top file drawer on the right side of the desk. Empty. Same with the one under it. Dylan Helmer was right; they had been thorough.

I heard the sound of a door opening behind us and turned toward the sound. The schlubby man exited the office and walked quickly past without saying a word or looking at us. The dark-haired woman followed him out. She was dressed in a smart black business suit with white pinstripes offset by a pink blouse. She smiled at Shreya and didn't look at me. I caught a glimpse of the schlubby guy through the window as he went down the hall.

"Ms. Bhandari?" The woman stuck out a cuff-linked hand to Shreya. "I'm Madolyn Cummings. I was Sara's supervisor. I'm so sorry for your loss. Sara was an important and much-loved member of our team."

Cummings was about five feet eight in two-inch square heels. She was thin and sharp featured. Small dark eyes and a long nose that anchored her face in an attractive way and gave the impression of forward momentum.

"Thank you." Shreya shook her hand. "I know Sara liked working here. Thanks for letting us have a look at her workspace."

"Of course." Cummings' smile managed to convey the same warmth and sympathy that Dylan Helmer's had. "Could we chat privately in my office?"

"Sure," Shreya said.

Cummings still hadn't acknowledged my existence. She would to Shreya when they talked in her office. She might even pull out a photographic exhibit. That was fine by me. I was confident that Shreya believed my innocence regarding the dick pic.

She led Shreya into her office and shut the door. Cummings took her perch behind her desk and Shreya sat in a chair across from her. I turned to Dylan Helmer, who was still standing next to Sara's old workstation instead of sitting down at her own.

"Thanks for getting all of Sara's things together." I smiled at Helmer. "The family is really broken up about her death."

"Yeah, it's terrible." Helmer held her hands in front of her, looking like she wasn't sure what to do. With me.

I didn't hear any noise coming from the prairie dog's cubbyhole on the other side of Sara's cubicle. No typing, no paper shuffling, no drawers opening and closing. My guess was that she was listening on the other side of the wall. The office gossip or just naturally curious? It didn't matter. I couldn't miss the opportunity to talk to Dylan Helmer alone. She probably wouldn't tell me much with her cubemate listening in. She might not tell me much alone, either, but I wouldn't know until I separated her from her office.

"It's been a long morning already," I said to Dylan. "I need a boost of caffeine. Do you have a Coke machine somewhere?"

"Yes. There's one in the breakroom downstairs. It's right across from the reception desk in the lobby." A hostess at a dinner party smile. "You can't miss it."

"Thanks." I took a step, then stopped, tilted my head, and rubbed my chin. "Would you mind going down there with me? I got some bad vibes from your security guard. I don't want him to see me wandering around here unescorted."

"I don't think it will be a problem. Steven already checked you in." Dylan looked even more uncomfortable. I had to get her isolated before Shreya came back out of Cummings' office.

"I'd really appreciate it." I gave her a needy smile. "Drinks and snacks on me."

"Ahhh, okay." I think she calculated the best way to deal with me was to go on this little errand and then, hopefully, her boss would be done talking to Shreya and we'd be gone.

"I'll take a Diet Coke and some Famous Amos cookies." A disembodied voice from the unseen prairie dog.

"You got it," I said and hurried over to the door and held it open for Dylan.

She exited the office in front of me and I glanced back at Madolyn Cummings. She was still seated talking to Shreya, but looked directly at me as I shut the door. I avoided looking through the Human Resources office window as I walked with Dylan Helmer down the hall.

"Thanks for doing this. I know you're busy," I said as we passed the accounting office.

"Oh. It's fine." Pleasantly placating.

"Hey, was that Trent Boswell coming out of your boss's office when we got there?" I was pretty sure it wasn't. I'd looked up Fulcrum Security's CEO when I first started doing work for them. It was two years ago, but the picture I saw of Boswell was of a man older than the one in Cummings' office. However, in better shape. I threw his name out to give Dylan the idea that I was somewhat familiar with her company in hopes that she'd be willing to give up a little information.

"No, that was Buddy Gatsen."

"The production manager?" I asked. Sara had mentioned Buddy as the person who recommended that Dylan use Leveraged Investigations for running background checks on the three new hires that had the temporary missing files.

"Yes." I caught her side-eyeing me. Wasn't sure what that meant.

"Hmm. I wouldn't expect the production manager and the VP of HR to have a lot of interaction." I shrugged my shoulders. "Shows you what I know."

She left that alone and was quiet on the rest of the walk downstairs to the breakroom. But she did side-eye me a couple more times. The breakroom was big enough for two small cafeteria-style picnic tables, two vending machines, one with snacks and one that held sugary drinks, a refrigerator, microwave, coffee maker, a sink, and two trash cans.

"What would you like?" I asked Dylan as I fed dollar bills into the soda machine and punched the keypad numbers for a Coke for me and a Diet Coke for my prairie dog friend. The cans banged down to the drawer of the machine and I pushed it open and retrieved the bounty. It hit me at that point that I had to drink the carbonated poison to give credence to my ruse. I hadn't had a soda in fifteen years. I popped the top and gagged a sip. I hadn't missed anything but an acidy swallow.

"I'm fine, thanks." Dylan's side-eye had turned into a head-on stare. "You're Rick Cahill, aren't you? Sara's background check guy."

"That's me." I shoved two bucks into the snack machine. I grabbed the tiny bag of Famous Amos chocolate chip cookies after they dropped from their shelf and fought off the urge to buy one for myself. "I actually did the background check on you before you were hired. Immaculate record. High recommendations. Everyone I spoke with had nothing but praise for you."

"That's nice." She squinted at me. "But why are you here with Sara's sister?"

"She needs my help." I took a look at the Coke in my hand and thought about taking another sip, but tossed it in the trash instead. The ruse was over. "With such glowing recommendations, I was surprised that Sara discovered that you either didn't do background checks on some new hires, or lost their reports. That doesn't sound like the excellent employee I ran a check on."

My time in the Fulcrum Security building was quickly coming to an end. I didn't have time to finesse Dylan Helmer into telling me what I wanted to know. I had to try brute force.

"That was just a mix-up with some files." Helmer's fair complexion flashed pink. "Why would you possibly care about it?"

Dylan Helmer seemed to me to be someone concerned about keeping her job, not about covering up some kind of conspiracy. She might have been guilty of shoddy work, but nothing more.

"I care about it because Sara cared about it." I set the Diet Coke and cookies down on the picnic table with a thump. "She asked me to look into it and a couple days later someone murdered her."

Dylan sucked in a quick, loud breath and her eyes opened wide. "What? The newspaper said she was raped. I don't understand. You think her murder had something to do with work?"

"I don't know. That's what I'm trying to find out and I need your help."

"My help?" Her voice fluttered. "What do you want me to do?"

"What happened with the background checks on the three new hires?"

"I don't know. I got them from Leveraged Investigations for all three applicants a couple months ago and sent the files to the production manager and he ended up hiring the applicants a couple weeks later." She rubbed the inside of her left wrist with her right thumb. A stress release. "Last week I was out sick on Monday and when I came back in, Sara asked me why the background checks were missing from those files. I searched my files and they were in there." She looked at the floor. "Except . . ."

"Except what?"

"They were in the wrong order in the file."

"What do you mean?"

She scanned the open doorway again before she spoke.

"I always put the background checks behind the proof of citizenship documents in the file and those were behind the applications."

"You couldn't have filed them out of order by accident on a busy day?" I asked.

"No. I have a set order. I'm kind of OCD about some things."

"So you think someone was in your files?"

Madolyn Cummings' voice drifted in through the door from the lobby. "If there's anything else you need, please contact me anytime."

Dylan froze, wide-eyed.

"Thank you for your kindness and your concern." Shreya in the lobby.

"I have to go." Dylan hurried out of the breakroom.

I picked up the prairie dog's goodies and followed her out. "Please give this to your cubemate upstairs."

Cummings and Shreya looked at us from the middle of the lobby. Dylan turned, pink-faced again, and took the Diet Coke and cookies from me and walked over to the two women.

"I'm really sorry for your loss," she said to Shreya.

"Thank you and thanks for taking such good care of Sara's things." Shreya put a hand on Dylan's shoulder.

Dylan's eyes turned glossy and she hurried up the stairs toward the HR office.

"She really looked up to Sara." Cummings opened her hands in front of herself. "Well, I'd better get back to work. So nice to meet you, Shreya. I wish it could have been under much happier circumstances."

"Nice to meet you," Shreya said.

Cummings turned and headed for the staircase without acknowledging my presence. Again.

CHAPTER TWENTY

WE EXITED THE Fulcrum Security parking lot in my Accord and headed for I-15.

"I'm guessing at least some of your private talk with Madolyn Cummings was about me," I said.

"Yes." Shreya stared straight ahead at the road, giving away nothing.

"Well?"

"She showed me some emails with inappropriate comments and she also said that you made veiled threats to her on the phone yesterday if she didn't give you high recommendations to any prospective new clients who contacted her about your work."

"I never sent Sara inappropriate emails. They're fake." I glanced at Shreya. Still couldn't read her. "And there was nothing veiled about what I said to Cummings. It wasn't a threat. I simply asked her not to continue to tell people that I sent the lewd photo and that if she did, she'd get a call from my lawyer. Not a threat. Just a fact. That was the extent of it. I didn't even raise my voice."

Shreya didn't say anything for a while as I got onto I-15 and headed south toward her home. The mansion. I was surprised that she didn't ask me if I got any information from Dylan Helmer. I had the sense she might be reevaluating hiring me. Did she believe what Cummings told her?

"Before you decide what to do going forward, you should know what I learned from Dylan Helmer."

"Oh?" Shreya seemed to come out of a trance and looked at me. "What did she tell you?"

I told her about Dylan's claim that she'd received background checks from Leveraged Investigations and sent them to the production manager, Buddy Gatsen, and that they were out of order when she produced them for Sara.

"Gatsen was the man Cummings was talking to when we walked into the Human Resources office," I said.

"She's sure that the report was out of order?"

"Yes. She claims to have a degree of OCD when it comes to work. I don't think she would have told me about the files if she wasn't sure about how she filed them."

"Maybe Madolyn checked to see they were there after Sara said they were missing and she put them back in the wrong order."

Madolyn. First-name basis. Fast friends?

"Dylan seemed a little spooked, like something wasn't quite right with the situation." I had my own first-name-basis friend. "I think if it was not unusual for someone to check her files, she would have mentioned it. I didn't get a chance to ask her anything else. She heard Cummings' voice in the lobby and panicked."

"She might just be worried about her job."

"I think she is worried about her job, but that there's more to it than that. I'm going to try and contact her away from work."

No response from Shreya. She was back in her trance. She didn't say anything for the remaining twenty minutes of the drive. I parked in Shreya's driveway and tapped the button under the dash to pop the hood of the trunk.

"Thanks for your help today." She stared straight ahead and seemed to choose the words carefully. The preamble to a verbal Dear John letter. "I'm not going to need your services going forward. You can cash the check, but our arrangement ends today."

She opened the door and got out of the car before I could respond. I swung my door open and jumped out.

"Whatever was on the emails Cummings showed you, I didn't write it. Someone at Fulcrum faked them."

"I'm going to let the police do their job." Shreya walked to the trunk of the car. "That's all. I shouldn't have hired a private detective in the first place."

"Bullshit." I met her at the trunk and grabbed the two boxes of Sara's things from it. "Cummings said something to you to poison the well. You've been the one pushing me to investigate and now, all of a sudden, the investigation is over? Something is off about Fulcrum Security. I saw it in Dylan Helmer's face when she was talking about the missing background checks. It may have nothing to do with Sara's murder, but it's worth looking into. Because of the timing of Sara's death, if nothing else."

"I'll take those boxes." Shreya reached out her hands.

"I'm going to drop them on your porch." I brushed past her on the brick paver driveway and set the boxes down in front of the multimillion-dollar home. "Whatever Cummings told you about me is a lie. Thanks for having my back."

I walked back to my car as Shreya passed by me without a word and wondered what kind of venom Madolyn Cummings had injected into her bloodstream.

And why.

CHAPTER TWENTY-ONE

MOIRA MACFARLANE'S WHITE Honda Accord was parked in front of her California Craftsman cottage on Fay Avenue in La Jolla. The small lot didn't have room for a driveway or a carport, much less a garage. Moira usually tackled paperwork, expense reports, and invoices at home at the end of the week. The best P.I. in San Diego always had a lot of paper to take care of because she never lacked for work. And she usually never lacked for wisdom, either. My, sometimes, missing ingredient.

I went through the white picket fence and up the short walkway that bisected her small front lawn and onto the porch. An idyllic setting that hadn't produced an idyllic life for Moira. She'd lost her husband to an early death. She'd almost lost her son to the same fate. She was still single in a lonely world ten years after her husband's death. And she'd adopted me as a younger brother, friend, and pain in the ass.

I knocked on the front door on the covered porch. A porch where we'd coughed tear gas out of our lungs and almost took our relationship in a wrong direction six years ago.

The door opened ten seconds later. Moira, all five feet, one hundred pounds of her frowned up at me. More sarcasm than irritation in her dark eyes. Her perma-puckered lips twitching away the beginnings of a grin.

"Your phone doesn't work?"

Neither one of us was a fan of the unannounced drop-by, but each had been guilty of it more than once.

"I was in the neighborhood." The neighborhood being all of San Diego County.

"Then, by all means, come on in." She smirked and swung the door open wide for me to enter.

The house's modern open floorplan was in direct contrast to its classic California Craftsman Cottage exterior, though it still maintained a dark wood interior. Moira walked to the head of the dining room table. Stacks of paper surrounded an open laptop. A mug with steam rising sat next to the papers. An herbal smell filled up the house giving it a lived-in, comfortable feel. And I didn't even like tea. Moira didn't sit down.

"Can I get you some refreshments?" She laced her fingers together in front of her, her voice thick with sarcasm. "Some tea? Fresh lemonade? I've got some lemons in the fridge. It will just take a moment for me to squeeze the juice out of them. Or can I cook you some breakfast? Is Eggs Benedict to your liking?"

I sat down at the dining table. "I get it, you're busy. I won't be here long."

She sat down and folded her arms in front of her. "What's the problem?"

I had more than one problem, but decided to keep my home life out of it.

"Sara Bhandari's sister hired me to look into Sara's death then fired me all within two days after she gave me a check for two weeks' work."

"Why did she fire you?"

I gave her the rundown of the last forty-eight hours, complete with the dick pic at Fulcrum Security.

"A dick pic?" A question of why, not what one was.

"Yeah, and Fulcrum's VP of Human Resources has already told potential clients about it."

"Hmm." She leaned back in her chair and pursed her lips.

"What?"

"Remember when I told you about Leveraged Investigations intimidating my client to get her to drop me from the case?"

"Yeah, but I also remember that you couldn't get her to admit that to you."

"That's not the important part." She shook her head. "What happened next is. Beginning about two weeks after the woman dropped me, three supposed ex-clients of mine bashed me on Google Reviews. Two posted under common first names and the other one was anonymous. They strung out the bad reviews over a couple of weeks so they didn't appear all at once, but I knew something was fishy about them.

The complaints were very general and I couldn't pin them to any cases I'd done over the preceding year. I complained to Google about them and actually got them to delete the anonymous one, but not the others. I wondered at the time if Leveraged Investigations might have had something to do with it, but convinced myself it was so petty that an agency doing well enough to have an office in the First Allied Plaza downtown wouldn't consider doing something like that. Now I think I was wrong."

"Me, too. They stink-bombed you, just like they did me." My stomach reminded me that I hadn't eaten breakfast before I picked up Shreya Gargano and drove up to Fulcrum Security. Eggs Benedict suddenly sounded delicious, even though it wasn't a real offer. "Do you think their thing is to try to hurt their competition or that they're just vindictive?"

"I don't know. Maybe a little bit of both." Moira leaned her elbows onto the table. "Do you think this has something to do with Sara

Bhandari's murder? I thought the police pinned it on the serial rapist they haven't caught yet."

"I don't know, but I told you Sara thought something that happened at Fulcrum Security was odd. The missing and then found background checks on three new hires.

"Yes, but like you said they were found. So case closed, right?"

"Nope. I got subtle confirmation this morning that something was off with them."

"What do you mean?" She edged closer to me across the table, her big round intelligent eyes already working on possibilities.

I told her what Dylan Helmer said about the background check reports being out of place in her strict filing system.

"And these were the background checks that Leveraged Investigations did?"

"Yeah."

"And Sara Bhandari told you about this and was murdered within a week, and a couple days after you discovered her body, someone attached a dick pic to an email you sent Sara?"

"Right, but the outlier is that the police are sure Sara's killer is the rapist. In fact, they're so sure that they're going to give a press conference about it tomorrow at noon." I told her what I'd gotten from Max Andrus, his upcoming article in tomorrow's paper, and that the rapist defiled his victims with toilet paper rods like what was done to Sara. I also told her about Sara's missing phone and computer.

"Sick bastard." Moira clenched her face, sat back into her chair and stared at me. She finally spoke after ten seconds or so. "You think there's a connection between the odd stuff that Sara Bhandari *thought* was going on at Fulcrum Security, the dick pic, and her murder and you're going to investigate whether you have a client or not, right?"

I didn't say anything because she could already read my mind. What was the point?

"And I'm guessing you came by here because either Leah doesn't think you should investigate or you haven't told her about what you're going to do yet and you need advice on how to be a good husband." She raised her eyebrows at me and flat smiled. "Right?"

She knew me well, but not well enough. No one knew me that well. If Leah hadn't taken my daughter and gone to Santa Barbara a week ago, I would probably be here for the reason she described. I wasn't a hundred percent sure why I steered my car toward Moira's house instead of my own. She'd been my North Star in times of uncertainty for the last six or seven years. Even after I married Leah.

I figured my subconscious had guided me to Moira because I was looking for confirmation. When it came to choices I made regarding my private investigative work, or choices I hadn't made yet, I looked to Moira for advice. Advice I didn't always take, but needed to hear, nonetheless.

"This isn't a Leah issue." I looked over her shoulder, not wanting to face her prying eyes.

"Then you came here because you want me to tell you to continue to investigate because, whether this is all connected to Sara Bhandari's murder or not, someone came after your livelihood and you want to stop it."

"And make them pay," I said just loudly enough to be heard.

"And make them pay." She squinted her eyes down. "So do I."

CHAPTER TWENTY-TWO

MOIRA SHOOED ME out of her house. She needed to get her paperwork done and make a few calls before she joined me on my quest. She'd joined me before. Almost always reluctantly, knowing the damage I could wreak when I thought I had justice on my side. She teamed with me in the past to be the brake to my accelerator and to try to keep me safe and out of trouble. Today she wasn't reluctant and her foot was firmly on the gas pedal. I just had to make room for her in the car.

I went up to my office when I got home and pulled up my case notes on Sara Bhandari's murder on my computer and added what I'd learned this morning at Fulcrum Security. The case I'd been paid to work, then not work anymore. After I was done, I deposited the check Shreya Gargano gave me into my credit union online with my phone. She'd told me to cash it even after she fired me and I couldn't afford to be gallant anymore when it came to money. Not with losing my Fulcrum Security gig and someone sabotaging my attempts to find new clients. Shreya was going to get her money's worth whether she liked it or not. Whatever I found, if that was anything at all, I'd take to the police. Getting them to listen would be the hard part.

Next, I called Fulcrum Security and got the automated phone system. When prompted, I punched in the numbers that corresponded to the first few letters of Dylan Helmer's name. I Google mapped

Fulcrum Security and looked for nearby restaurants or bars while my call was being transferred. A phone rang and was answered.

"Dylan Helmer, how may I help you?"

"Dylan, this is Rick Cahill. I need to finish the conversation we were having in the breakroom this morning."

Silence.

I waited. If she hung up, I'd just call back. She may have been weighing that possibility in her head. Thus, the silence and not a dial tone.

"I'd like to help you, but that's not something that's possible." Overly pleasant, possibly a code, like someone was close enough to hear the conversation and I was a Fulcrum customer. Probably the prairie dog.

"Let's find a time and a place where it can be possible." I scanned the area around Fulcrum on Google Maps. "There's a Starbucks across the 78 in the Nordahl Marketplace. What time do you get off? Five? Five thirty?"

Silence.

Finally in a hushed voice. "Five thirty."

Bingo. Dylan Helmer had more to say. And whatever it was bothered her enough that she'd probably be risking her job to tell me about it.

I pulled away from my desk and went downstairs. Midnight scrambled after me. He beat me to the kitchen door that led into the backyard, but waited for me to open it instead of using the doggie door. I led us both outside. He pranced over to the picnic table on the deck. Tail wagging, big open-mouthed Lab grin. He knew me well.

We both could use a break from the dark cloud hanging in our empty home. I grabbed a tennis ball off the table and tossed it twenty yards along the grass. Midnight bolted after it, snatched it in his mouth on the bounce, and pranced back, head held high. We repeated the simple, yet favorite, routine for a few minutes until Midnight dropped the ball on the grass mid-trot, coming back and growling, his head pointed at the house.

I quieted him, then heard the gong of the doorbell. I was tempted to let whoever was out there knock and ring all they wanted. The world could take a breath; Midnight and I were enjoying the afternoon. A knock on the door or a rung bell was rarely good news. But I'd found over the years that it was best to take bad news head-on.

The longer you avoided it, the worse the news got.

I put the ball on the picnic table and wiped Midnight's slobber off my hands with a towel I kept there just for that purpose and went inside the house. Midnight clung close to my side, ears and hackles spiked.

I looked through the peephole. I was right. Bad news.

I opened the door. Detective Skupin looked like he hadn't slept or changed his clothes since I saw him at Sara Bhandari's house three days ago. His partner looked better rested. The other detective I'd seen at the crime scene. Latino, early forties, short-cropped brown hair, lean. Looked like he worked out to stay in shape, not to bulk up. His slacks and blazer were tailored but, thankfully, the pants weren't skinny.

I was pretty sure I knew why Skupin knocked on my door. But not why he didn't call instead.

"Cahill." Skupin, weary.

Midnight growled. Maybe he sensed something worse than bad news. Danger.

"Outside." I snapped my fingers toward the kitchen and Midnight slunk away, through the living room, kitchen, and out the doggie door. He stood sentry outside the sliding glass door in the living room, staring inside.

"Detectives." I didn't move from the door. "What can I do for you?"

"It'd be easier to talk inside." Skupin. A frown below basset hound eyes and a multi-creviced forehead.

"Okay." I swung open the door and let the two SDPD homicide detectives into my empty sanctuary.

We walked into the living room and Skupin nodded at Krista's toys corralled in a playpen in the corner.

"I see you weren't lying about having a kid." He gave me half a smile.

"Why would I lie about that?" I folded my arms, splayed my feet, and didn't offer the detectives a place to sit.

Skupin sat down on the sofa opposite my La-Z-Boy anyway. His partner did the same. I remained standing.

"People lie for all sorts of reasons." Full smile now, but without any warmth. "Sometimes innocently. Sometimes not."

I didn't say anything.

"You wanna sit down, Cahill?" Skupin. "So we can keep this friendly?"

"Keep what friendly?"

"We're just here to talk." An extra wrinkle in his forehead. "Sit down."

I didn't like being told what to do. Especially from uninvited guests in my own house. Even if they were SDPD homicide detectives. But sometimes it was better to just play the game than try to win it. I sat down in my recliner.

"You going to introduce me to your partner?" I asked.

"Detective Ramos." Skupin.

I looked at Ramos. He kept his eyes pinned on mine. Like he had since I answered the door. He wasn't mean-mugging, just studying me.

"Does he talk?" I asked Skupin, but kept my eyes on Ramos. His expression didn't change.

"He listens." Skupin scooted forward on the sofa. "How about you tell us about your relationship with Sara Bhandari?"

Yep. I knew exactly why two homicide detectives knocked on my door. So did Madolyn Cummings.

"As I told you earlier, it was strictly work related. She was my contact with Fulcrum Security. I do background reports on potential employees for them." Did background reports.

"And you weren't seeing her on a social basis?"

"Nope. Like I said on Tuesday, she invited me for lunch last Thursday to talk about work. That's the first and last time I ever talked to her in person." I rehashed what I'd told him at Sara's house sitting in his detective car about Sara's concern regarding the missing files. I added what Dylan Helmer told me this morning about her files being in the wrong order.

"Did you keep up an email correspondence with her?"

Here we go.

"Only through work."

Skupin frowned. Ramos stared. The world turned.

"What about on the phone? Ever call her personal cell phone?"

"Only after I couldn't get a hold of her at the office this week when I was following up on a report I'd sent her."

"How did you happen to have her private cell phone number?" He made the word private sound salacious.

"She used it to call me last Thursday to set up the lunch." I kept my calm, even as agitation stirred inside me. "I'm sure you can find the call on her phone records, as well as the only couple calls I made to her cell."

"Did you have a casual, jokey kind of relationship with Ms. Bhandari?"

"We had a work friendship. We'd been conversing via email and occasionally the phone for two years." The heat started to boil out. But, controllable. "I didn't send her a dick pic and I never sent anything remotely indecent to her."

"Who said anything about that?" Skupin made a big show of being surprised. High school drama club overacting.

"I know you talked to Madolyn Cummings. She's been spreading lies about me to potential clients and I'm going to sue her for slander if I have to." My ears burned hot. "I never sent Sara anything disgusting like that. I can show you every email I sent her if I have to. But the fact that someone at Fulcrum faked them should make you curious about what's going on over there."

"Do you remember where you were last Saturday night?" Skupin, nonplussed by my mini speech, tried to throw off the question like he was asking about the weather.

"I was right here. All night."

"Can your wife verify that?"

"No." My face burned hotter. "She's up in Santa Barbara with my daughter visiting her parents."

"Oh." This seemed like genuine surprise. "When did she leave?"

"Last Thursday." More heat. The day was getting worse.

"The day Ms. Bhandari asked you to lunch." He didn't put a question mark on the end of it.

"My wife and daughter left about nine. Sara called me around eleven thirty." I stood up. "Anything else, Detective?"

"No. We got what we need."

"I hope part of what you need is the information I gave you about the odd goings-on at Fulcrum Security." I led them to the door. Skupin stopped when I opened it.

"Ramos, I'll meet you at the car."

Ramos paused on his way out and raised his eyebrows. His first show of emotion since I'd met him. Then he nodded to Skupin and left my house.

"Why don't you just come clean about you and the Bhandari girl, Cahill." Skupin tilted his head to the side. "So you messed around, that doesn't make you a killer. But the longer you hold out on it, the more guilty it makes you look about everything else."

"I thought your theory was that a serial rapist killed Sara." More heat and an edge to my voice. But a slow build, controllable. Not a CTE explosion of rage. "Are you now going to try to pin some rapes on me? My wife's only been out of town for a few days, not a few months. Pretty sure I'll be good on alibis for whenever they happened."

"Who said anything about a rapist?" Skupin's face showed some heat of its own.

"I've got my own sources."

"Stay the fuck out of my investigation." Face now full red. "Your kinky emails have already diverted too much attention away from the real killer's track. I told my LT that you're a foul ball, but your performance today doesn't help your case." He jabbed a finger into my chest. "Smarten up, Cahill."

Skupin slammed the door behind him.

CHAPTER TWENTY-THREE

I ARRIVED AT the Starbucks at 5:20 p.m. It was in a retail mall with big-box stores and a lot of empty parking spaces in San Marcos, just over the border of Escondido. The Starbucks looked like a Starbucks. A scattering of individual people in their twenties sat in uncomfortable wooden chairs and tapped on laptop keyboards or stared at their tablets or phones. The modern village square.

I bought a $2.40 bottle of water and sat on a wooden stool at a raised two-top table in the back of the coffee shop and waited. And waited some more.

Dylan Helmer finally walked through the door a little after 6:00 p.m. Her eyes found me right away and she walked back to my table, but not before she warily glanced around the coffee shop.

"Sorry I'm late." She slung a tan leather shoulder bag down into her lap. "Madolyn held me after work to talk to me."

"What about?" I asked after she didn't offer more.

I was pretty sure I'd been the topic of conversation in Madolyn Cummings' office. She'd ignored me while in my presence as if I didn't exist this morning, but glared at me when I escorted Dylan out of the HR office.

"She asked me why I walked downstairs with you to the break-room." Dylan brought a hand free from the purse clasped against her chest and fidgeted with a hoop earring.

"What did you tell her?"

"Mostly what you told me, that you asked me to take you to the breakroom because you wanted a Coke and didn't want to be seen walking around the building alone. And I said we talked about Sara and how sad it is what happened to her."

"That doesn't take a half hour. What else?"

"I had to wait while she talked to Buddy first."

"Gatsen?" The production manager seemed to spend a lot of time in the VP of HR's office.

"Yeah."

"Is that normal for her to have two meetings with him in her office in one day?"

"Not really, although he's been in there a lot lately over the last few weeks." She set her purse on the table and straightened her posture. The tension seemed to be leaving her body. "I think I'm going to get a latte. Do you want anything other than your water?"

"No thanks." I took out my wallet and pulled out a ten-dollar bill. I hoped lattes were less than that. My water was more than two bucks, so maybe I should have pulled out a twenty for the latte. I pushed the money at her. "Here. It's on me."

"Thanks." Dylan took the bill from my hand without argument. An honest person. I appreciated not having to go through the usual reluctant banter before the proffered money was finally accepted. She scooted off her stool and went over to the counter and returned with change a minute later.

"Back to our conversation in the breakroom this morning." I tried to make it sound offhand and as nonthreatening as possible. "You said the background checks in your files on those three recent hires were out of order. Did you tell Sara that at the time?"

"No." She frowned and glanced down at the table.

"Why not?"

"Because I wasn't a hundred percent sure. I didn't want to come off as paranoid or have Sara make a big deal out of it. I've only worked at Fulcrum for a few months. I need the job."

"But now you're certain the paperwork was out of order?" I knew memories rarely improved with time, but there were occasional exceptions. Was this one or did I want it to be so I could wedge in a confirmation that something was wrong with Fulcrum Security and my quest was not a fool's errand.

"Yes." Dylan nodded her head and stared at me. Studying me. I'm not sure what she saw. "Why are you doing this? None of this probably has anything to do with Sara's murder. Are you just investigating so you can feel good about taking Shreya Gargano's money?" Her tone didn't carry the accusation of her words. She seemed to be trying to figure me out without judgment.

The judgment could come later.

"I was looking into Sara's murder before Shreya hired me. I don't feel good or bad about taking her money." I air-quoted *taking*. "That's my job. People pay me for the work I do. Incidentally, Shreya fired me after she talked to your boss this morning. She told me to keep the money and I didn't argue. But I'm still working the case. If the police are right about the serial rapist, then I'm wasting my time. But if they're wrong, I'm giving them a head start they don't know they need when they finally realize they've been running down the wrong path."

Dylan's left eye slowly blinked and her head did a slight slow-motion nod. She believed me.

"Someone took the background reports from my files and then returned them," she said.

"Can you think of any reason someone would do that and who that person might be?" I had my suspicions on who, but not on why.

"First, regarding who, it would have to be someone with access to my files when I'm away from my desk." Some of Dylan's father's cop

DNA beaconed in her posture and voice. She sat upright and spoke with certainty. "One would be Sara, who we can rule out. The others are Bridget, who you bought the cookies for this morning, Madolyn, and maybe Buddy, because he's in the office a lot and works late. Mr. Boswell for the same reasons and the cleaning crew that comes in twice a week after we're gone."

Madolyn Cummings seemed like the most likely option, but I pulled out my notepad and wrote everyone's name down, including the CEO, Trent Boswell.

"What about the why?" The linchpin that had to explain the office intrigue that Sara got me involved in. The fuse she lit that led to her murder or trivial office politics that added up to nothing? And somehow led to someone trying to damage my career?

"That's the part I can't figure out." She sounded like she'd been thinking about who grabbed the reports, then replaced them, long before I asked her about them. "If someone wanted to take a look at the background reports, they could have just asked me or looked at them on their computer if they had access to the files."

"Who would have access?"

"Madolyn, of course, and any of the managers of the different departments who do the hiring. And Mr. Boswell."

"What about Sara and Bridget? Would they have access to your files on their computers?"

"No, only the managers of the departments do. Seems kind of stupid because we all do the same jobs. It's just a matter of who's assigned which prospective hires."

"Dylan?" The barista behind the counter.

"I'll be right back." She went to the counter and returned with something that smelled like coffee and had frothy steamed milk or cream on top. She took a sip and smacked her lips.

I picked up where I left off.

"Sara said Buddy Gatsen told you to use Leveraged Investigations for those three hires whose background check reports were missing then found. Is that true?"

"Not exactly. Madolyn told me to use them, but she said that Buddy had recommended them to her."

Slightly different from what Sara told me, but could have just been a shorthand to the truth.

"Is it usual for the Production Manager to make suggestions to the VP of Human Resources about which private investigative agency to hire?" I asked.

"It seemed a little strange. As far as I know, it's the first time they started using someone other than you and Brady Investigations to run background reports. Maybe Buddy's involved because most of the people who are hired work in production."

"Do you have higher turnover in production than the other departments?"

"A little, but that's the biggest workforce and we're taking on more and more clients."

"On the cruise ship and luxury yacht side?"

"No, defense contracts." She looked around the coffee shop, leaned forward, and spoke in a hushed tone. "But we recently got a contract with a big Canadian defense contractor for our new LIDAR system."

"LIDAR?"

"It's short for Light Detection and Ranging. It uses light in the form of a pulsed laser to map out terrain in 3D. It's very useful on the battlefield to locate enemy weaponry."

"You seem to know a lot about it for working on the civilian side of Fulcrum Security."

"My boyfriend was a Marine and used LIDAR on the battlefield." Her face lit up when she mentioned her boyfriend.

"What's different about your new system?"

"It's smaller, lighter, and more accurate. It's perfect for the new, more maneuverable drones."

"Is that supposed to be a secret?" I asked.

"No. There was a press release about it right after I started. It's supposed to be better than any other system available."

"The background checks for everyone hired to work on defense contractor projects have to be vetted by DCSA, right?" The government agency. "So, I'm guessing that wouldn't really affect anyone on the retail side."

"Actually, it does because Buddy likes to use workers who have already been working on our radar and sonar systems for defense contractor projects. The contractors pay more money than retail so it's a promotion for the workers who he chooses. They still have to go through DCSA background checks, but we have to fill their spots on the retail side, so we've been accepting a lot of new applications."

"Do you use Leveraged Investigations for all the background checks on applicants that you're responsible for?"

"Not all, but more and more now."

"Is that on Madolyn's instructions?"

"Yes." She took a sip of her latte and smacked her lips again. It must have been good.

"How long has that been going on?"

"About two months."

"Did she tell Sara the same thing? That she needed to use Leveraged Investigations?"

"I don't think she told Sara that she had to use them, but I know she told her to try them, and Sara did with one applicant, but she said they took longer than you did and the information wasn't as extensive."

"Did Sara have the autonomy to decide who to use for background checks?"

"I don't know, but after she complained about the work Leveraged Investigations did, I don't think Madolyn ever asked her to use them again."

Dylan was almost done with her latte and she'd glanced at the screen on her phone a couple times. Probably checking the time. Mine was running out.

Dylan had been more open and helpful than I could have hoped for. I thought I knew why, but wasn't a hundred percent. "Why are you helping me?"

She was about to take a sip of coffee, but set the cup down instead and looked at me. Studying me again like she had when she asked me the question about why I was investigating Fulcrum. Piercing green eyes squinted down into lasers.

"Because my dad was a policer officer and he taught me about right and wrong. He turned his partner and four other cops into Internal Affairs for extorting money from drug dealers. Instead of being honored for doing the right thing, he was ostracized by other cops and given a new beat in the worst part of town by his commander. He was shot and killed on a domestic disturbance call a few months later." Her mouth tightened, but her voice trembled. "There was an investigation into his new partner's actions, or lack thereof, that went nowhere. If my dad hadn't done the right thing and turned those bad cops in, he'd probably still be alive. But he always did what was right.

"Something not right is going on at Fulcrum. I've kept it to myself because I need the job. And I'm ashamed. I'm not acting like my father's daughter. Sara found something wrong and she didn't let it go. That's who I want to be. Someone my father would be proud of again."

"I'm sorry about your father. He sounded like a great man. My dad was a cop, too. I think both would be proud of you."

"Thank you." Dylan wiped a tear from her eye.

"Sara asked me to find out what I could about Leveraged Investigations a couple days before she was murdered. I didn't learn much about them, but what I did isn't good." I told her about Moira's experience with them, including the suddenly bad reviews from three supposed ex-clients. "And I'm pretty sure they went after me."

I told her about the dick pic, but used more delicate terms.

She didn't say anything for a while and I thought that I'd made a mistake by being completely honest.

"Who did Cummings have go through Sara's emails after she died?" I asked.

"She didn't ask me or Bridget, so she must have done it on her own."

"Who's your contact at Leveraged Investigations?" One piece of information that was tangible. A name. Something I could take a deep dive into online instead of dealing with gossamer supposition that dissolved when you tried to put your hands around it.

"There are two. Mark Fields and Jeff Grant." Bingo. Dylan Helmer was all in.

Mark Fields and Jeff Grant. I wrote the names down. Both common names that weren't memorable.

"Have you ever met them?"

"No."

I pulled up the photo of the guy from Leveraged who Moira'd tangled with. I looked at the blank canvas face and showed it to Dylan. "Have you ever seen this man at the office or anywhere else?"

Dylan looked at the photo. "No. Who is he?"

"He works for Leveraged Investigations, but I don't know his name. I was hoping he's one of the two investigators you deal with."

"I couldn't tell you if he's either one of them. Sorry."

"No worries." I smiled and patted her hand. "You've already been a big help. But I have two last asks. Would you be able to get into Sara's email and send me a copy of the email I sent her that has the added attachment?"

"I don't think so. Her computer is in Madolyn's office now and everyone's computers are password protected anyway. What's the other thing?"

"Can you get me copies of the background reports for the three hires that disappeared then reappeared?"

"I wouldn't feel comfortable making copies and sending them to you. Management can monitor my emails and you have to put in your personal code when you print something on the printer. Everything could be traced back to me." She frowned, then bit her lower lip. "How about if I text you the names and social security numbers of them instead when I'm back to work on Monday?"

"Perfect." I pulled a business card out of my wallet and handed it to her. "My phone number's on there. If anything else strange happens at work and you want to talk about it, call me."

"Thank you." Dylan opened her purse and put my card in it. When her hands came back out, she was holding another business card and a pen. She wrote a phone number on the back of the card and handed it to me. "That's my cell number. Please call me if you find out anything else or can think of something I might be able to help you with."

"Thanks. I will." I put the card in my wallet.

We both slid off our stools to leave.

"Sara was sort of sarcastic and hard to get to know when I first started working at Fulcrum." Dylan slid her bag over her shoulder. "But she helped me a lot with work and we were finally kind of becoming friends. I want whoever killed her to get caught and go to jail."

"So do I."

Or worse.

CHAPTER TWENTY-FOUR

THE NEXT MORNING, I grabbed the newspaper off the driveway barefoot in cotton workout shorts and a T-shirt. My newspaper delivery person—an adult in a car now instead of a kid on a bike—has yet to land a paper on the porch. Plenty under my car, though.

I took the paper inside and sat down at the butcher block island in my kitchen, my most cherished piece of furniture in the house, and opened it. Max Andrus's article made the front page, just above the fold. The headline read: "Police Intensify Investigation of Murdered Sabre Springs Woman."

I doubted Shreya Gargano and the rest of Sara Bhandari's family would be happy when they read the headline. It suggested that SDPD wasn't going full bore from the beginning. Which, despite my reservations with the direction of their investigation, was misleading. I never doubted their intensity in the hunt. But, the headline itself created a sense of urgency and the hook the paper hoped would grab readers' attention. It would have grabbed mine even if I wasn't already investigating Sara's death. Or knew her in life.

The second thing that may have bothered Sara's family was a picture of Sara below the headline. She was beautiful, or had been beautiful, and that fact would attract eyes, too. I was on the fence between thinking the photo was exploitative or beneficial. While the photo of a beautiful dead woman would attract readers to sell newspapers, it would also bring attention to Sara's case and possibly help unearth new information. A mixed bag that tilted me toward the side of beneficial.

Andrus didn't bury the lede in the article. He put it right in the first sentence: *San Diego Police Department Homicide Detectives investigating the murder of Sara Bhandari of Sabre Springs believe that her death may be related to a string of rapes that have been committed throughout San Diego County over the last six months.* He went on to mention the dates and places of the first three rapes but didn't name the living victims, which was the accepted procedure for the press. Thankfully.

Also thankfully, there was no mention of me or my supposed creepy emails. Maybe Andrus' source wasn't as tuned in to the investigation as I thought. Or, hopefully, Skupin and crew had already moved on from me.

In the article, Andrus also mentioned that the police concluded that all the rapes and the murder had similar M.O.s but didn't give specifics. There was no mention of the rapist's signature. Holding back that information was Crime Investigation 101. The police saved that to corroborate a confession from a good suspect during an interrogation and for a trial.

The best cops and prosecutors, the ones who were truly seeking justice, and not just a win, understood that confessions had to be supplemented with evidence. If they were able to break down the real murderer/rapist and get a confession, him admitting to his sick actions with the toilet paper holders would slam the prison cell door on him for life.

I put Detective Skupin in that class of cop. A justice seeker. We had our differences in the past and again with Sara Bhandari's death, but I knew he wasn't in it for the glory. Justice meant something to him. And so did the victims and their families. I just hoped I could get him to listen if I came to him with information that might not jibe with his serial rapist theory. Or have him listen to any new information at all. Sometimes my prior actions left scars on more people than only those I meant to injure.

Andrus mentioned that SDPD would hold a press conference at their headquarters on Broadway. I doubted the local TV stations would carry the news conference live. There'd probably only be snippets of it later on the nightly news. I wanted to see all of it, not just the parts a TV news director thought were important.

For the first time in my life, I wished I had a press pass.

Andrus didn't say where the press conference would be held at SDPD headquarters. Most of the footage of the ones I'd seen on television had been held in their press room, but a couple had been done outside in front of the building. If they did do it there, I might be able to get close enough to hear it. But I'd have to be incognito so Skupin didn't recognize me. I didn't want him to think I was meddling with his investigation. Or have him think I was worried about what the police might have on me. I was, a little, but that was secondary to what I wanted to learn about their serial rapist theory.

CHAPTER TWENTY-FIVE

AFTER BREAKFAST, I got onto an online pay people search database on my computer. Midnight settled in at his favorite spot under the desk. Familiar spots for both of us over the last couple years. But today felt different. I wasn't going through the mundane task of checking histories of Fulcrum Security and other businesses' potential hires. I was on the chase of an elusive target. And the information I found sitting in front of my computer would be ammunition I would use when I was out on the street tracking down the people trying to ruin my business and who may have had something to do with Sara Bhandari's death.

Mark Fields and Jeff Grant. Dylan Helmer's contacts at Leveraged Investigations. Not surprisingly, there were a lot of Mark Fields and Jeff Grants to search online. Nothing came up for either when associating them with Leveraged Investigations, San Diego.

I started doing individual searches on each of the Mark Fields. There were ten. One was seventeen years old and two were over seventy-five. Of the remaining seven, one was a choreographer, one was a teacher, a restaurant worker, golf salesman, cardiologist, grocery store manager, and the last was a retired cop. Bingo. Worked at SDPD from 1996 until 2018. The year 2018 rang a bell with me. I googled Leveraged Investigations and saw that their establishment year was 2018.

Private Investigator was the go-to second career for retired cops. I was one myself, although the retirement wasn't my choice and there was no gold watch ceremony or party at a cop bar with all my brothers and sisters in blue. You don't get those when you're fired after less than three years on the job. Or a pension.

I found a copy of Mark Wilson Fields' California Driver's License. Fifty-seven years old, six foot two, one hundred eighty five pounds. Lived in Santee, a city in the eastern part of San Diego County. His CDL photo didn't match the one Moira had given me of the Leveraged Investigation P.I. Made sense as that man looked to be in his early forties and not late fifties like Fields.

The narrowing down of the Jeff Grants was more difficult as all but one fit into an age group that made sense for a private investigator. No private investigators or ex-cops or any field that would be a stepping-stone to P.I. in the bunch. Electrical engineer, technical writer, high school principal, pharmaceutical salesman, web designer, and mailman. I had no choice but to pull up all of their California drivers licenses. None was a dead ringer for the photo I had of the guy from Leveraged Investigations.

I found Dylan Helmer's card and called the number she'd written in ink.

"Hello?"

"Dylan, Rick Cahill." I tried to sound cheery, like invading someone's weekend was something fun. "I'm texting you a photo of someone."

"Okay." She strung out the word in skepticism. "Who is it?"

"Mark Fields'. I want to know if you've ever seen him around Fulcrum Security or anywhere else." I pulled up the photo of Field's driver's license and texted it to her.

A couple seconds later, "He doesn't look familiar. You say he's the Mark Fields with Leveraged Investigations who has been running the background reports for me?"

"Pretty certain."

"Well, I'll keep an eye out, but I don't think I've ever seen him."

"Thanks. Talk to you Monday."

CHAPTER TWENTY-SIX

MOIRA CALLED ME an hour later.

She started right in without a greeting. Normal for her when she was mad at me or had information about a case we were working together. So, just normal for her.

"I found another P.I. that Leveraged Investigations stink-bombed, as you say." Her croaky voice was on assault rifle full auto. Fast and on target. "She was investigating possible intellectual property theft for a biotech company in town. The target was one of the company's vice presidents. He found out that he was being investigated and hired Leveraged Investigations. A week later the biotech company told my friend to halt the investigation. She told the company founder, the guy who hired her, that she thought the VP was guilty, but that she couldn't prove it yet. The founder didn't care and told her to stop the investigation immediately.

"Investigating for biotech firms is her specialty, but she hasn't gotten another contract with one of them since the founder of that company halted the investigation. A few weeks later one of her former clients who'd left his company told her that she suddenly had a bad reputation in the field. She never found any proof, but had the feeling that someone had put out lies about her to potential and former clients."

"That someone being Leveraged Investigations."

"No proof, but that's what she thinks now and so do I."

"Me, too. That sounds like their M.O. Not just blowing up a stink bomb on the P.I., but the client suddenly dropping her. Leveraged is all about intimidation and scorched earth."

"Yup."

"There's something else you should know." Moira was my partner on this journey. She needed to know everything. "Madolyn Cummings told Detective Skupin about the dick pic and whatever else I supposedly said on other emails. He stopped by my house with his partner yesterday."

"What did he say? Does he think you sent the picture?"

"Yeah, I think he does. You sure you still want to take this ride with me?"

"Hell, yes. Leveraged Investigations came after me before you. But I didn't put it together at the time." More edge on the rapid-fire words. "And Skupin's an idiot if he believes you sent that email."

Partners.

"What's the endgame if we can prove Leveraged is guilty of trying to ruin our reputations?" My knee-jerk reaction was vengeance and retribution. What that looked like, I hadn't figured out yet. Moira wasn't big on vengeance and her knee rarely jerked.

"We sue them. Juliet Fisher, the P.I. I just told you about is in, and I already talked to Angus." Angus Buttis, a lawyer Moira sometimes did work for and who let her use his office to meet clients. "He thinks, if we can prove all of this, we can sue for slander. Also, Juliet and I are putting feelers out to see if any other P.I.s have experienced the same thing. Angus thinks if we can find twenty of them, we could file a class action lawsuit."

"Twenty? You'd be lucky to find twenty licensed P.I. agencies in San Diego that earn enough to pay their bills. Even if you could come up with that number, how much money do you think a court could squeeze out of one agency? And even if we won, which is questionable at best, we'd have to split the money twenty ways, which probably wouldn't cover the cost of a lawyer."

"Class action or not, Angus would take the case on a contingency basis. And it's not about the money, anyway. It's about putting Leveraged Investigations out of business or at least shining a spotlight on their practices so people know who they are."

"Some clients are looking for a P.I. agency that uses those exact practices. This could ultimately give them the kind of PR that could help their business." I'd turned down jobs from a few people looking for those kinds of underhanded practices. Even when I needed the money.

"This is about doing the right thing, Rick." Older sister voice. "These people need to be stopped and I'm going to help do that. Are you?"

My late father, before he was kicked off the police force for allegedly being hooked up with the mob, lived by a credo that he verbalized to me when I was ten years old. Sometimes you have to do what's right even when the law says it's wrong. I didn't understand what that meant at the time. He was a police officer and was supposed to protect the law. Later in life, when I became a cop myself, I saw that there was gray between black and white. A lot of it. I finally understood what my father meant and adopted his credo as my own. But it had always been inside me, anyway. Transferred through my father's blood into mine and into my psyche by the actions he took. Nature and nurture, I was my father's son.

If Moira's right didn't pan out using the courts, I'd do what was right. My right.

"I'm in."

"Good, because it turns out that there might be more going on than just bad behavior." Her voice perked up. On the chase. "I've been trying to find out who pays for the lease on Leveraged Investigations' office in the First Allied Plaza building since yesterday. I contacted a friend in commercial real estate to get the answer and he's only been able to track it to one shell corporation after another. Holding companies that seem to be nothing more than a name. It looks like the one that the checks are written on is called Obsidian Holdings. It's located in Monterey."

"Mexico?"

"No, the one next to Carmel. You know, in California?" Talking to me like I was the dumb kid in class. I knew there weren't any dumb kids now. Just different thinkers. Maybe that's what I was.

"Yeah, I've heard of it." Monterey is located along the rugged central coast of California, four hundred–some miles north of San Diego. Just to the south of it is the city of Carmel, where I spread my late wife Colleen's ashes eighteen years ago. The central coast was an area we both loved and where I was able to filter some good memories past the lone bad one. "But I didn't know that it was a center of corporate high finance. Plus, I thought shell companies didn't have brick-and-mortar addresses. Just paper entities to move around anonymous money and limit tax liability."

I'd been paid by a third party once for services rendered. I didn't know at the time if it was a shell company, but later suspected that it must be. But the work I'd done for the client had been legal so I didn't worry much about it. Whatever Leveraged Investigations was doing may have been legal, too. But it wasn't legit.

"I don't know what kind of business goes on in Monterey, but the address for Obsidian Holdings is in a real building up there. Not some P.O. box. I looked it up on Google Maps." Moira rolling in the energy of the chase. "And according to my real estate guy, the checks for the lease on the First Allied Plaza office are from the Pacific Coast Bank, which is also in Monterey. Signed by a Mr. Samuel Chen."

"You ever hear of a P.I. agency having their office rent paid by a shell company?" Moira had been in the game over twice as long as I had and knew more about the ins and outs than I did. I tended to look straight ahead, one step at a time. Even if there was a brick wall in front of me.

"Nope. I've never actually checked up on an agency before to find out how the rent is paid, but I'm pretty sure all the ones I know of in town pay out of their own bank accounts here in San Diego with checks that have their own signatures on them."

"What did you find out about Obsidian Holdings and Samuel Chen?"

"I didn't find anything out about Obsidian Holdings. Just what I already told you. A name, an address, and nothing else." An edge of irritation ran along her voice. "Samuel Chen is a Taiwanese business-man who has dual Taiwan and U.S. citizenship and lives in Pacific Grove, which is right next to Monterey. Pacific Grove has some of the most expensive real estate in California. So, Chen makes a lot of money, but doing what is difficult to figure out."

"Rap sheet?"

"Only a single 236. False imprisonment. Misdemeanor. Probably pled down from something else. Something just short of sexual as-sault. He probably came on to a woman, got rebuffed, and wouldn't let her leave his house for a while. A high-priced lawyer gets a plea down and Chen avoids being listed as a sex offender."

"Charming. He and Leveraged Investigations are a good fit," I said. "They seem as shady as the dark side of hell. No history about the agency or testimonials on their website. No reviews. They have the least amount of information on their site that I've ever seen, yet they supposedly generate enough business to afford the lease on their office at First Allied Plaza, which is paid for by some rich CEO of a company that doesn't do anything through a shell corporation four hundred miles away. And there's no indication that they have offices in any other city, which might explain the third-party lease payment."

"I agree. And my radar says they're probably involved in some sort of criminal enterprise." Moira had radar, I had my gut. Both had helped us solve cases in the past. Sometimes together. My gut was used more often, but her radar had been more accurate. "But right now, all we have is that when Leveraged Investigations is involved, opposing P.I.'s tend to drop their investigations and have their reputations besmirched."

"Stink-bombed."

"Okay, stink-bombed." Older sister tone. "Have you found out anything new regarding Leveraged Investigations and Fulcrum Security that could lead to something criminal against them?"

"Not yet, but something funky is going on over at Fulcrum and I'm pretty sure Leveraged has something to do with it." I told her about my phone call with Dylan Helmer and the two Leveraged P.I.s whose names were on, then off, the background reports.

"She's one hundred percent sure about that?" Her voice conveyed her skepticism.

I told her about my internet searches and finding information on Mark Fields but coming up with nothing on anyone named Jeff Grant that would make sense as a private investigator.

"But this Dylan couldn't verify that the Mark Fields you found is the same person who is her contact at Leveraged Investigations?"

"No. Like I said, she's never met either one of them and didn't recognize the photo on Fields' driver's license or the photo of the guy from Leveraged you sent me." I texted her the picture of Fields' driver's license. "I just sent you a copy of Fields' CDL. You ever seen him before?"

"No, but he does have that cop look."

"Yeah, he's the best candidate for Dylan's contact at Leveraged from all the Mark Fields in San Diego I found, but I can't even say I'm a hundred percent sure. Nothing but shadows with that agency. What's your next move?"

"Continue to put feelers out about Leveraged Investigations with other P.I.s and then drive up to Monterey on Monday morning to have a talk with Samuel Chen. What about you?"

"I'm watching a press conference in about an hour." I told her about Max Andrus's article in the *Union-Tribune* and SDPD's press conference at noon.

"I read the article, too. The police seem pretty attached to the serial rapist theory." Wary, like she was getting ready to approach a delicate subject. "But you still think this business with the missing reports at Fulcrum Security has something to do with Sara's death?"

"I'm not a hundred percent sure of anything. I'm just going where my gut tells me to and pulling loose threads to see what unwinds." My turn to poke the bear. "My car or yours for the drive to Monterey and what time do you want to leave Monday morning?"

"You weren't invited."

"Well, I'm sending an RSVP anyway. These fuckers went after my livelihood. That can't stand. I've got a family to support."

"If you're coming uninvited, then you drive. Get to my house by five a.m. so we can get in front of some of the L.A. traffic."

"Roger."

"What's Leah going to say about you going away to Monterey with a cougar like me?" A tease in her voice that I'd normally welcome and poke back at with a snarky rejoinder.

"Nothing." My funny bone was broken when it came to Leah.

CHAPTER TWENTY-SEVEN

I CALLED MAX Andrus as soon as I hung up with Moira. He picked up on the fifth ring. Maybe he saw my name on his phone and needed time to make a decision.

"I take it you read the article." His first words to me. Nobody said hello anymore.

"I did. Congrats on the scoop." I wasn't sure what you were supposed to say in celebration to a reporter whose story made the front page.

"Thanks, but I'm sure you didn't call me to congratulate me on the story." His voice was wispy like he was walking quickly. "What do you want?"

I admired his directness, so I went with my own. "Can you get me a press pass for the press conference at SDPD today?"

I figured I could hide somewhere in the back under the bill of a hat and avoid being seen by Detective Skupin. Or any other discerning cop.

"You're kidding, right?" He didn't sound like he was in a jocular mood. "They don't hand them out like face masks at a hospital during the pandemic. You don't get a badge that says 'press' that you stick in the band of your fedora like a 1940s Barbara Stanwyck movie. You have to go through a process."

Andrus was younger than me, but he knew who Barbara Stanwyck was. Like me, he must have been a Turner Classic Movies buff.

"Meet John Doe?" I asked.

"Hmm. One of my favorites." His voice lightened and he stopped huffing and puffing. He must have arrived at his destination. "You're in luck, Cahill. The press gaggle is taking place in front of SDPD Headquarters, not inside it. You don't need press credentials to attend an outdoor press conference given by the police."

"Good to know. Thanks, Max."

"I guess I'll see you here, but good luck getting close."

* * *

San Diego Police Headquarters was located downtown on Broadway a couple blocks from San Diego City College. The structure was six stories of hard angles that the architect tried to soften by making the pillars outside the building and the lower panes of the numerous windows baby blue. It gave the building kind of a weird beachy vibe and made the whole police experience incongruent with the hard facts of a cop's job and the surrounding environment. Strangely, I kind of liked the look.

I hustled over from a parking garage to the press conference just as it was starting. There was a crowd of about fifty to sixty people grouped together on the cement courtyard in front of police headquarters. I stood at the back of the crowd, my Padres cap pulled low over my eyes and tried to blend with the other looky-loo civilians at the event. There weren't any chairs in front of the podium, signifying that the press conference wouldn't be very long.

A middle-aged woman in an SDPD navy blue uniform stood at a portable metal podium. Her ginger hair was in an old-fashioned bobbed haircut, sun-creased face like an aging surfer or a cop who served many years on patrol. She introduced herself as Deputy Chief

Connie Bristol in a husky voice. A phalanx of uniformed officers and plain-clothed detectives stood behind her. One of the detectives was Brian Skupin. He looked like he'd rather be anywhere else but where he stood. His normal resting expression.

"Thanks, everyone, for coming. The purpose of this news conference is to update you on the investigation of Sara Bhandari's murder and a series of rapes that have taken place throughout the county." She proceeded to introduce the eight people who stood behind her and their various duties.

One I took as a plain-clothed detective was actually a police spokesman. Two were detectives from the San Diego County Sheriff's Department. There was also a lieutenant from the Sheriff's department. Their inclusion must have meant that an interdepartmental task force was being put together. Each cop gave a slight nod as their names were announced. No hints of smiles. This was a somber event. The weather disagreed. Sunlight beamed straight down from overhead, casting no shadows, but bathing the event in warmth and necessitating sunglasses for us all. Even the deputy chief.

After the intros, the Deputy Chief talked about the extent of hours and overtime that was being dedicated to Sara's murder and the rapes. She was warming up to something. Something that might put the department in a bad light. I was pretty sure I knew what it was. And so did Max Andrus. I saw the back of his head in the front row of the press. He stood next to someone I was pretty sure I recognized, too. Even from the back. Cathy Cade from Channel 6 News. We had a history. Not a good one.

The deputy chief finally got down to the nuts and bolts: SDPD and the Sheriff's Department had just formed a task force to investigate Sara Bhandari's murder and its connection to a series of rapes that had taken place around San Diego County for the last eighteen months.

Heads turned and a murmur went through the press corps in front of the deputy chief. Eighteen months was a lot longer than the six Max Andrus had told me about. His hand shot up a millisecond before Cathy Cade's.

"Max Andrus, *San Diego Union-Tribune*." Andrus spoke quickly and loudly enough for the whole crowd to hear and to cut off Cade. "How many rapes have been committed and are you saying that they were done by the same person who murdered Sara Bhandari?"

He already knew the answer to the second question. That was a layup for Deputy Chief Bristol. Maybe a way to stay in SDPD's good graces while he asked the harder questions. The first question was because he was shocked by the revelation that the rapes had been going on for a year and a half, not six months.

"How long has the San Diego Police Department known that there's been a serial rapist victimizing innocent women?" Cathy Cade piggybacked on Andrus.

Others in the crowd shouted questions.

"Wait a second. Hold on." Bristol raised her hands, palms down, and maintained her command presence. "I'll take questions in just a minute, but we have more information to give you before I do."

A few more shouts, but Bristol stood resolutely until the crowd quieted down. Cathy Cade's question, as usual, had struck to the heart of the matter: Why hadn't SDPD alerted the public that there was a serial rapist on the loose for a year and a half?

Bristol gave out a task force hotline phone number then introduced Lieutenant Shames from the Sheriff's Department. He wore the olive-green pants and beige shirt uniform instead of his street clothes, probably to project authority. Shames had a dark cop mustache to go with his close-cropped dark hair. He said his department had been investigating four rapes that were committed in Solana Beach, Del

Mar, and two in Encinitas over the last year and a half that had a particular modus operandi that he wouldn't get into. The Sheriff's Department conferred with detectives at SDPD in the past few months and saw similarities in the rapes of three women in Carlsbad, La Jolla, and Pacific Beach over the last six months.

More buzzing in the press corps. Max Andrus's head moved toward the end of the line of the cops behind the speaker where the SDPD spokesman stood. I wasn't a hundred percent certain that's where Andrus looked, but the spokesman looked at the ground after Andrus' head turned in his direction.

Could he be Max's source? Wouldn't be a bad one if you wanted to know what the brass in the department was thinking. Probably less so for the rank and file. But the spokesman probably sat in on weekly, if not daily, meetings with the chief and other police brass. They, no doubt, gave him his talking points, but he was certainly privy to more information than he disseminated to the public.

If he was Max Andrus's source, he'd been holding back some information and Max's head turn was a not-so-subtle way of calling him out. I wondered if anyone else noticed. Of course, I could have been completely wrong and Max might have looked at someone or something else.

But I doubted it.

Lieutenant Shames finished up and threw it back to Deputy Chief Bristol. She stated publicly for the first time that there was evidence that one rapist committed all the rapes they just mentioned and that he could be responsible for Sara Bhandari's murder. She then opened it up to questions and called Max by name for the first one.

He didn't go with the question he asked earlier because Deputy Chief Bristol had already answered it. SDPD believed the rapist and the murderer were the same person.

"Why did it take so long for the police and the sheriff's departments to confer about the cases if they are all so similar?" I texted Andrus as he spoke. "Is there some sort of jurisdictional turf war going on?"

Andrus's head dropped for an instant. He must have looked at my text.

"Not at all." Bristol winced a smile and shook her head. "The Sheriff's Office and the Department have a long-standing history of working together. Detectives at the Sheriff's Office reached out to the department before any rapes with similar characteristics were committed in our jurisdiction. It wasn't until there was a rape in Pacific Beach that had similar characteristics as the ones in the North County area that our detectives realized that we were looking for the same perpetrator. The two agencies have been trading information for a while now and have formed the Coastal Rapist Task Force, as I mentioned."

"If I might follow up?" Andrus pushed forward as Bristol looked at Cathy Cade for the next question. "Sara Bhandari lived in Sabre Springs, which is significantly inland. Has the rapist expanded his hunting grounds along with now murdering his victims?"

The question I texted him to ask.

"Yes, it would appear so."

Bristol answered questions for the next fifteen minutes, then brought back Lieutenant Shames to answer a couple questions about the rapes that took place in San Diego County jurisdiction. Neither he nor Bristol gave up much useful information. The press conference seemed to me to be a defensive ploy. They knew that Max Andrus's article would be in the *Union-Tribune* that morning, which forced them to come out in public and show that they'd been diligently working the rapes and the murder. The press conference was for public relations and very little else. The only new news to the assembled reporters, including Max Andrus, being that there were a total of seven rapes committed, plus the murder of Sara Bhandari, over the past year and a half, not the three rapes over six months that Andrus told me about.

Jeremy Thalen, the SDPD spokesperson, stepped up to the podium after Bristol cut off questions. Thin, late-forties, short blond hair, gently receding. Gave off a metrosexual vibe and was immaculately dressed in a skinny-legged blue suit and colorful polka dot tie.

I should have discerned at first glance that he wasn't one of the homicide detectives who'd been lined up behind Deputy Chief Connie Bristol at the beginning of the press conference. No bags under his eyes and his suit was neatly pressed. The detectives all looked like they were wearing the same clothes they'd left on their bedroom floors the night before or they'd slept in the SDPD quiet room when they got their first three-hour nap in five days that morning.

Thalen introduced himself, gave the Coastal Rapist Task Force tip hotline number again, and told the media they could contact him with any questions about the case going forward. He shot a quick glance in Max Andrus's direction before he stepped away from the podium and went inside SDPD Headquarters. Or the glance might have been at Cathy Cade next to Andrus.

The crowd broke up and a man in a white T-shirt, cargo shorts, and a Padres hat off to my left caught my eye. He looked familiar, but I didn't recognize him. Late-thirties, early forties. Short brown hair below the cap, neatly trimmed sideburns. Sunglasses that blocked his eyes. No visible tattoos or a distinctive look. He could have been me off the clock. Or even on the clock working surveillance. He looked like a hundred thousand other men on the streets of San Diego. That's when it hit me.

I took my phone out of my pocket and pulled up the image of the guy from Leveraged Investigations that Moira sent me. I looked at the photo then back at the man, who was now walking down Broadway. The angle on the photo was three-quarters straight on and I only got a glimpse of the man's profile before he passed in front of me. He could have been the man in the photo. And he could have been just one of those other hundred thousand men walking the streets. The height seemed about right. Moira's stealth cell phone photo caught him coming out of the Leveraged Investigations office and the door was in the frame for reference.

If he was the same man, like me, he was at the press conference incognito. What did he have to hide?

He kept heading west. Toward West Broadway. So did I, fifty feet behind him.

CHAPTER TWENTY-EIGHT

I PULLED UP First Allied Plaza on Google Maps on my phone as I followed the man in the shorts and Padres hat, thirty feet behind him. First Allied was a straight shot about a mile down Broadway. The man's pace was leisurely. He stopped at crosswalks and waited for the red Do Not Cross lights to turn into white walking stickmen. He wasn't in a hurry. At one point, the man pulled a cell phone out of his pocket and appeared to be talking on it. After about a minute, he put the phone back in his pocket and continued his stroll.

I gave him plenty of space and he never looked over his shoulder like he was worried about being followed. No panoramic look when he stopped at crosswalks. I didn't think he made me. But if he wasn't the man in the photo Moira sent me, he'd never even consider that he was being followed.

We passed the Hall of Justice across the street on the right, which held the County Courthouse. First Allied Plaza loomed off to the left after fifteen or twenty minutes of following Padre Cap. A twenty-three-story wedge of a building, First Allied Plaza was a mishmash of materials, angles, and designs. Its structure was mostly made of steel and glass, but its first few floors were stone and cement and it had a sixteen-floor pale cement inset, plus a sloping roof, part of which was open scaffolding. The juxtapositions all seemed to work in a postmodern way.

I decided I was going to follow Padres Cap inside the building to be certain he went up to the floor that housed Leveraged Investigations. Except he went right on walking and passed First Allied. He crossed West Broadway going north on Kettner Boulevard. Three blocks later he turned left on Ash Street and walked a couple blocks until he arrived at the Waterfront Park Playground.

The playground had some jungle gyms for kids and a wide strip of lawn next to wading pools fueled by spraying water spouts near the cement walkway. The San Diego Harbor was in full view a few hundred yards to the west. A couple families with small children frolicked in the wading pool, while others picnicked on the grass and tossed Frisbees. San Diego's idea of bucolic. A pang reverberated in my chest. I thought of Krista and Leah and prayed my family would soon be whole again. Healed and whole.

I wondered where Padres Cap fit in. He walked to the side of the wading pool, sat down, and took off his shoes and socks and dangled his feet in the water. Now I was the one who didn't fit in.

The *Star of India*, the world's oldest active sailing vessel, was docked on the Embarcadero right across Harbor Boulevard. Sunlight danced along the water next to the ship. I kept walking and went onto the lawn and gazed at the *Star of India*. Just another sightseer.

I gave myself an angle where I could shift my eyes between the ship and the wading pool and not be in the direct line of vision of Padres Cap. I took out my phone and pretended like I was reading something on the screen and snapped a shot of him. Even zoomed, the picture was too far away for great detail.

A couple minutes later, I took out my phone again and pretended to be talking to someone. I sold the fake call by meandering around absent-mindedly as people do when they're in lengthy phone conversations.

I kept an eye on the man as I got deeper into my conversation with no one. A few minutes in, a woman approached Padres Cap. She was smiling, and he stood up to greet her. She was tall, wore sunglasses above sculpted cheekbones, had long blond hair, and looked to be in her late twenties. She wore blue slacks and a matching vest that revealed athletic shoulders like a tennis player. The outfit and her blue stiletto shoes looked like she was on her lunchbreak from a nearby office building. Or just walked off a model shoot for the young executive look. The two embraced and kissed the way couples do when they greet each other. There was a bit of an age gap, but who was I to judge? The woman looked at Padres Cap's bare feet and laughed, and he put his arms out to his side and shrugged. She hugged him, then picked up his shoes and his socks and they ambled off arm in arm toward Ash Street.

I followed them out of the park, no longer tailing Padres Cap, only exiting the park to reenter my day. The surveillance had been a bust. Mr. Padres Cap was just another San Diegan out for a stroll, not the nefarious man in the photo from Leveraged Investigations. I watched the couple get into a Tesla Model 3 in the parking lot and drive away, and cursed myself for not making better use of the last forty minutes of my life.

*   *   *

I called Max Andrus after I started the long trek back to the parking garage east of SDPD Headquarters where I'd left my car over an hour ago.

"I saw you made it to the press conference." His greeting. "Did you learn anything interesting."

I did. That SDPD spokesperson Jeremy Thalen was probably Andrus's contact with the police. But I decided to keep that under my fedora for the time being.

"How did you see me? I was behind you."

"After the gaggle was over, I saw you walking down Broadway when I was leaving."

"Were you surprised about the four rapes the Sheriff's Office is investigating and that the rapist has been operating for a year and a half."

"Yes. That was new information."

"Thanks for asking my question about this coastal rapist suddenly going inland and committing murder." I hit Kettner and turned right toward West Broadway. "Do you think that's kind of strange? That he'd change his M.O. twice on one rape? Change geographic locations *and* start killing his victims?"

"Maybe a little, but don't forget about the toilet paper holder."

"I couldn't if I wanted to."

The vicious signature of the rapist. The mention of it brought me back into Sara Bhandari's bedroom and her ravaged body splayed out on her bed like a depraved calling card. The six-inch circular rod protruding from her rectum.

Gruesome. Heinous. Malevolent. The stench and stillness of death. The residue of evil still in the room. The taste of decay from Sara's bedroom that day crept down my throat.

Death discovered in a confined space seeps into your pores and never leaves you.

I quickened my pace, pushing against an afternoon breeze, trying to cleanse my mind and body of the memory. I couldn't and never would. Just like all the other death I'd seen in my life, it never goes away. But time could blur the edges and distance the disruptions in my mind. Still, they'd occasionally spike into my thoughts as clear as the day I saw them. Every single one of them.

"Hmm, sorry." Andrus' voice softened. "But you know what I meant. The signature."

"I do. That's a hard one to overcome unless Sara Bhandari was killed by someone with intimate knowledge of the serial rapist's crimes." My gut, that weathervane that sometimes spun in the wrong direction, told me that Sara's death was tied to Fulcrum Security and Leveraged Investigations. Not the serial rapist that the allied law enforcement agencies of San Diego saw as the number one suspect. About 4,500 cops to one private eye. A former cop who couldn't last three years on the job. But the 4,500 cops didn't know what I did and their lead detective didn't want to know.

"What?" His voice pitched high. In tune. "Are you saying a cop killed Sara Bhandari and tried to make it look like the Coastal Rapist did it?" Seemed like Andrus liked having a nickname for the rapist. The media love nicknames for serial predators. Makes for great headlines and chyrons along the bottom of TV screens. Grabs your attention, your imagination. Your dark imagination.

"I'm saying someone who knew the rapist's M.O. and signature." My mind clicked in and I started walking even faster. The puzzle pieces were in front of me on the board, and I hadn't seen the connection until now. "Doesn't have to be a cop. Could be an ex-cop buddy who a detective on the case might bounce theories off of."

The photo from retired cop Mark Wilson Fields' driver's license billboarded in my mind. Retired in 2018, the same year Leveraged Investigations began.

"You're way out on a limb, Rick. Sara Bhandari's murder fits the Coastal Rapist's M.O. and signature. To a T." Again with the nickname.

I hit the corner of Kettner and West Broadway and saw the First Allied Plaza edifice across the street to the left. Leveraged Investigations. Mark Fields.

"Not quite to a T. In the rapes before Sara Bhandari, he entered the victims' houses while they were out and raped them when they came home." I crossed Broadway and headed toward First Allied. "Sara's phone was at her house the whole night she was murdered, until the killer turned it off and took it, so she must have been home when the killer entered the house. Plus, there's the location. Sabre Springs is fifteen miles from the beach. All the other rapes, including the ones that Lieutenant Shames revealed today, were all close enough to the coast to be able to smell the ocean from the crime scenes. And the most important difference, Sara was murdered. He left all the other victims alive."

"You were a cop, Rick. You know that serial rapists can graduate to murder. Look at Joseph DeAngelo, the Golden State Killer. He raped fifty women before he started murdering people. It's hardly unusual."

"Some do and some don't. But there are too many other issues surrounding Sara's murder. Loose threads that need to be examined." I decided against telling Andrus about what I'd learned from Dylan Helmer yesterday. I didn't want to put her job in jeopardy if Andrus decided to call Fulcrum Security and start asking questions. At least not until I absolutely had to. "Did you know of a cop at SDPD named Mark Wilson Fields? Served for twenty-three years and retired in 2018."

Andrus had written the article about me solving my wife's cold case murder in Santa Barbara in 2019. He was working the crime beat then. He was young, but I guessed that 2019 wasn't his first year on the beat.

"Maybe. I remember a homicide detective named Mark Fields. He used to partner with Detective Skupin who's heading the Coastal Rapist Task Force for SDPD."

Shit.

Skupin's ex-partner. The Brotherhood of the Blue. There was no way Skupin would even entertain my evolving theory if I put Mark Fields in the middle of it. Worse yet, Skupin might be Sara Bhandari's killer's unwitting source of information on the Coastal Rapist. I had to make sure Mark Fields the ex-cop was the same Mark Fields who worked for

Leveraged Investigations and emailed Dylan Helmer the revised background checks. And that he was the same ex-cop Skupin worked with. Fields was a common name. So was Mark. There was one way to find out if he was Skupin's partner. I texted the copy of Fields' driver's license to Andrus.

"Twenty-three years on the force. Why did he retire before he could collect his full pension? Was he dirty and Internal Affairs couldn't prove it?"

"I don't know. I think I remember some talk going around that he might have been dirty. I don't think anyone on the crime beat ever looked into it. I was new and didn't really know the ropes yet."

"I just texted you a picture of the Mark Fields I'm interested in. Is he the same guy who worked with Skupin?"

Silence.

"The driver's license picture is a little grainy, but I think it's the same guy. Why all the interest in Mark Fields?"

"Involved in an infidelity case I'm working. Trying to get all the dirt I can." I lied. "Thanks."

The Mark Fields I'd tagged as working for Leveraged Investigations had a possible source for information on the Coastal Rapist. The bad news was that that source was Detective Skupin.

I got off the phone with Andrus and entered First Allied Plaza.

CHAPTER TWENTY-NINE

THE LOBBY OF First Allied Plaza was sterile chic. Cement walls with twenty-foot-high thin light fixtures running up them vertically. Hard-lined geometric shapes on a huge accent wall. I found the listing for all the businesses in the Plaza. Leveraged Investigations was on the seventeenth floor. Not quite the penthouse but far from the madding crowd.

I didn't have a game plan. I didn't even know if Leveraged had office hours on Saturdays. The biggest agency in town, Brady Investigations, was open on Saturdays, but a lot of one-man or one-woman P.I. shops closed for the weekends unless they were working an active case. Even then, their offices would be closed. I didn't have a business office, so I was open 24/7. If I needed to meet a client, I had a booth available for me at Muldoon's Steak House.

Game plan or not, I got into an elevator and hit the seventeenth-floor button. I wanted to get a look at the office. Get a feel. A vibe, if there was one. A quick trip up and the elevator door opened into a foyer. The first office I saw was a law office that had a plate glass window in its waiting area. If all the offices had windows, at the least, I'd get a look into Leveraged Investigations.

They did and I did. And saw the young blond woman I'd seen with the guy in the Padres cap at the Waterfront Park Playground. She sat behind the receptionist's desk overlooking a small waiting area.

A coincidence that I just happened to see her at the park with her older partner who looked a lot like a private investigator that Moira confirmed worked for Leveraged Investigations?

If he wanted to attend the press conference because he was concerned about the progress of the investigation into a business contact's death, why the subterfuge with the ball cap and shorts and the walk past his office to the water park?

Because he made me.

He saw me at the press conference before I saw him. When he started walking back to the office and I followed him, he had to change it up. He didn't want me to see his connection to Leveraged Investigations. Even if he thought I knew he worked there, he wanted to try to convince me that two and two equaled five. He failed that test.

The Leveraged Investigations private eye who intimidated Moira's client and pushed Moira off her case had gone incognito to the press conference about the murder of Sara Bhandari who his agency had a connection to. Why?

The woman looked up and our eyes met. A micro flash of recognition in hers, then she tried to camouflage it with a pleasant receptionist smile.

Decision time. The woman recognized me. I was certain of it. But how? I didn't see her look my way when I spied her and Padres Cap at the water park playground. It's possible that she eyeballed me when she walked up to greet her supposed partner, but I doubted it. And I was wearing sunglasses that blocked my eyes in the park. I was sixty feet away from Padres Cap and at an angle, not behind him. If she didn't see me at the park, she had to have recognized me from somewhere else. My picture hadn't been in the newspaper or on local TV in years. And now I wore eyeglasses, which I didn't back when my face showed up in the paper or the news. Even if that was where she'd initially seen me, why would she remember me after so long?

She didn't. She'd recognized me because someone brought me to her attention. She knew who I was before the park. But why?

Time to find out. I opened the door to Leveraged Investigations and went inside. The belly of the beast was elegantly furnished in an understated way. Mahogany reception desk. Wainscoting. Textured coastal landscape oil paintings with adobe skies and rugged sea cliffs on the walls that looked like they'd been done by Kristen Schumacher, a rising star in the La Jolla art world whom I'd met at the San Diego Festival of Arts a couple years ago.

There was a nameplate on the reception desk that I couldn't see from the window outside. It read JASMINE STRECK. She kept up the polite smile. Her hazel doe eyes popped below dark prominent eyebrows and long blond hair.

"Hi, Jasmine?" I asked.

"Yes."

"Have we met before?" I gave her my friendliest smile. A creepy come-on for almost any situation, but even more creepy from someone fifteen years or more older than her. But in this circumstance, a legit question not meant as a come-on.

Her brows furrowed convincingly. "I don't think so."

"My bad. It's just that when you looked at me through the window, it seemed like you recognized me."

"Nope." Now tiring of the game, probably like she had many times in her life sitting in bars, the grocery store checkout line, or about anywhere else. Beautiful women are magnets to the male libido. Some are able to grow a hard shell to ward off such probes. "How can I help you?"

Hardened calcium.

"Is Mark Fields in the office today?" I glanced down the hall to the left, which I assumed led to individual offices and a conference room.

"No, I'm afraid he's not." A spark of triumph in her voice. She looked at me and waited for my next attempted disruption of her day.

At least I got confirmation that there was a Mark Fields who still worked at Leveraged Investigations matching the name on the background checks sent to Dylan Helmer at Fulcrum Security. A minor victory. I was tempted to pull out my phone and show her the photo of the ex-cop's driver's license and ask if it was the same Mark Fields. But that would be giving away too much. I'd be showing my hand, and that it was weak.

"How about Jeff Grant?"

A couple quick blinks. I struck a nerve, but she recovered quickly. "There's no one here by that name."

She was almost believable. If I didn't know what I knew.

"Not here today or no one by that name works here at all?"

"Would you like to make an appointment with one of our investigators?" The business smile again, like we weren't going through a game of tug-o-war. "The earliest I could have you meet with someone is next Tuesday. Would you like to fill out a questionnaire here or would you prefer to do it online at your convenience?"

"Oh, you mean there are no investigators here on Saturdays?" I put my hands on the reception desk and leaned forward, invading Jasmine's space. "What about the guy in the Padres hat you met at the water park playground on Ash Street about a half hour ago? Is he hanging around the office on his day off?"

"If you don't want to make an appointment with one of our investigators, I'm going to have to ask you to leave."

The gig was up. For both of us. I had to leave and Jasmine didn't even try to hide the fact that Padres Cap worked at Leveraged Investigations. Another confirmation. One that further cemented my belief that I was on the right track. Their P.I., who intimidated Moira's client, watched the police press conference about Sara Bhandari's murder incognito, then pretended that he didn't work at the agency.

Why go to the press conference? He could have watched the highlights on TV later that night. Did he just want to walk the mile to Police Headquarters for the exercise or did he go so he could see who was in the audience instead of at the podium? Searching the audience for someone like me.

He must have already known who I was. Was he there looking for me? Was he the one at Leveraged Investigations who planted the dick pic on my email to Sara? If so, he'd known about me for almost a week. Maybe longer. Why? Because something was going on at Fulcrum Security. Like Sara thought before she was murdered and what Dylan Helmer believed now. And Leveraged Investigations was somehow in on it.

They were dirty and I was going to prove it. But what would I be able to do with that proof once I got it? Detective Brian Skupin, lead detective on the Coastal Rapist Task Force, wouldn't be open to hearing a theory about how the private investigative agency his old partner worked for was somehow tied up in Sara Bhandari's murder. Especially a theory that Skupin may have inadvertently fed the crooked P.I. information that helped conceal their part in it.

And he certainly wouldn't want to hear the theory coming from me.

What were my options beyond the leader of the Coastal Rapist Task Force? Go over Skupin's head to his lieutenant? Maybe, but the thin blue line thickened up when there was information that could make the police department look bad. The FBI? Nothing federal at this point.

Max Andrus and the press might be my only option. At least at first. I'd worry about that, and what might follow, when I found the proof I needed. That I knew was out there. Somewhere.

"Thanks for your time, Jasmine." I turned and walked to the door but was stopped by Jasmine's voice.

"Who should I tell Mr. Fields was looking for him?" The triumph returned to her voice.

I turned to face her.

"You already know the answer to that question, but you can tell him whomever you want was looking for him." A little triumph in my own voice. "And you can tell the same to Jeff Grant."

I exited the Leveraged Investigations office knowing about as much as I did when I entered. But I replaced everything that had had question marks before my visit with exclamation points afterwards.

And, if the operatives at Leveraged Investigations didn't already know it before today, I'd shown them that I was on their tail.

And put a target on my own back.

CHAPTER THIRTY

LEAH CALLED ME around seven as I sat on the deck drinking a beer in the backyard.

"How's Krista?" I asked. Our daughter and Leah's interior design work were the only acceptable topics of conversation since she took Krista to Santa Barbara.

"She's fine. Mom and Dad are spoiling her rotten and she chases Spritz around the house all day." Spritz was the Landinghams' little white fuzzball dog. "She misses you and Midnight, though. She says 'Dada' and 'Night' a lot."

The edge I'd heard in Leah's voice on her infrequent phone calls over the last couple days had been smoothed down. Almost back to normal. That's where I wanted to go. Back to normal. If we got there, I had to figure out how to make it permanent. How to squelch the rage that went from simmer to volcanic with one wrong word or look. I had an appointment with my neurologist on Thursday. I prayed science could quell the rage and slow my inevitable decline into CTE dementia and death.

Leah might have been trying to cheer me up by talking about Krista, but it had the opposite effect. There was a vacuum in my soul that could only be filled by seeing Krista. Holding her in my arms. Looking into her sapphire blue eyes as they locked onto mine. Hearing her say "Dada." Leah telling me Krista said my name without hearing it live and that she missed me just reminded me of what I was missing.

"When are you coming home?" I asked. I could hear the need in my own voice. "The house feels empty without you here. Both of you."

"Thursday. Probably late afternoon." Her voice went soft. "We have a lot to talk about."

"Yes, we do. I'll be driving back from Monterey on Tuesday or Wednesday with Moira. She could drop me at your parents' house and we could drive home together."

"Monterey?" Concern. "What are you doing there? With Moira?"

"I'm not there yet. We're driving up Monday morning." Silence on the other end. So, I filled it. "We're working on a case together."

I didn't want to go into too much detail. Most of it would be hard to explain and Leah wouldn't approve of any of it.

"You have to drive to Monterey for a case? On a background check?" Her voice picked up momentum. "Do you have a new client up there? And why is Moira going with you?"

I'd sworn an oath to myself a year and a half ago that I'd always tell Leah the truth. I'd broken that oath in principle, if not in practice, regarding the progress of the disease and the depth of my rages. Lies of omission. Rationalized and justified, but I knew better.

"There isn't a new client and this isn't about background checks. We're following up on a lead and we have to go to Monterey. I can tell you more about it when I see you on Tuesday or Wednesday in Santa Barbara."

"I'm confused." Tension unmasked. "Is this a case that Moira asked you to help her with?"

"No. I asked for her help." Leah was used to me not telling her too many specifics about my cases. Even on background checks. I believed in P.I. client privilege. But I had a family I was trying to hold together. "Sara Bhandari, my contact at Fulcrum Security, was murdered last week and I'm looking into it."

"Murdered and you're looking into it?" A high-pitched jab. "Why? Aren't the police investigating?"

I promised to be truthful. Even when it hurt.

"Yes, they are, but they're locked onto one theory and not looking at other possibilities." Or so I'd convinced myself. "I'm looking into something they're ignoring."

"Why, Rick? That's not your job. Why can't you just leave it to the police?" Anger crowded in on the anxiety in her voice. "I'm sorry about this poor woman, but your job is not to find her killer. Your job is to work with whoever the next person is that Fulcrum Security assigns to you. Why do you have to get involved in a murder investigation?"

Why? A fair question. Why did I do what I did? Years on a therapist's couch might provide an answer, but I'd never been on one. I fought for people who couldn't fight for themselves. Surely, the therapist would conclude I was filling some emotional or psychological need. I didn't search for the why, I just did what I thought was right. I had to.

"I found her body." An edge to the defensiveness in my voice. "I'm going to make sure the right person is brought to justice for what he did. Like I said, we can talk about it when I see you."

"We do need to talk, but not up here. So, please don't stop by."

Leah hung up.

I looked forward to seeing Krista and Leah again soon. But I didn't look forward to the talk. I had a mea culpa to confess. I was ready for that. I had an obligation to tell Leah the whole truth that I'd put aside for too long. I'd deal with the ramifications as they came. But I feared it was something else that Leah wanted to talk about. Something new that I didn't have an answer to. Something that was completely outside of my control.

I couldn't wait for Thursday to come. And I feared its arrival.

CHAPTER THIRTY-ONE

MOIRA WAS ON her porch when I arrived at her house at 4:55 a.m. Monday morning. She wore jeans, tennis shoes, an ivory-colored heavy wool sweater, and a Padres hat. The hat looked better on her than on the guy at the park Saturday. And better than I did in the one I was wearing.

I had a Giants cap in the trunk of my car that would blend in better with the locals of the Monterey Peninsula, which was only a hundred and twenty miles from San Francisco. I had hats for all the West Coast teams for surveillance jobs from my old days as a P.I. Even some out-of-state teams for when I wanted to play tourist in my home town.

Moira traveled light. Lighter than any woman I'd ever known. She had a single sport duffle bag and a laptop case in her right hand and a coffee travel cup in her left. I'd left my laptop at home because I knew she'd bring hers and take meticulous notes.

Her duffle bag maintained its normal shape. It wasn't overstuffed with unnecessary fashion choices. Moira didn't do unnecessary. I hit the latch below the dashboard to pop the trunk and she deposited her bag and closed the lid. If I'd gotten out of the car to put the bag in the trunk for her, she would have looked at me like I was from Venus instead of Mars.

Moira required less maintenance than she had clothes in the duffle bag. She got into the car and grunted good morning. I did the same.

I pulled a folded check out of the inside pocket of my bomber jacket and handed it to Moira. "Your half."

"My half of what?" She took the check and unfolded it.

"The money Shreya Gargano paid me to investigate her sister's murder. Before she fired me."

"I can't take this." She pushed the check back at me. "I'm investigating Leveraged Investigations, not Sara Bhandari's death. If they overlap, so be it. But I'm in this to bring down those bastards at Leveraged. They can't be allowed to continue to ruin other P.I.s' reputations. Not in my town."

"I agree, Marshal MacFarlane." I ignored her hand and pulled the car away from the curb. "But you're helping me with my case, and we're investigating the same people on this trip. It's only fair. Keep the check."

"Life's not fair. You lost your main source of income because of some venal bastards at a P.I. agency. That's not fair." She ripped up the check and put the scraps of paper in the glove compartment. "You keeping all the money is more than fair. It's the only thing to do. You have Krista to take care of. My son is all raised and an adult now and making more money than either one of us. I'm not taking money away from that little nugget God somehow thought you deserved. I couldn't live with the guilt and I'm not going to let you lay it on me. You can pay for my hotel room."

Moira turned her head toward the windshield and looked out at the moonless morning.

The mention of Krista pulled a lump up into my throat.

* * *

The morning was pitch black except for highway light stands and red dot brake lights on the backs of cars I soon passed and the low beams of vehicles heading south on I-5. Sunrise was an hour and a half away and so was the beginning of L.A. traffic.

"Which way are you going?" Moira asked.

"What do you mean?"

"Are you taking the 5 or the 101?" California freeways.

"I'm taking the 5. It's quicker."

"By how much?"

I'd checked Google Maps after I deposited Midnight in my neighbor's backyard so her daughter could look after him as she often did when I lived alone and had to travel. Google gave the 5 a twenty-minute edge over the 101. We'd planned to make this a short trip so any minutes we could shave off travel and add to investigating were vital.

"Twenty minutes."

"Then let's just take the 101. It's not like adding an extra two hours by driving up Pacific Coast Highway. We could use a little scenery. I don't want to have to stare at your profile the whole time."

I had another reason for choosing the 5 over the 101, but I didn't want to verbalize it. And I didn't want Moira to nag me for four hundred miles as we drove up the monotony of the Central Valley.

"Okay." I'd handle my issue with the 101 the best I could. In silence.

I'd already given Moira the rundown of the SDPD press conference and my tail of the Leveraged Investigations agent on the phone Saturday afternoon. Moira'd agreed with me that Padres Cap had been trying to hide that he worked for Leveraged Investigations that day. Neither one of us was sure what his attendance at the SDPD press conference meant, but we figured whatever it was wasn't good.

We didn't speak again for the next forty-five minutes, examining our own thoughts in our heads. An easy silence that didn't need to be interrupted for the sake of small talk. Country tunes from Sirius radio's The Highway filled in the gaps.

Moira finally spoke after we were north of San Clemente.

"I learned some interesting facts about Obsidian Holdings and Samuel Chen yesterday." She turned toward me and I caught the excitement in her eyes. "There are three other businesses with the exact same address in Monterey as Obsidian Holdings."

"Why are you just telling me this now?" I turned down the radio.

"I wanted to give us something to talk about on the drive other than you pointing out your idea of landmarks along the way that I couldn't care less about."

"San Juan Capistrano coming up," I said. "Home of the mission and the returning swallows."

"Exactly."

"What type of businesses are the other three at the Obsidian address?"

"One is a real estate investment company called . . ." She took out her phone and pulled something up. "Celestial Shores Real Estate. Another one is called Enviro-Strategies, which has something to do with studying the environment. And the last one is Bio-Ethic Strategies, which, according to its website, consults biotech companies on ethics relating to research. That's the one that really caught my eye."

"Why?"

"Remember the domestic case I was working that the Leveraged Investigations guy shut down?"

"Yeah, Padres Cap."

"What?"

"That's the name I gave him when I was tailing him Saturday. He was wearing one."

"Whatever." She shook her head. "Anyway, the cheating husband I was surveilling was a founding partner in a biotech firm in Mira Mesa.

The firm had something to do with biofuels like algae. And, Juliet Fisher, the other P.I. I told you about who ran up against Leveraged Investigations, was investigating possible intellectual property theft by a vice president of another biotech firm."

"So, Leveraged Investigations, which has ended investigations by other P.I. agencies into executives who worked in biotech, has its rent paid by Obsidian Holdings at an address in Monterey where a company connected to the biotech industry is also located?"

"Exactly." Moira bobbed her head for emphasis.

"Is it possible that these other companies are located in different suites in the same building? I looked up the address online after you gave it to me and the building is part of a small office complex."

"I asked my real estate friend the same question and she assured me that all the businesses are located in the exact same suite."

"Is Samuel Chen's name connected to any of them?" Samuel Chen, the name on the checks that paid the lease on the Leveraged Investigations office at First Allied Plaza and the only officer listed with Obsidian Holdings.

"No, but the founder and CEO of Bio-Ethic Strategies is a doctor and professor at Taipei Medical University in Taiwan named Albert Chen."

"Chen is a fairly common Chinese name, right? That could just be a coincidence." Now I was being the cautious one, unwilling to immediately jump on a possible conspiracy. Role reversal. Or a by-product of my antagonistic relationship with Moira. We constantly played devil's advocate to the other's theory. Or it was just to be annoying, but ultimately, it forced us to narrow our focus on cases we worked together. Today reminded me how much I missed working cases with Moira. Cases that required putting puzzle pieces together and testing theories. And getting out of the office to investigate.

"Yes, but Samuel Chen of Obsidian Holdings is also from Taipei."

"I'm sure along with hundreds of other Chens who live in the city. It's Taiwan's capital, right? Probably their biggest city, too."

"This coming from the guy I have to constantly pull down off conspiracy theory ledges that pop out of his head every time we work together." Moira turned her entire torso to face me. "Wait, you're just being contrary to be a jerk. Aren't you?"

"The thought never crossed my mind." I smiled but kept looking straight ahead. "Only trying to keep you and your flights of fantasy in check. It's a full-time job."

"Shut up." She turned back and faced the windshield, but I caught the corner of her mouth turn upwards. "Even if there is no connection between the two Chens, it doesn't change the fact that Leveraged Investigations is being funded by an organization that is connected to the biotech industry and has intervened in cases where biotech executives were being investigated. And has tried to ruin the reputations of every P.I. it's gone up against who worked the other side."

"Agreed. Five years in business and Leveraged doesn't have a single review on any lists that I've seen." The top edge of the sky through my windshield lightened enough to foreshadow the coming sunrise. "Is it possible that the only clients Leveraged Investigations has are Samuel Chen and the entities he's associated with?"

"Certainly seems like a possibility. Hopefully we'll find out after we talk to him," Moira said.

"If that's the case, why is Leveraged Investigations hooked up with Fulcrum Security? They don't have anything to do with biotech."

"I don't know, but there has to be some reason. I think Leveraged Investigations is a criminal organization or just bent enough to work for criminal organizations."

"Agreed." I glanced over at her then back at the miles of freeway ahead of us. "And that means whoever hired them at Fulcrum Security is bent, too. They've been working with me for two years. With Brady Investigations even longer. Then, all of a sudden someone hires Leveraged to start doing background checks. Why? It's not like there aren't other, more qualified options listed online. Whoever chose them did it for reasons other than just hiring a new agency to run background checks. Something illegal."

"And that someone is the production manager, right?" Moira asked. "Billy something?"

"Buddy Gatsen," I said and tapped my breaks to match the string of brake lights on cars ahead. Orange County at 6:20 a.m. and the traffic was already backing up. "But I'm not certain that he's responsible. It could be Madolyn Cummings, the Vice President of Human Resources, too. Or both. Sara thought Gatsen was responsible, but Dylan Helmer thinks it could have been Cummings."

"Whoever made that decision, on its face, it's not criminal," Moira said. "A corporation can hire whoever they want for whatever reasons they want as long as what they're doing is legal."

"Radar, sonar, and LIDAR." It was starting to make sense.

"What are you talking about?" Moira's cheeks pinched up into a squint. "And what's LIDAR?"

"Light detection and ranging." I told her about the technology Dylan had explained to me. "It uses pulsating laser light to measure the exact distance away an object is on the earth's surface. I imagine it would come in handy for military weapons systems. Fulcrum has contracts with the Department of Defense for their radar, sonar, and LIDAR systems. These are different from their civilian products and I'm sure contain proprietary information that U.S. adversaries, like China for instance, would like to get their hands on."

"Somebody got smart all of a sudden. Not like everybody says." A smirk in her voice. Nonetheless, an internal hat tip from me for the nod to Fredo in *Godfather II*. "But are you maybe jumping the gun here because the guy paying the bills for Leveraged Investigations is Chinese? You know, Taiwan is its own country and an ally to the U.S."

"China doesn't think so. The scenario fits. I'll bet the one thing Fulcrum Security has that's worth Samuel Chen and his shell corporation getting involved in are military secrets. And hell, we know China has spies all over the world. They even had one sleeping with a U.S. congressman. You don't think it's possible they have one who's a Taiwanese American businessman?"

"You don't think we have spies all over the world?"

"I know we do, and if they're involved in Sara Bhandari's death, I'm going to find them and bring them to justice. But I doubt that's the case here. Radar, sonar, and LIDAR. Those are keys. It makes too much sense. And it has to be connected to one or all of the three new hires at Fulcrum that Leveraged Investigations did the background checks on. The ones that were missing then found."

"Is there any way to find out?"

"I don't think so. Dylan said the original reports weren't attached to the new ones like they're supposed to whenever a report is revised."

"Wait a second." Moira shook her head. "I remembered that when you first started working with Fulcrum you told me that you were only allowed to do background checks for their civilian side. Yachts and cruise ships. That some U.S. agency handles all the background checks on employees that work on defense contracts."

"Right, the DCSA."

"And the three new hires with the wonky background check reports were for the civilian side, right?"

"Yes."

"Then that shoots a hole right through your international intrigue theory. The new hires wouldn't even have access to the defense contractor side. Right?"

"In theory, but someone went to a lot of trouble to replace those background check reports. Why?"

"I don't know, but cool your jets, James Bond. Let's follow the leads we have before we cause an international incident." Moira reclined her seat, toed off her shoes, and put her feet on the dashboard. Her short legs left her plenty of room. She pulled the brim of her Padres cap down over her eyes. "I'm going to take a little nap. I didn't get to sleep until after one this morning. Wake me before you decide to nuke China."

"Will do, Moneypenny."

"Shut up."

CHAPTER THIRTY-TWO

I LEFT THE music low and swallowed the expletives I wanted to shout at drivers who concentrated more on their cell phones than the road and made the traffic even worse. Occasionally a purred snore would come from Moira until she shifted her position. They were barely audible over the music and road sounds. Midnight's nightly snorts at the foot of my bed were much louder.

My phone rang through my car's entertainment system at 7:05 a.m. Dylan Helmer. Moira woke up, wiped her mouth, and looked at me. I answered the phone on speaker through the car.

"Rick, it's Dylan." Energy crackled from her voice. "I'm texting the names and social security numbers of the three new hires that Leveraged Investigations did the background reports for. But I found something else."

The speaker pinged the arrival of her text.

"Are you in the office?"

"Yes, but there's no one else here."

"What did you find?"

"Something I didn't notice at first. Jeff Grant was the name on the background reports on the three recent hires when they were emailed to me. I'm sure of it. But I just checked them and the name's been changed to Mark Fields on all of them. On both my hard copies and the ones stored in our computer system."

The ping along my spine echoed in my ears.

"Are you sure?"

"Yes."

"Could Fields have sent revised reports in place of Grant's earlier ones and they went to someone else in your department, maybe Madolyn, and she replaced them in your files?" A rare occurrence for me when doing background checks, but I'd revised reports a couple times as I learned new information. I did it on the last week that Sara was in the office. The last week of her life.

"I really doubt it. Someone would have told me about it and only Madolyn or someone else in upper management would have been able to access my computer files." Concern clung to her words in a hushed echo. "And even if someone did put a revised report in my files, they would have attached it to the existing one. That's the procedure we're supposed to follow with any revised reports or new ones."

"And the name Jeff Grant isn't on any other background checks or any other emails?"

"No."

"Why do you think someone would replace the reports or change the name of the person who sent the originals?"

She was quiet for ten, fifteen seconds. Finally, "Because they didn't want Jeff Grant to be affiliated with the reports?"

More of a question than an answer, but the same one I came up with.

"If you looked over the report, do you think you could tell if anything had been changed?"

"I already did. I can't swear to it, but I think all the information is the same."

"Could someone at Leveraged Investigations have re-sent the reports and attached Fields' name to them so that he'd be the person for anyone in Fulcrum HR to follow up with?"

"They could have, but that wouldn't explain why there isn't a copy of the first report in my hardcopy files or my electronic files in our computer system. Someone here had to replace them and delete the old reports."

"And the person it makes most sense for that to be is Madolyn Cummings?" I made it a question, even though in my mind it wasn't.

"Yes." A reluctant whisper. "But I don't think she'd do something like that. She'd tell me about the new reports and attach them to the old ones. She does everything by the book. And she's . . . she's just not like that. Madolyn's a very honest person. I like her and she's been very fair to me."

"But something in your gut, in that cop DNA inside you, is telling you that something's off at Fulcrum Security and you don't trust Cummings enough to ask her about it."

"It could be anyone in upper management who has access to the online files." Fighting for her boss.

"But they're not in your office every day twenty feet from your desk."

"Buddy's been in there a lot lately and he's the one who suggested we start using Leveraged Investigations."

"So says Madolyn." I let go a relaxed breath. "Look, we don't know why someone changed the background reports, only that they did. There could be an innocent explanation, but we need to find out who did it and why. You wouldn't be talking to me right now if you didn't want the same thing I do. Right?"

"Yes."

"And we will figure it out. In the meantime, keep using those cop instincts you got from your dad. But be careful. I'll be in touch."

"I will." Not as resolute as her words. The call ended.

I took a quick glance at my phone and the three names Dylan texted me.

Charles Alfred Parme, Andrew Thomas Burke, and Milton Joseph Aksne. The names meant nothing to me.

"You want to get started on the three hires that Leveraged did the background checks on?" I handed Moira my phone with Dylan's text message still on the screen.

She took the phone then pulled out her computer from her backpack on the floor of the passenger seat. She typed a few things into her computer, handed me back the phone, and continued to peck at her laptop keyboard.

"Hotspot?" I asked.

"Huh?" She looked over at me.

"Getting an online connection on your laptop from your iPhone?"

"Duh."

"Anything interesting?"

"You're interrupting my flow. I'll let you know if I find anything." An annoyed look and a pause. "When I'm finished."

"You make long drives fun."

"Shut up."

Neither of us said anything for the next half hour or so.

As the exit to the 101 Freeway approached, I thought about just staying on the 5 like I originally planned. Moira was right, the 101 was much more scenic than the 5 and, in the current traffic according to the GPS on the entertainment center on the dashboard, only nineteen minutes slower.

But the 101 had one big negative to me. It passed through Santa Barbara. The urge to stop by Leah's parents' house and see her and Krista would tug at me. I hadn't seen either of them, except for a few Skype calls, in almost two weeks. The longest I'd been away from either since Krista was born before this was five days.

I only had to wait three more days until I got to see them both again. Stopping by today would be a mistake. Leah had been clear about not going to the house. She wanted to see me on her timeline, not mine. She needed the extra time to let the anger dissipate. But I wanted and deserved to see my daughter. And my wife. On my timeline. But I'd wait.

Seeing them both meant Leah and I would have to talk about my progressive disease. And she said there was something she wanted to talk to me about.

I took the exit onto the 101 and decided to risk temptation. Santa Barbara was only a few exits on the highway. They'd go by quickly. At seventy-five miles an hour.

CHAPTER THIRTY-THREE

MOIRA FINALLY LIFTED her head up from her laptop. The sun was up outside the car, but camouflaged by the heavy marine layer that gave the morning a gray tinge. The ocean spread out to the horizon on the left, rolling hills tight above the freeway on the right.

She'd spent the last ninety minutes tapping away on her laptop, running her own background check on the three Fulcrum Security employees who'd been the subjects of the missing background reports. Using their social security numbers to dig up what she could online.

"Where are we?" Moira tipped up the bill of her cap and looked past me at the ocean.

"Ventura."

"Oh, yeah. This is where we get closest to the ocean." She tucked her feet up underneath herself. "I drove up to San Luis Obispo to visit Luke a couple times when he was in school. Seems like a long time ago now."

A wistfulness to her voice. Moira's relationship with her only child had been rocky ever since her husband died of a heart attack ten years ago when Luke was fifteen. Moira hid the turmoil from me until the emotion all came boiling out eighteen months ago when Luke got involved in a dangerous situation. A vulnerability I'd never seen in her before. A vulnerability I'd foolishly thought couldn't exist. Not in steel-spined Moira.

We're all vulnerable no matter how hard we work to hide it. Now, as a father, that vulnerability was tattooed onto my heart. I'd felt it more in the last twelve days than at any other time in my life. Even more now than when I was a scared kid with a distant mother and a father crumbling to sand right in front of me.

But I kept moving forward. Forward momentum wasn't a cure to vulnerability, but it helped ease the anxiety that came from it. Even as my mind slipped into the past, I moved forward. It had taken me over a decade after the death of my first wife to learn that lesson, but I'd made it my life's propulsion. Forward. Always forward.

"Anything interesting about the three guys background-checked by Leveraged Investigations?" I finally asked since Moira didn't volunteer.

"Potentially. Charles Parme and Milton Aksne have both worked in factories assembling electronic products for years. A lot of background material to wade through. They check out." She turned in her seat and faced me as I drove along the coast. "Andrew Burke is a systems analyst and his history is less dense and dead-ends in 2004. Just his birth certificate before then. Born on March 20, 1987, to Tony and Maryanne Burke in San Pedro, California. He graduated from Stanford in 2007 and had a handful of computer programming–type jobs in the Bay Area. The last, before Fulcrum Security, was as a systems analyst for three years for a now defunct Silicon Valley startup called SeaSonic that was supposed to be developing some new sonar that didn't interfere with whale sonar. It went out of business last year."

"Did you get anything from his former employers?"

"I sent them emails, but no one replied yet." She turned back and faced the road. "It's still early, in case you haven't noticed. But the email I sent to the whale sonar place bounced back, which makes sense since they went out of business."

Moira spent the next half hour commenting on the scenery, justifying her choice to take the 101. When we passed into Santa Barbara County and veered slightly inland toward Carpenteria, my heart shifted into a higher gear. Fifteen minutes outside of Santa Barbara. I took a sip from my water bottle in the console to coat my dry mouth.

Santa Barbara had good memories for me. Where I married my first wife, Colleen. Where I fulfilled the goal I'd had ever since my father died. To become a cop. And, later, where I met Leah. But bad memories outweighed the good. Santa Barbara. Where Colleen was killed and I was arrested for her murder. Where the Brotherhood of the Blue turned against me. Where I failed Colleen irrevocably and defiled our marriage the night she died.

And now where Leah fled with my daughter to get away from me.

I stepped on the gas and pushed the car up to eighty-five, weaving through traffic on the two-lane northbound highway. Racing past exits I knew too well.

"Wow." Moira straightened in her seat. "You trying to make up time for not taking the 5? Twenty minutes is not going to kill us."

I didn't say anything and continued to weave as I got closer and closer to the exit that led to Leah's parents' house. I whipped past the West Mission Street off-ramp. Los Positas was a mile and a quarter ahead. I eased off the gas a quarter mile south of Los Positas. The exit sign loomed on the side of the highway. My hands gripped the steering wheel. A few hundred feet more and Leah and Krista would be in my rearview window until Thursday. Forward, always forward.

I whipped the car across traffic, cut off a driver in the slow lane, and took the Los Positas exit.

"What the hell?" Moira jammed her hands against the dashboard and shouted above the blaring car horns. "What are you doing?"

"Going to see my daughter." My voice, tight in my throat. My lungs short on air.

"What? Krista is in Santa Barbara?" She shifted to face me. I turned left onto Los Positas at the light. "Is she visiting her grandparents?"

"Yes. She and Leah are at Leah's parents' house." The words were sharp and brittle in my mouth.

"Why didn't you just tell me we were going to visit them instead of the stealth bullshit and scary driving? I don't mind."

Moira deserved an explanation, but I wasn't ready to give her the messy details. Just the results.

"Leah took Krista up here almost two weeks ago." Guilt and shame clung to my voice.

"Oh." For all her brashness and direct inquiry, Moira knew when to let what was written between the lines speak for itself. One of the reasons we were friends. Best friends.

A couple minutes later I turned onto Portesuello Avenue, drove up the hill, and stopped in front of the driveway that led up to the Landingham ranch-style home on a bluff. I let the car idle and looked at Leah's Ford Escape parked in the driveway. The marine layer still washed the morning in gray.

"Does she know you were coming up?" Moira read the situation perfectly.

"No." I let go a long breath. "And she probably doesn't want to see me. She and Krista are driving home Thursday."

We sat in silence with the car idling for another minute.

"Well, what do you want to do?" Moira finally asked.

"I want to see my daughter."

"Then you should."

I pulled into the driveway, punched off the ignition, and took out my phone and texted Leah.

I'm outside in the driveway with Moira.

HERE?

Yes. I wanted you to know before I knocked on the door.

You can't come in. Krista's still asleep. We shouldn't wake her.

Why is she still asleep?

Krista usually woke up around 7:30 a.m. It was 8:25 a.m.

She caught a little cold and was up late last night.

I need to see her.

Wait outside.

"You should probably wait here," I said to Moira.

"No problem." She nodded and patted my leg. "Take as much time as you need."

I got out of the car and walked over to the covered red brick porch.

The front door opened immediately. Leah stood holding the door. Anger in her blue eyes. Her mouth, a tight line. She wore shorts. And a T-shirt. One of mine that she sometimes slept in. The T-shirt sent a warm pang to my heart. Even with her anger up front now and the residue of it from twelve days ago, she'd taken a little piece of me with her. And wore it close to her skin.

I ached to see Krista. But I ached for Leah in a different way. In many ways. Leah had given my life a second chance. And given us both Krista. We were a family, the three of us, and we needed to be together.

"Hi." I fought the urge to touch her arm. To pull her close. To feel her against me.

"Hi." The tension around her mouth loosened a fraction. "Why didn't you tell me on the phone the other night that you were planning on stopping by here?"

"I just decided five minutes ago. I planned to drive up the 5, but Moira wanted to take the scenic route. I thought I could drive through Santa Barbara without stopping. Drive right by my family who I haven't seen in almost two weeks. I couldn't. Not when you and Krista were within reach. I had to see you. See you both. I miss you."

Leah let out a breath and stepped out onto the porch, closing the door behind her. Her shoulders slumped. Her eyes glistened with moisture. Dazzling even in pain.

"You think this has been easy for me?" Her voice quavered and I again wanted to reach out and touch her. But we were on her timetable, not mine. "I miss you too, be we can't go on with you shutting me down all the time. Married couples need to talk things out. Whenever I want to discuss something, even some tiny disagreement we're having, you freak out and storm off in the car or go into the garage and pound your punching bag. Your face turns red and your eyes . . . your eyes . . . so much anger. I don't even recognize you. It frightens me. I can't sleep in the same bed with someone I'm scared of. What's going on? Why won't you talk to me?"

"I'm sorry. About the anger and shutting you down. About everything. I know it's not fair and I need to fix it. But . . ." All the energy left my body. Staying upright took all the strength I had left. "The CTE is getting worse. A rage comes over me that I can't control. I have to leave when it happens. To go away. I . . . I'm afraid of what might happen if I stay."

Leah wrapped her arms around her chest and her torso edged backwards. Away from me. Unconsciously. A reflex. Survival instinct.

"What about medication? Is there something you can take?"

"I've been taking Prozac and mood stabilizers, but they stopped working." I blinked away tears welling in my eyes. "They made me listless and I had a hard time concentrating when I was working on the computer. When I got angry, my adrenaline burned right through them and I'd be just as agitated as before I started taking them. I'm scheduled to see Doctor Andrews on Thursday. I'm hoping we can try something else."

"Why did you hide this from me?"

"I didn't want you to worry." My voice caught. "And I was embarrassed."

Tears ran down Leah's face. I grabbed her and pulled her toward me. She collapsed into me. Huffing breaths and tears on my neck. My own tears slipped from my eyes. I tucked my head against hers and held her body against mine.

She was my lifeline. Krista, my eternal flame. Together, my reason to live. To battle the rage and the brokenness of my soul.

Life had been cruel to Leah. Her sister, Krista, our daughter's name-sake and my training officer when I'd been a cop, had been killed four years ago. And then Leah fell in love with me.

I was imperfect like everyone else who'd ever walked the earth, but one. More imperfect than many. I'd done evil cloaked in the shroud of righteousness. Just like many others. But I wasn't evil. Broken but worth redeeming. I deserved to be happy and I deserved to be married to Leah. But there was a time bomb ticking inside me that neither Leah nor I knew about when we fell in love.

My disease may or may not have been fair. I'd lived a life of violence, first through sports, then as a cop, and finally as a private investigator. Knowing what I know about the disease now, CTE was a likely out-come. Maybe its sudden progression was unfair, but every sane adult knew life wasn't fair. Its unfairness manifests itself differently in ev-eryone's life. But mine had splashed over onto Leah and that could have been avoided if I'd known I had the disease earlier. Now my life's sentence was hers, too. She'd accepted me with my faults and loved the good in me. But she was stuck to deal with what she hadn't known.

Even if we didn't stay together, I was the father of her child and my decline would affect Krista.

"We'll find a way to get through this." Leah pulled her head back and looked at me. The sparkle of her beauty gashed a whole in my heart. "But you need to be honest with me. About everything. I need to know how the disease is progressing. You can't keep hiding things from me."

"I know. There are some things I need to tell you, but I have to see Krista." I put my hands on Leah's shoulders. "Even if I just get a glimpse of her sleeping. I need to see her."

"Okay." She took my hand in hers, opened the front door, and led me into the foyer.

CHAPTER THIRTY-FOUR

THE KITCHEN AND living room were to the right, the bedrooms to the left. Leah's parents, Spence and Myriam Landingham, sat at the kitchen table in bathrobes with coffee mugs in front of them. Not a hello or a smile from either. Not even a head nod. Slightly cooler than normal. They didn't like me and never had. Only after the birth of Krista did they put a façade on their hostility.

Leah led me down the hallway to Krista's bedroom. The door was ajar and I could see the back of Krista's head through the slats in her crib. The same model crib as the one in her bedroom at home.

I quietly nudged the door open and walked inside. Leah put her index finger up to her lips. As much as I wanted to hold Krista, ached to hold her, it wouldn't be fair to wake her. To show up after being away from her for so long and then quickly disappear again would be too confusing to her. I needed to see her for my own sanity, but I wasn't so selfish that I'd risk possibly traumatizing her just to hold her in my arms.

I edged toward the foot of the crib to get a look at her face, which was turned toward the wall. She slept on her tummy. A tiny pink blanket, matching the one at home, was wedged under her arm. I stood still and watched her sleep like I did in the early morning hours at home. Her little puckered lips open, her tangle of fine dishwater blond hair matted to her head. The quiet wisps of her breath. My heart filled up and warmth spread throughout my body. Finally, I was whole again.

I stood entranced until a hand grabbed my arm and gently pulled. I turned my head and saw Leah. I'd forgotten she was there. Concern in her eyes as she tugged harder on my arm. I took one last look back at Krista, then relented and let Leah lead me out of the room.

Leah led me down the hall into her childhood bedroom. The room where we slept together on the few occasions I came up with Leah and Krista and stayed for the weekend in the Landingham home. It probably hadn't changed much since Leah lived there as a teenager. Her softball and soccer trophies lined a bookshelf. There were a lot of them. A stack of yearbooks on the bottom shelf. At least the queen-size bed was new. Bought by the Landinghams, along with the crib, when Krista was born. Perhaps a concession so there'd be room for me to sleep when I came up with Leah and Krista. I knew it was just one less excuse the Landinghams didn't want to have to overcome in their effort to see their daughter and grandchild as often as possible.

I also knew they'd rather not see me at all. That didn't bother me too much. They loved Krista and were good to her. Spoiled her, but not too excessively. The fact that we'd named her after their deceased oldest child was one of the few points in my favor. That and the fact that they had to grudgingly give me credit for being a good father. Those were the only checkmarks on my plus side. There were plenty of marks on the negative. Spence Landingham had been a cop in his earlier years and he still considered me a bent one even though I'd finally been exonerated for the death of my first wife. By me.

My relationship with my in-laws was a minor irritation to be weathered once every couple months. Doable. Especially since my mother had come out from Phoenix to visit exactly once since Krista was born. Also the first time she'd met Leah. An hour flight and only the one time. She'd never invited us to come to Phoenix for a visit. So, I was happy that Krista had loving grandparents to see her every once in a while. I just wished their love didn't turn to hate when it came to me.

Leah closed the door to her bedroom and I braced myself for the other thing she wanted to talk about.

"Do you know how long you were in there?" Leah searched my eyes.

"What?"

"You stood over Krista's crib and stared at her without moving a muscle for over five minutes."

"What?" I shook my head. "She's my daughter. I haven't seen her in twelve days. I've never been away from her this long. I miss her."

"I know." She blinked and nodded and her voice softened. "But it reminded me of what you do every night at home. I know you worry about her, but she's fine. She's a well-adapted, smart little girl."

"I . . ." The same discussion that had started our last argument and caused the early exit to Santa Barbara. I hadn't expected that. "Is that what you wanted to talk about? How I look at my child?"

A spark of heat itched along my skin. No, not now. I closed my eyes, took a deep breath, and let it out slowly.

"No." She stood with her arms wrapped around her chest. Her tension shrunk the room. "You said out front that you had something you had to tell me."

I concentrated on my breath. My skin was still warm, but not on fire. No red rage.

"Yeah. Do you want to sit down?" I flipped the wooden chair in front of her little high school homework desk and sat in it. She looked at her bed, then back at me, and finally sat down on it, locking her fingers together in her lap. "I told you about my contact at Fulcrum being murdered."

"Yes." She absentmindedly tapped her thumbs together, waiting for the bad new she was sure I would convey. I wouldn't disappoint her.

"Well, I'm not going to get any more contract work from them and someone is trying to ruin my reputation with potential clients." I told her about the dick pic and much of what Moira and I had learned about Leveraged Investigations. She sat quietly the whole time and tried unsuccessfully to hide her dismay at what I'd told her. She waited ten or fifteen seconds before she spoke. It seemed like an eternity.

"Why do you think this other private investigative agency wants to ruin your reputation?" Her tapping thumbs picked up velocity.

"I don't know. They like to hurt the competition. It's their M.O. Whenever they get involved in a case that's being worked by another P.I., they do the same thing. The dick pic was something new, as far as we can tell."

"Is all of this why you're going to Monterey? What does it have to do with the murdered woman?"

"I'm not sure Leveraged Investigations has anything to do with Sara's murder." But my gut told me different. "They may not be connected, but the company that pays the very expensive lease for Leveraged's office at First Allied Plaza is a shell corporation in Monterey. Moira's talked to a lawyer and he thinks we might be able to sue Leveraged and maybe whoever is pulling their strings."

"Is that why you're involved in this? Because of a potential lawsuit?" She folded her arms again. Tightly against her chest.

"No. Whoever is behind this may have murdered Sara and they came after my livelihood. The thing that supports my family. I can't let that stand."

"You can't let it stand? That's your damn pride speaking!" She shot up from the bed and started pacing across her childhood bedroom. "It always gets you into trouble. There are other jobs, Rick. Your health is more important than your job. Your family will survive. In fact, it could survive on my income alone if I went back to work full-time. It would give you a chance to rest. Relax and enjoy things for a change."

Supporting and protecting my family was my life. And, as this case reminded me, so was finding the truth and getting justice for those who had nowhere else to go to get it. Those were the only things I cared about. And they both kept me moving forward. Always forward.

"I thought you wanted to wait until Krista was at least two years old before you started working full-time. And even when you do, it's going to take you a while to build up a client base in San Diego like you have up here. In the meantime, we need my income."

And I needed to be needed. Not just placated. Not indulged to think that the work I did mattered while my disease progressed toward its inevitable conclusion. The work had to matter and I had to matter. While I still could.

Leah paced back and forth without saying anything for thirty, forty seconds. Maybe a minute. Bad news was coming. For me.

I finally couldn't take the wait anymore and stood up. "What is it? Tell me what you need to say."

"Theo's not working out up here." The man she brought in to run the business in Santa Barbara while she took time off to raise Krista and eventually start an office in San Diego. "I can't do nothing and let the business I built from scratch die."

"Can't you fire him and hire someone else?" I knew what was coming, but grasped for a way to make it not happen.

"I couldn't fire him. He was a partner, not an employee. I had to buy him out. He's gone now."

"When did this happen?"

"Last Tuesday."

"This didn't just come about in the last few days." I snapped off the words. Heat sizzled along my nerve synapses. "You must have had this in the works for weeks and didn't tell me about it. And you're upset with me for not telling you about things?"

"I knew things weren't going well, but I thought they were fixable. I didn't know how bad it was until I got up here and talked to my associate designers and a couple longtime clients." Defensiveness in her voice, but she didn't avoid my glare. "I didn't come up here intending to make the change, but when I got here, I realized I had to. You knew things weren't going very well with the office. I mentioned it to you more than once."

She had told me there were issues at the office, but had downplayed them. I asked her about the specifics a couple times, but couldn't remember what she said. Memories lost to my disease or self-centeredness about my own work? Whichever, it didn't change the current circumstances.

"It's your business, you can do what you want." Now I stood up and edged past Leah and stood in front of the bookshelf that held memories of her childhood in the bedroom her parents had frozen in time for over twenty years since she left their house. I concentrated on steadying my breathing and stared at Leah's accomplishments as an athlete. "But this decision affects your family. Krista and me. I'm sure you're going to have to come up here much more often now, which means I'll be separated from Krista more or you will if you leave her at home with me. It's going to get confusing for her."

Leah didn't say anything, but I could hear her pacing behind me. I turned around and looked at her. Her face was locked in pain. Then it hit me. Like a kidney punch with a sledgehammer. My stomach knotted and my breath went short. "You're planning on moving back up here."

She continued pacing and wouldn't look at me. My face went blast furnace. I stepped in front of Leah and grabbed her forearms and stopped her.

"You can find work up here, Rick." A strained smile on her face. "You just lost your biggest client in San Diego. You can start over up here and find new clients. Or you don't have to. Only work when you want to. And you wouldn't even have to worry about this business with Leveraged Investigations and Monterey. You can let Moira handle all of that. There's new business waiting for me up here now that Theo is gone. I already have a new project. We can start fresh again here. Where we fell in love. We can stay here until we find a new home. Krista loves playing with her cousin Spencer. She loves it here."

Here. Santa Barbara. Where Colleen was murdered and where I dishonored our marriage. Where her ghost would always have dominion over me. And in the Landingham house, where I'd never be good enough for the daughter whose room her parents had bronzed, like baby shoes. I'd be despised or, at best, tolerated.

I was done being tolerated.

"We fell in love up here, but Krista was born in San Diego. We've built a life there. We have a home there. We don't need to live in your parents' house. We can get your business going in San Diego, no matter how long it takes. But I'm not quitting my job. And I'm not walking away from a threat to my family's livelihood." The fire along my skin burned hotter. "I'm not going to run away when someone challenges me. I'm not going to be some house husband. That's not who you fell in love with. That's not the father I want Krista to see. And I'm not going to sit in front of a computer, cocooned away in my office for the rest of my life. I'm going to live my life doing what I'm meant to do while I'm still capable of doing it."

"What do you mean, *what you're meant to do?*"

"Helping people that need it. Not hiding behind a keyboard all day."

"I thought you liked doing background checks." Leah's eyes question marks.

I'd kept my growing restlessness with desk work to myself. More dishonesty or not bitching about a sacrifice to try to make my marriage work? Leah had moved to San Diego and paused doing the work she loved to be my wife and raise Krista, so I'd done what I thought was the right thing to do and shut up about my unease. Spouses made sacrifices for each other and their children. It was the unwritten clause in the contract. But it had started to chafe and affected me more than I knew until the death of Sara Bhandari brought it into stark reality.

"It's a job. And I'll continue to do it, but I need to take other cases, too. And I need to stop the people who are trying to ruin my reputation."

"So you're going to put your pride and your ego ahead of your family?" Leah snapped her hands to her hips. "How are you helping your child when you're chasing bad guys and going after private eyes who offended you?"

"They didn't offend me. They came after all of us." The room turned red. "And if I die protecting my family, Krista will know I wasn't a coward who hid from danger in his office upstairs!"

"Ssshh. You'll wake Krista up."

"Me? I'm the problem? I'm not the one trying to break up our family. That's on you!"

The bedroom door snapped open. Spence Landingham stood in the doorway. His once tall, angular frame now slumped and softened. Pajamas showing under his open robe. Blue hatred in his eyes.

"What's going on in here?" He straightened up as best he could, pulling from cop memories decades old. "I'm not going to let you come into my house and yell at my daughter when her baby is down the hall."

"Her baby is my daughter, too, asshole."

"Rick!" Leah's eyes went round.

Wails from Krista echoed down the hallway and into the bedroom.

"Get out of my house!" Spence Landingham took a half step inside the room. His hand raised pointing toward the hall, mouth in a snarl.

A challenge. My breath shotgunned in and out of my mouth. Rage raced past reason. I took a step toward him.

"Rick." A pleading voice. Someone grabbed my arms. My eyes were targeted on Spence Landingham. I yanked my arms out of the grasp and took another step toward my aggressor. "Rick! Rick! Look at me!"

Two hands wrapped around my face and pulled it downward. Terrified blue eyes stared up at me. I blinked, ten, fifteen times. The face around the eyes came into focus. Leah. Terrified.

"I . . ." I shook my head and looked at Spence, a step back from the doorway now. Fear in his eyes. Krista wailed in the background, Myriam Landingham's gentle voice trying to quiet her. The rage ebbed, lost its grip, and slipped back into the shadows. The soul-crushing weight of shame took its place. "I . . ."

"You need to go." Spence. "Now."

"Krista . . ."

"You need to go, Rick." Leah dropped her hands from my face. Disgust replaced terror in her eyes. She'd seen my rage at its full uncontrolled fury. The slip of the mask I'd been trying to hide from her for the last two months. The violence that was closer to the surface than she could ever imagine and that I would ever admit. Until now.

I stepped away from Leah toward the door. Spence moved backwards into the hallway and I walked out of Leah's bedroom. Wails still coming from Krista's room down the hall to the left. I turned right and kept walking.

CHAPTER THIRTY-FIVE

MOIRA DIDN'T SAY anything when I got into the car. My look must have said everything.

I wanted to yell at her for convincing me to take Highway 101 instead of Interstate 5 up to Monterey. But the decision, ultimately, was mine, as was the choice to stop at the Landinghams'. I held my tongue, punched the ignition, and sped out of the driveway in reverse. Moira eyeballed me until we got back onto the freeway. I found the restraint I couldn't in Leah's bedroom and kept the car under seventy-five the rest of the way to Monterey.

The drive along the 101 north of Santa Barbara calmed me a bit. The muscular rolling hills dotted with oak trees reminded me of my grandparents' ranch in Northern California when I was a kid. Before everything turned to shit and I had to grow up a lot sooner than I wanted to. Sooner than an adolescent kid should have to.

Signs for San Luis Obispo showed up along the highway about an hour and a half after we left Santa Barbara.

"Do you want to stop in San Luis Obispo?" I asked Moira. The first words either of us had spoken since we left the Landinghams' driveway. Home to University of California at San Luis Obispo where her son went to college. "Look at any of Luke's old haunts? The campus? Anything like that?"

"No. Thanks." She spoke again a few seconds later. "I only visited him here a couple times. That's all he could stomach. Something for you to look forward to when Krista goes to college."

Moira knew about my disease and its ticking clock. She knew about it before Leah did. Not that I had CTE, just that there was something wrong with me and that I was seeing a neurologist. She was the first person I told about the specifics after I told Leah. She knew that I might not be mentally cognizant or even alive when Krista was old enough for college. Her remark had been an entreaty for me to open up about what happened at the Landingham house. And it was a dose of optimism, conveyed in a way that only she could deliver, to a friend. When I really needed one.

"Leah wants to move back to Santa Barbara." It didn't feel good to say out loud, but it was nice to be with someone who would care. "She wants me to try to make a go as a P.I. up there. Either that or let her be the breadwinner and sit in a rocking chair while the disease steals pieces of my brain one day at a time."

"I'm sure that's not what she said."

"Close enough."

"How did you end it?" She meant the discussion. She might have been asking about my marriage.

"I almost attacked my father-in-law, terrified my wife, and left the house listening to my daughter crying in the background." The shame crept back up into my chest and strangled my heart. Krista's wails, Leah's eyes. The terror, the disgust.

"What?" Moira snapped her body toward me. "What happened? What did you do?"

"It's what I almost did." Even as I stared straight ahead out the windshield, I could see Moira's mouth hanging open. My brain wouldn't let me not see it. "What I wanted to do."

I told her what happened when Spence Landingham whipped open Leah's bedroom door. As best I could remember through the red haze that enveloped me at the time.

"Rage is a symptom of the disease. It's not an excuse, just a fact," I said after I recounted what happened.

"How long have you . . . have you noticed it?" Moira's voice, normally a gravelly, machine-gun assault, now cushiony and deliberate.

"A few months. It's getting worse. I can't control it." Tears welled in my eyes. Not for me. Or not only for me. For my family and the bliss we lived during our first few months together. Even with a death sentence hanging over me and our family unit, we lived life fully. It couldn't last forever, but it didn't have to end this way. "They tried antidepressants and mood stabilizers, but they don't work. I'm seeing my neurologist on Thursday, hoping we can try something new."

"Does Leah know about your doctor's appointment?"

"Yeah."

"Is she going to go with you?"

"Don't know."

"If she doesn't, I will." A quiet tenderness that almost made me feel worse. I appreciated the gesture, but didn't like the fact that she thought she needed to treat me with kid gloves. Or maybe I just didn't understand how to accept kindness anymore.

"Thanks."

*　*　*

About an hour south of Monterey we started talking strategy. Moira felt certain that she'd made the Samuel Chen who lived in Pacific Grove as the same person who signed the checks with the Obsidian Holdings address on them. However, she hadn't been able to find a

copy of his California Driver's License online or a license from any
state that made sense for someone living in Pacific Grove. So, we had
no photo that we could definitely count on as being the Samuel Chen
we were looking for. However, Moira was reasonably confident that
she found someone on social media that fit the bill.

He went by Samchen007 and posted a lot of photos of a sixty-foot
motor yacht christened *Sea Stud* tooling around Monterey Bay with
bikinied women in their twenties and thirties on Instagram. Maybe
that's where the 007 came in. A lower-case James Bond wannabe.

Chen also took plenty of pictures of himself, especially with said
women. He looked to be around my age, early forties. He was a bit
pudgy and had an adolescent look to him. Like a kid who aged but
never grew up.

A motor yacht the size of the one Samchen007 posted on Instagram had to cost well over a million dollars. Even if he only leased it,
it would be a huge chunk of change. But judging from the dates of
comments on his posts, the photos were taken over the last three
years, so he probably owned it. And if he was the same Samuel Chen
who lived in Pacific Grove, he also owned a home recently appraised
for $3,700,000.

After seeing Samchen007's pictures on Instagram, it was obvious
that he liked pretty ladies. Moira, although possibly aged out of his
preferred demographic, certainly qualified. Thus, I knew there was a
bikini and a black cocktail dress in the lone duffle bag she toted with
her on this trip. The Moira honey trap was a backup if our first gambit
didn't work.

We made it to Monterey by 12:30. Our lost time in Santa Barbara
offset by only stopping for gas and eschewing a meal. Monterey and its
Cannery Row immortalized by John Steinbeck's novel of the same
name were once the center of the sardine packing industry. Now

Monterey was known more as a tourist hub, although you could still get a waft of the past on Old Fisherman's Wharf.

Monterey was a small town with a small-town American vibe to it. Most of the buildings still had a Steinbeck-era feel to them. Quaint, nostalgic, comforting. Not that unique from many small towns across America. Except that it's right on the ocean and close to Carmel and Big Sur, the most spectacular stretch of coastline in California if not in the entire United States. Unfortunately, Moira and I didn't have time for sightseeing.

CHAPTER THIRTY-SIX

AFTER WE MADE a quick pitstop at a nearby Best Western, Moira parked on the street about a hundred feet down from Obsidian Holdings with a view of the parking lot. She wore a black cocktail dress, sling-back heels, and tasteful makeup and wine-red lipstick that accented her natural attractiveness. Her facial features, taken individually, wouldn't seem to go together, but they meshed into exotic beauty. Large round dark eyes, full lips, and a dainty button nose.

I'd only seen her in makeup and lipstick two other times in the eight years I'd known her. In both instances we were working a case together. She didn't give much thought to her appearance, but she didn't have to.

"You sure you don't think I should come with you?" Moira asked.

"Not for the preliminary. You're the second act."

"Easy, buddy, you're hardly a headliner yourself."

"That's not what I meant."

"Go, dummy."

I tapped on the recording app on my phone, got out of the car, and started walking. The deal with Moira was I'd record my conversation with Samuel Chen, which she'd be able to listen to later. I welcomed her discerning ears listening to some nuance I might miss. I was pretty good at ferreting out subtleties, but my specialty was blunt frontal attacks.

Obsidian Holdings was located in a faded mustard yellow two-story office building with a red tiled roof on Munras Avenue in the heart of downtown Monterey. The building had some architectural interest to it in that it wasn't just a rectangle block. It had a recessed wing, pillared walkways, and a bell tower without a bell. There were eight or ten cars in the parking lot of various makes and ages. A black late model Mercedes-Benz Z class had a vanity license plate that read: MR SKPR.

Mr. Skipper? Samuel Chen, proud yacht owner? It looked like the person who signed the checks for the rent for Leveraged Investigations in San Diego was in his office in Monterey. I went inside the building.

Obsidian Holdings was on the second floor of the wing that fronted the parking lot. Its name was the only one on the placard next to the door. No Celestial Shores Real Estate, Enviro-Strategies, or Bio-Ethic Strategies listed.

I opened the door and walked inside to a plush modern lobby area. Marble floor, with a blue flatweave area rug. Large coastal landscape oil paintings on the wall that looked like Krista Schumacher originals. Unless Chen or whoever decorated the office found the paintings through social media, he must have gone down to La Jolla and San Diego at some point. And connected with Leveraged Investigations while he was there?

There was a long hallway to the right with two closed doors on either side and an open one at the end. I caught a glimpse of the edge of a desk and a blown-up photo on the wall. Of a yacht.

I'd yet to get a look at the Samuel Chen of Obsidian Holdings, but I felt certain he was the same person as Samchen007 who posted photos of himself and pretty women in bikinis on a yacht on Instagram. Progress.

There were more than enough offices in the suite for each to represent all the individual businesses that shared the same address. I wondered if there were any people behind the closed doors or if everything funneled down to the big office at the end of the hall.

A middle-aged Asian woman sat at a sleek black desk with chrome finishings. No nameplate on the desk. Her hair was up in a tight bun. She wore a tailored executive blouse and jacket. The corners of her mouth turned down into a permanent frown. She eyed me suspiciously and said nothing. No greeting whatsoever. We played a silent game of blink until I got bored.

"I'm here to see Samuel Chen." I said it with cop command presence. I dressed for the part at our brief stop and check-in at our hotel. Dark slacks, blue sports coat. Even shaved that morning before I picked up Moira. My first read on the woman was that polite and friendly wouldn't work. She read as an experienced gatekeeper. Flattery wouldn't get me over the moat and neither would a complicated ruse.

She looked me up and down like I was a mathematical equation she needed to solve.

"Who are you?" The woman spoke with a moderate accent. She had her own command presence.

"Rick Cahill." I went with the truth and looked for a reaction.

Her expression didn't change. Still dour. She'd either never heard my name before, didn't care, or was a practiced actress. I didn't have a favorite among the three.

"Why do you want to see him?" She gave nothing. I appreciated her directness. Let me know where I stood. Which was on the outside looking in.

"That's between Mr. Chen and me."

"He's a busy man. You don't have an appointment. Come back next Wednesday at four o'clock. That's the next time available. "

"I'll wait for him here until he's done with all of the other important things he needs to do." I sat down on a beige wool mid-century modern sofa against the wall. If there'd been a coffee table in front of the sofa, I would have put my feet up on it. "Then we can talk."

The woman looked at me, still giving away nothing. Just the same dour expression she wore when I walked through the door.

"You are very rude." She eyeballed me a couple beats then picked up the phone receiver on her desk. She tapped the phone console and started talking almost immediately. I was pretty sure the language was Mandarin. Back in my restaurant days, I prided myself in being able to differentiate accents, but it was tougher when you didn't understand the language. The only words I understood were Rick and Cahill. They received harsh emphasis.

After a little animated back-and-forth, the woman hung up the phone and looked at me. Same look.

A minute later, a man appeared at the end of the hall. Asian, six feet, lean, dark hair and glasses. Black fitted suit and tie with a white shirt. Could have been a well-dressed accountant or undertaker. Or anything in between. He walked straight at me, smiling with an outstretched hand.

"Mr. Cahill?" He spoke perfect English with the slightest trace of an accent. British.

"Yes." I extended my hand for a quick pump. "And you are?"

"David Liu. Why don't we talk in my office?"

"I'd rather talk in Mr. Chen's office. With Mr. Chen."

"Let's start in my office." He took a step toward the hall and turned back to me. "Humor me."

"Sure." I followed him into the first office down the hall on the left. The door at the end of the hallway was now closed. Someone else knew I was there.

David Liu's office had nothing in common with the lobby fifteen feet away from it. Rudimentary metal desk. The kind you'd expect to see in a shop foreman's office on a working warehouse floor. Armless rolling office chair behind it. Nothing on the stark white walls. The only things on the desk were an Apple MacBook Pro laptop and phone console. No paper anywhere and no file cabinets. Only a wire trash can with nothing in it.

Liu closed the laptop when we entered the office. Company secrets or private ones? The laptop had some wear to it. Like it got a lot of use and maybe a lot of miles on airplanes.

"Please, sit down." Liu gestured to the lone old-time wooden desk chair opposite him. He sat in the cheap armless roller in his tailored suit.

Not only didn't the office match the lobby, it didn't match David Liu. I figured it was merely a cubbyhole for him to use while he was in town. In town from where, I didn't know. Taiwan? Hong Kong? Mainland China? Could have been any or L.A. or San Francisco. Or San Diego.

Whatever the case, I knew it wasn't his main office. I had the feeling there was the same setup behind all the other doors in the hall but the one at the end. Or, the other offices had nothing at all in them. The emptiness inside of a shell corporation. But someone was doing business out of this address and signing checks for a lease on office space in San Diego. Samuel Chen. The man who didn't want to talk to me.

I sat and made a show of looking around the room before I spoke. "Quite a place you have here."

Liu faked a polite laugh. "I will admit, it's a little spartan, but it serves its purpose."

"And what purpose is that?"

Another forced laugh.

"Work. Commerce. It's what makes the world go round." A smile. "Now, how can I help you?"

"I don't think you can." I smiled. "I'm just sitting here to humor you. Remember. I'm here to talk to Samuel Chen in the office down the hall."

"And what would you like to talk to Mr. Chen about?"

"That's between him and me, Mr. Liu." I leaned over the desk. "What exactly do you do here, anyway? Are you part of Celestial Shores Real Estate, Enviro-Strategies, or Bio-Ethic Strategies?"

The tiniest of flickers in his dark eyes. I'd struck a nerve. Made a tiny crack in the shell of the shell corporation.

"I'm afraid I'm not going to be able to help you unless you tell me what it is you'd like to talk to Mr. Chen about." This smile was strained. "He is a very busy man and doesn't have time to talk to just anyone who comes in off the street."

"I'm not anyone just off the street, unless the street you mean is West Broadway in San Diego." Another flicker in Liu's eyes. "Tell him I'm here to talk about Leveraged Investigations."

He stared at me for a couple ticks, then looked at the phone on his desk. Possibly debating if he should call the office down the hall.

"If you'll excuse me for a minute." He stood up. "I'll be right back."

"Sure."

Whatever Liu had to talk to Chen about, he didn't want to do it in front of me on the phone. Didn't even want to risk it in Mandarin.

He walked out of the office and turned left down the hall. Towards the office in the back. He left the door open behind him. I quietly slipped out of my chair and hurried around to the front of the desk. I hovered over Liu's laptop, stared at the door, and listened for movement outside the office. Nothing. I flipped open the laptop and hit *Enter*. The screen illuminated. With a password prompt. Shit. What I expected, but worth a try. I closed the laptop and went back to my chair.

Liu returned five or so minutes later, which was about the maximum my rear end could have remained in the uncompromising wooden chair.

"Follow me, please." He led me down the hall to the office at the end.

Samchen007 from Instagram sat behind a Scarborough House solid wood mahogany desk. I recognized the claw feet and lion heads on the corners. A wealthy client of mine from my earlier P.I. days had one that looked similar. Probably cost fifteen to twenty grand. Chen's chair was equally grand. He sat in a red velvet high-backed throne chair.

He looked a little older and paunchier than he did on his Instagram posts. Probably used a filter on the photos because many of them were recent. He wore a navy-blue silk blazer and a collared shirt with two buttons opened revealing a tanned, hairless upper chest. A thin gold rope chain hung around his neck. He looked more like an after-hours club manager than a titan of industry.

"Please, sit." He pointed at one of two leather wingback chairs in front of his desk.

The door closed behind me, and I assumed that David Liu had left the two of us alone.

The office was bright and modern and had a couple large oil land-scapes similar to the ones in the lobby to go along with some photos of his yacht, *Sea Stud*. None of which matched the dark mahogany desk and red velvet throne. Incongruous. Kind of like the fashion sense of Samuel Chen in relation to his being the face of the shell cor-poration, Obsidian Holdings.

"What is so important that you need to interrupt my day without an appointment?" He spoke in perfect, unaccented English and raised his left hand in the air dismissively. No wedding band on his ring finger. Only a bulbous gold pinky ring. His fingernails looked manicured.

Whatever Obsidian Holdings was involved in, it seemed to be mak-ing Samuel Chen a lot of money. Thus, he had a lot to lose. Especially if Moira and her lawyer, Angus Buttis, sued Leveraged Investigations and him. A good lawyer is going to find a connection with deep pock-ets in any corporate malfeasance civil suit. Obsidian Holdings had those deep pockets and Angus Buttis was a good lawyer.

And as much as I now needed the money we might win in a civil suit, suing Obsidian Holdings wasn't my top priority. Finding out how deeply Leveraged Investigations was involved with Fulcrum Security and possibly the death of Sara Bhandari was. If I had to forfeit the civil suit and a big payday to find the truth, so be it.

"What's your association with Leveraged Investigations in San Diego?"

Chen frowned deeper and pushed his head backwards, adding an extra chin to the two he already had.

"I don't discuss my business with strangers. Particularly ones who barge into my office off the street." He folded his arms while he sat on his throne.

Both Liu and Chen had a problem with people walking in off the street. Where else would you come from? A helipad on top of the building? Obsidian Holdings didn't have one. And I didn't have a helicopter.

"I'm trying to do you a favor, pal." I gave him my best reptilian smile. "I know Obsidian Holdings pays Leveraged Investigations' rent and your signature is on the checks. You have great penmanship, by the way."

"How would you know that?" Chen might as well just have flipped his cards over. Not a face card in the bunch. His non-answer revealed more than he wanted it to. That Leveraged Investigations was under the umbrella of Obsidian Holdings.

"Obsidian Holdings has positions in many businesses." David Liu's voice from behind me. I spun around in my chair to look at him. He stood next to the door. Same strained smile from his cubbyhole down the hall. "Think of it as a mutual fund like in the stock market."

"I didn't know you were still here." I smiled. "A mutual fund? So why would investors who pool their money put it into a private investigative agency? Seems like a bad investment with limited returns. If any."

"We like to keep things diversified." Liu.

"Would you mind sitting down over here so I don't have to keep straining my neck to look at you." I then turned back and faced Samuel Chen, still speaking to Liu. "Since you seem to be the one who's doing all the talking now."

Chen snarled a lip at me. Good. I wanted him angry. More likely to crack out of turn to show me he was in charge. Which I was pretty sure he wasn't. I was now convinced my read on him from his social media posts was right. He was a dilettante, not an astute businessman. He was the figurehead of Obsidian Holdings, not its brains.

If he was somehow in charge, would he need Liu in the room with him when he talked to me? And have Liu do most of the talking? The fact that I knew he signed the checks on the lease for Leveraged Investigations shouldn't have surprised him. Particularly after Liu must have told him I knew Obsidian Holdings was connected to Leveraged. Even if he was somehow surprised, a man in charge would never let me know that. Not a competent one, at least.

Liu walked over and sat in the wingback chair next to me. "We've answered your questions about Leveraged Investigations. Mr. Chen is quite busy. Do you have any more questions before we ask you to leave?"

"Actually, you didn't really answer my question about Leveraged Investigations. You hedged and avoided telling me the truth. Why does a shell corporation in Monterey have any connection to a crooked P.I. agency in San Diego?"

"Crooked?" Chen slid his eyes from me to Liu. Nervous eyes.

"Leveraged Investigations has a spotless reputation and maintains the highest ethical standards." Liu, silky smooth.

"They use intimidation to bend people to the will of their clients and try to ruin the reputations of other private investigation agencies. And that's just on the surface." I looked at Chen the whole time I spoke. He glanced at Liu, more worried with each word that came out of my mouth. Leveraged's tactics were news to him. "They've done worse and broken the law. But here's what should interest you, Mr. Chen. If some sharp lawyer gets to them before the police do and decides to sue them, your connection to them is going to be a problem. For you. An expensive one."

"Are you—" Liu started to speak, but Chen cut him off.

"What are you talking about?" Chen looked at me, his face pink.

"Obsidian Holdings pays the rent on Leveraged Investigations' office. Your signature is on the checks. If they get sued, any smart lawyer would discover your connection and your deep pockets and name you in the lawsuit."

"What lawsuit?" Chen looked at Liu. "What is he talking about?"

"Is this some kind of shakedown, Mr. Cahill?" Liu ignored Chen and looked at me. The silk in his voice turned to sandpaper.

"I'm just letting Mr. Chen know what's going on outside the cocoon of his office. Obsidian Holdings is connected to some bad people." I turned toward Chen. "Your little piece of paradise with your throne and your yacht and your house in Pacific Grove is sitting on a foundation of Jenga blocks. When the wrong block gets pulled out, everything is going to come tumbling down. No more bikini boat rides on Monterey Bay."

Chen's face went from pink to red and he started shouting at Liu in Mandarin. Liu seemed to be trying to placate him in a soothing voice, but Chen continued to shout and gesticulate. Liu's body language changed and he snapped off some words in a husky timbre and slammed his hand down on Chen's twenty-thousand-dollar Scarborough House desk. Chen whipped backwards like he'd been slapped. His eyes went big and his mouth stopped talking.

Liu stood up and turned to me.

"It's time for you to leave, Mr. Cahill." He buttoned his jacket and snapped his cuffs. "I can assure you that if you try to extort money

from Obsidian Holdings or Mr. Chen on the grounds of these specious allegations, we will get the authorities involved."

"Which ones?" I stood up. "The authorities here or the ones in Taiwan, Hong Kong, or Beijing?"

Liu went to the door and opened it. "You must leave now."

"I'm pretty sure you don't want any U.S. authorities involved." I
didn't move from the front of Chen's desk. "They might ask questions
that I have answers to. Not specious allegations. I think I have your
connection to Leveraged Investigations figured out. I'm still working
on where Celestial Shores Real Estate, Enviro-Strategies, and
Bio-Ethic Strategies come in. But I'm getting close. Particularly with
Bio-Ethic Strategies and Albert Chen." The Taiwanese citizen who
owned the company whose name Moira had dug up online. I looked
at Samuel Chen. "Relative?"

Chen looked at Liu again. All the color washed out of his face.

"I'd be happy to introduce you to the Monterey Police, Mr. Cahill."
David Liu, still holding the door. "I don't need international authorities to have you charged with trespassing."

"Deep pockets get picked, Mr. Chen."

I snapped my own cuffs then left Samuel Chen's office.

CHAPTER THIRTY-SEVEN

I PLAYED THE recording of my conversations inside Obsidian Holdings for Moira back in the car. She frowned after it was over.

"Didn't get much," she said.

"They're dirty and obviously hiding something." I tried to keep my irritation at bay. She was just mad that I'd convinced her to let me go it alone. But I had a reason for that.

We sat in silence until Samuel Chen left the Obsidian Holdings parking lot in his MR SKPR vanity-plated Mercedes-Benz Z at 2:55 p.m., less than a half hour after I was kicked out of his office.

Mission accomplished. I'd rattled him. His carefree playboy life just got disrupted. After my talk with him and David Liu, two things were clear to me. The first being that Obsidian Holdings was dirty and Samuel Chen was a prop. A dupe. The public face for a business that was really a criminal enterprise. The other thing was that Chen didn't know the depths of Obsidian's criminality, if he even knew they were criminal at all.

David Liu knew. He may or may not have been the brains behind the operation, but he knew what Obsidian was about and had a hand in what they did. I was sure of it. But he'd be a tough nut to crack, if not impossible. Chen, on the other hand, had a soft shell.

Moira and I followed his Mercedes. Moira still wore the black cock-tail dress she had on when she dropped me off, but I'd changed into a different set of clothes from my duffle bag. Jeans, gray sweatshirt, ten-nis shoes, sunglasses, and a San Francisco Giants baseball cap. Close enough to pass for a local and different enough from what I wore in Samuel Chen's office that he wouldn't recognize me on a tail.

Chen headed toward the ocean on Figueroa Street. His house was to the northwest in Pacific Grove. It looked like he was taking the scenic route. I couldn't blame him. The sun shone brightly down on the day from a mostly cloudless sky in cleansing rays. Chen's soul needed some cleansing. So did mine.

He drove past Del Monte Avenue, which led west to Pacific Grove, and continued toward the ocean.

"Shit. He's going to the marina," I said. "Probably going to take his yacht out on the water and wonder how he can get his suddenly upside-down life back on track."

"That's okay. I'm prepared." Moira pulled her dress over her head and shimmied out of it, exposing a black bikini against her tan skin. She carefully rolled up the dress and put it in the duffle bag at her feet. She slipped off her heels and replaced them with flip-flops, then wrapped a short purple sarong around her hips. The whole costume change took less than thirty seconds.

"I guess you are."

She took out a cloth shoulder bag from the duffle that had a beach towel and a bottle of sunscreen in it, tapped the screen of her phone, and dropped it inside. My phone rang. I answered the call from Moira and muted it. I'd be able to hear her conversation live with Chen. Hopefully, there'd be one.

"Did you turn on the recording app?"

Moira tilted her head and frowned at me. "Armed."

Chen pulled into the Municipal Wharf 2 parking lot, not to be confused with Old Fisherman's Wharf, and parked near the walkway to the marina and the boat slips. There weren't many cars in the lot on a Monday afternoon in May, so I didn't have a lot of cover. Moira needed to be within hailing distance of Chen when he got to the locked gate on the pier that led down to the docked boats.

Chen got out of his car and walked toward the pier. I parked ten or so spots away and Moira jumped out of the car and hurried after Chen. I stayed put and watched through binoculars and listened through my phone's earbuds. Moira was within ten feet of Chen when he got to the gate and unlocked it.

"Could you hold the gate for me, hon?" Moira added a little purr to her normal throaty voice. Most men are malleable to a woman with a sexy voice calling them hon.

Chen turned and looked at her. Sunglasses hid his eyes, but a tiny smile cracked his lips. His day had just taken a turn for the better. Or so he thought.

"Sure." Bigger smile now as he held the gate open. "Out for a day of sunbathing on the water?"

Chen's voice was faint and a little muffled over the phone, but I could make out what he said. His smile was a little too big after he said sunbathing. Creepy. A wannabe playboy without game, but with a big yacht.

"I'm meeting some friends." Concern in Moira's voice. She passed through the open gate. "But I'm late. They were supposed to wait for me in the parking lot. I think they might have left without me."

Moira looked around the marina to sell it.

"What's the slip number to their boat? Let's go see if we can find them." He shut the gate behind Moira.

"I don't know. I think it was supposed to be somewhere in front." She gestured with her hand to an open slip in front of them. They both started walking down the wooden pier toward the boat slips. I tracked them easily with the binoculars through the chain-link fence.

"We were supposed to meet in the parking lot. I've never been on their boat before. I don't know the person who owns it. He's a friend of Brittany, one of my girlfriends. I tried calling her, but she must have turned off her phone or something because it went straight to voicemail."

"It looks like your friends have already left." Chen shook his head.

"Darn it." Moira slumped her shoulders. "I was really looking forward to this. You have no idea how much I needed a relaxing afternoon in the sun out on the water."

The hook was baited. We just needed the fish to swallow it.

"Well, we could go out on my yacht. It's a 60 Cantius." Pride in his voice as he gobbled the bait.

"That's very nice of you to offer, but . . ." Moira looked around in an Oscar-worthy performance. "We don't really know each other . . ."

"Everyone here knows me. I've had the *Sea Stud* here for three years. Everyone knows the *Sea Stud*."

How could they forget?

"Well . . ."

"We can cruise around the marina, if you like, or even just sit in the dock. Sometimes I come down to the *Sea Stud* and just sit at the helm to feel the rocking of the water."

"Okay. Sure." Moira bobbed her head. "That's really nice of you."

"My pleasure. What's the point of having a sixty-foot yacht if you can't share it?" Big smile. "Here, I can carry your bag for you."

Chen reached his arm out to Moira.

"That's okay. Thanks." Moira held the strap to her shoulder. "Where's your boat?"

"It's a yacht." Pride of ownership. "It's down here. What's your name?"

"Moira. What's yours?"

"Sam. That's a pretty name, Moira."

"Thanks."

They started walking and went down to the third row of boat slips. The parking lot was slightly higher than the marina, so I could still follow them until they turned left down the row of anchored boats, which blocked my view.

Moira and Chen chatted about some of the boats they saw as they walked. Moira feigning interest in his knowledge of seafaring vessels.

"Here it is." Chen almost giddy. "The *Sea Stud*."

"It's beautiful." Awe in Moira's voice. "And so big."

I wished I could have seen Chen's face when she marvels at the size of his yacht.

"Thank you. Here, let me help you aboard."

"Oh." A rustle like she lifted her arm with the canvas bag holding the phone. "Thank you."

It sounded like Chen gave Moira a guided tour along the yacht for the next few minutes, starting on the upper deck. The cockpit, the upper salon: "This is where I entertain." The helm: "This is where I captain the yacht. I'm the skipper." And the bow, which he called the bow lounge, complete with two reclining sun pads.

"You can sunbathe here." Again, a little too much eagerness in his voice. I had the feeling he was ogling Moira behind his sunglasses. "And if it gets too hot, I can put a screen overhead like a cabana."

Although Moira was small in stature, she was tough and could handle herself, but there was no way I was letting her go out alone on that boat with Chen. Not with his false imprisonment conviction.

The tour progressed inside to the three staterooms. In other words, bedrooms. The master, the VIP, and the less eloquently named third stateroom.

"I have plenty of sleeping areas for guests when I set sail for a weekend of adventure." He tried to make a weekend of adventure sound mysterious. It just sounded creepy. And I hardly knew anything about sailing, but I figured you actually needed sails to set sail for somewhere. I guess it sounded more romantic than saying, "When I drive the boat."

Chen finished the tour of the master stateroom in my ear.

"See? An ambient rain showerhead. Very soothing after a day in the sun." Things were getting creepier.

"Good to know. Let's go back up to the upper deck. It's a beautiful day, we should be outside."

"Of course, of course." A hint of frustration in Chen's voice. "Let's go up to the bow lounge."

The shuffle of movement as they must have been heading back up to the main deck.

A six- or seven-year-old Jeep Cherokee pulled in between Samuel Chen's Mercedes and my Honda. Three college-aged males wearing swim trunks and T-shirts got out and headed for the gate to the marina. Two were also wearing Giants ball caps.

My chance to get inside without scaling the fence. I got out of my car and walked quickly after the young men, getting to within three feet of them, when one of them keyed the gate open. He went through and turned to hold the gate for his buddies. After they went through, he held the gate open for me, too.

"Thanks." I walked through the gate.

"Go Giants!" the other kid wearing a Giants hat said.

"Go Giants," I parroted and gave a thumbs-up. The words sour in this Padre fan's mouth, as I walked down the pier toward the third row of boat slips and Samuel Chen's yacht.

The Giants fans veered off to the first row.

"Let's get out on the open water so we can enjoy this beautiful day." Chen through my earbuds.

"Why don't we just sit in the dock for a little bit. I'm still getting used to being on a boat."

"Okay." Disappointed. Then a few seconds later, "I haven't been on the yacht for a while and I need to run the engines. If you let engines sit idle for too long, the seawater can make the propellers seize."

I didn't know if that was true, but according to his last Instagram post, Chen had been on the boat in open water on Saturday, two days ago.

I hurried down the pier.

"Okay, as long as we don't leave the dock." Moira's voice.

"I'll be right back."

A few seconds later, I heard the whir of engines. I turned onto the third row of slips and scanned the boats docked there. Mostly sailboats and yachts. And one cruiser yacht at the end of the dock, it's upper deck visible above the other boats. The *Sea Stud* was backed into the slip, like a few other boats I saw. All the rest were bow in.

I was twenty or so slips away from the *Sea Stud* when I saw Chen exit it from the stern. Now wearing a windbreaker instead of the suit jacket I saw him wearing in his office. His attention was directed over his shoulder at the bow as he hurried to a metal cleat on the dock and untied the line connected to the boat. His movements were practiced and swift. Swifter than I'd expect from the pudgy playboy wannabe. He scurried back onto the stern of the boat and disappeared inside the main deck.

He wasn't just running the engines for maintenance, he was planning to leave the dock. I bolted down the pier at a full sprint. A shuffle of movement through the earbuds.

"What are you doing?" Moira to Chen five seconds later.

"I'm taking the boat out for a spin around the marina." Chen playing innocent. "The harbormaster won't let me sit in the dock and run my engines. Other owners complain, so I have to take the *Sea Stud* out of the slip and take a trip around the marina. It will only take about fifteen minutes."

"Let me off." A command. "Now."

"It's just for a few minutes and then we come back . . ."

The sound of the engines changed when I was five slips away from Chen's boat. Water churned below the stern and the boat started to move slowly forward, out of the slip. I hit a gear I didn't know I still had and leapt at the boat. I landed on the swim platform on the stern, tumbled forward and almost slid off the other side into the water.

"Stop the damn boat!" Moira in my ears and through the air.

I scampered up the four steps onto the main deck and the cockpit area. I could see Moira shouting at Chen through the salon as he sat at the helm of the boat. Both Moira's and Chen's backs were to me.

"It's fine, really. Fifteen minutes around the marina. It's fun."

I entered the salon.

"Where we going, Sam?" I spoke loudly enough to be heard over the hum of the engines.

Chen's body lurched forward over the boat's wheel. Moira snapped her head toward me. I nodded at her and her shoulders relaxed.

"What are you doing on my yacht?" Chen's shoulders and head were now turned toward me. The *Sea Stud* idled in the water just outside of its slip.

"I think the better question is what are you doing on your yacht?"

Chen stood up and pulled a phone out of his windbreaker pocket.

"I'm calling the police. You're trespassing."

"Good idea. We can talk to them about you holding Moira against her will and about your connection to a woman who was murdered in San Diego."

Chen's mouth fell open and he dropped the hand holding the phone to his side.

CHAPTER THIRTY-EIGHT

"WHAT WOMAN?" CHEN'S eyes still wide and his voice rose an octave. "I've never killed or hurt anyone in my life. And I haven't been to San Diego in months."

He sat on the covered bench seat behind a dining table. Moira and I were on a small sofa across from him. I wanted him behind the table so he'd feel somewhat confined. The boat was back in its slip. Moira had gone down and tied it to the cleat on the pier. Chen could refasten the line correctly after we left. The important thing was, the boat wasn't going anywhere right now. And neither was Samuel Chen.

As creepy as Chen had been with Moira, I was still convinced that he didn't know much about Obsidian Holdings' connection to Leveraged Investigations and whatever nefarious enterprises they were involved in. But I needed to scare him to get him to tell me what he did know.

"Sara Bhandari." I gave Chen a stone face. "She worked at Fulcrum Security who your investigative agency, Leveraged Investigations, did background checks for."

"I don't know this woman. Leveraged Investigations is not my company." Adamant. His voice more confident.

"Your signature is on the Obsidian Holdings checks that pays their rent." Moira, an edge to her voice that didn't come out often. Her dislike for Chen after he'd tried to get her alone in the middle of the ocean showing. "You're involved with Leveraged Investigations and they're involved in some bad things. That makes you involved in bad things."

"Who are you?" Chen looked at Moira. "Why are you and this man trying to set me up?"

"You set yourself up. You invited me onto your boat, promised that we'd stay docked, then you tried to isolate me alone with you out on the ocean." Moira's machine gun voice picked up momentum. "Sounds a lot like false imprisonment. Like on your rap sheet. You seem exactly like the kind of creep who would have something to do with people who'd murder an innocent woman."

"I was only going to sail around the marina like I said." His voice went up again, his face burned red. "And I don't know anything about this Sara woman. I just sign the checks for the rent. I don't know anything about Leveraged Investigations. I sign a lot of checks."

Bingo.

"A lot of checks to whom and for what?" I asked.

Chen pressed his lips together like a child who got caught saying something he wasn't supposed to.

Too late.

"I don't have to tell you anything about my business." He folded his arms across his chest. "Now it's time for you to get off my yacht."

"Why don't you tell me what you were planning on doing to me once we were alone at sea." Moira grinned at Chen. I hoped she never grinned at me that way. "I don't want to have to embellish too much when I talk to the police."

"You liar!" Chen raised up and bounced his thighs against the table and dropped back down.

"Who are the police going to believe? Me or a man who has a conviction for false imprisonment and is the owner of a boat with the name *Sea Stud*? I'll bet that conviction was a plea bargain down from something much worse. Something that happened out on the open water with no one around but you and your victim." Moira stood up and thrust a finger at Chen. "And quit lying about taking the boat for a cruise around the marina. You know what you were planning to do, you little creep."

Chen started to say something, then sealed his lips again.

"What else do you write checks for?" I asked calmly.

Chen kept his mouth shut and looked out the window at the ocean. Maybe wondering how much longer he'd be able to do that from his own boat.

"Sooner or later, you're going to be talking to the police, Samuel." I kept my voice as soothing as possible. Just a sensitive guy trying to help out. "And, with your priors, I doubt you want the first time to be about the . . . let's call it a misunderstanding for now, that you had with Moira. I don't think you know everything that goes on with Obsidian Holdings. I think you were put up as the face of the corporation and given a nice life. While it lasts. Ultimately, you were set up to take the fall when the time came and that time is fast approaching. Like an ICBM pointed at your chest."

"I didn't do anything wrong. I only do what I'm told." Sweat pebbled along Chen's hairline. "What do you want to know?"

"Who tells you what to do?" I asked. "David Liu?"

"Yes. Eh . . ." He looked down at the table. He had more to tell.

"Who else?"

He kept staring at the table.

"Albert Chen? Do you get orders from him too? Is he related to you?"

Samuel Chen still wouldn't look at me, but he nodded his head.

"Yes, Albert Chen is related to you, or yes, he tells you to do things?" Moira jumped in.

"Both." Chen, head down.

"How are you related to Albert and what does he ask you to do?" I asked.

"He's my uncle." Chen finally lifted his head. "He tells me what he wants me to do through David and comes here three or four times a year."

"From where? Taiwan?"

"Yes."

"How did you come to be the CEO of Obsidian Holdings?" I asked.

"My uncle offered me the job. My family used to be a major manu- facturer in Taiwan. Plush toys." Chen leaned against the back of the bench seat. "My father built the company from nothing. We lived a good life back home. We were a very important family in Taipei. Then my father got sick, and I took over as CEO. I'm the only son. But busi- ness slowed down and my father died. The market changed and I didn't have my father's guidance. Too much cheap competition. China. Vietnam. The Philippines. We couldn't compete with the cheap labor. The company went out of business five years ago. I had no way to help my family. My mother, my sisters, they were used to a certain kind of lifestyle. I had to help them."

From what I'd seen on Chen's Instagram posts and in his office and his boat, he was helping himself very well, living that certain kind of lifestyle. Whether he sent any of his wealth across the ocean was be- tween him and his family.

"So you helped your family by becoming the CEO of Obsidian Holdings?"

"Yes."

"Your uncle is a doctor and a professor, right? Back in Taipei?"

"Yes."

"I'm sure doctors and professors do well in Taiwan, but I didn't know they did well enough to put together an entity the size of Ob- sidian Holdings. Does he have other investors?"

"I don't know. We don't talk about that part of the business."

"Samuel." I waited a beat after he looked at me. "This boat has to be worth one or two million dollars. You bought a house in Pacific Grove four years ago that's been recently appraised for three-and-three-quarter million. The desk in your fricking office is worth twenty grand. You ran a manufacturing plant in Taiwan and you don't know if your uncle has investors because you don't talk about that part of the business? You expect us to believe that?"

"He has connections that he doesn't like to talk about. Maybe they have ownership in the corporation, maybe not. I don't know."

"Don't you look at the financials? Don't you want to know if your golden goose is going to keep laying eggs and who the other eggs go to?"

"My uncle is very secretive. He doesn't like to be questioned. If I ask too many questions, I'll lose this job. I can't afford to try to find a new job. I just do what he tells me to do."

"Yeah. You'd hate to lose a job like this." Moira, the edge back in her voice. "One that pays enough to own a house in Pacific Grove and a boat you can cruise around in and take women out to sea. Whether they want to go or not."

"Why does your uncle have you pay the rent for Leveraged Investigations?" I jumped in to get the conversation back on track.

"I don't know. I only do what I'm told."

"I don't believe you." Moira, back on the right track.

"Neither do I," I said.

"I'm telling you the truth." Chen.

Moira stood up and unwound the sarong from around her waist, then stepped in front of Chen and draped it over his head. He recoiled and yanked off the sarong.

"What are you doing, you crazy bitch?" Chen, red-faced.

"Give me that back." Moira held out her hand.

Chen threw the sarong at her, and she deftly caught it. She then picked up a knife from one of the place settings on the dining table and sawed a slit into the waist of the sarong.

"What are you doing?" Chen asked, but he looked like he'd figured out the game. His face turned even more red. Moira had gotten his DNA on the sarong.

"Embellishing." Moira tossed the knife onto the sofa next to me, then turned back to Chen and ripped the sarong where she'd made the slit.

"You crazy bitch! I didn't touch you!" He looked at me. "You're my witness. You know I didn't touch her."

"I don't know what happened before I got here." I opened my hands, palms up. "Just that you were about to take Moira out to sea against her will."

I'd seen Moira walk up to the edge of breaking the law a few times before. But she only crossed over it when I gave her a shove. The torn sarong was all her idea. I admired her commitment, but wondered if years of working with me had rubbed off on her. And not in a good way. She'd adopted my zeal to find the truth no matter the cost.

"Why are you trying to set me up?" Chen directed this at me. "What did I do to you?"

"It's not you, it's the people you associate with. They came after my livelihood and that's the same as going after my family." I stood up and walked over to Chen, pressed my hands down on the table, and leaned toward him. "And I take that personally. So, I need you to tell me everything you know about Leveraged Investigations or life is going to get very uncomfortable for you. Even here in paradise."

Chen let go a long breath and seemed to relax for the first time since I surprised him at the helm. He was ready to spill. Unload the weight he'd been carrying around. Probably all by himself.

"I don't know how long Obsidian has had a relationship with Leveraged Investigations, but I started signing checks to them about two years ago."

"Checks to them or checks to First Allied Plaza for the lease on their office?" Moira asked.

"Both."

"How much do you send them and how often?" I asked.

"They're on retainer for Obsidian. I send them a check for twenty-five thousand every month."

Moira and I looked at each other. Twenty-five K a month would be life-changing money for either one of us. Even half of it.

"Why does Obsidian Holdings need a private detective agency in San Diego on a monthly retainer?"

Chen lifted his hand and shook his head. "I just sign the checks."

"There's more to it than that, though." I leaned even closer down into Chen's personal space. "I saw the back-and-forth you had in Mandarin with David Liu this afternoon. You didn't just roll over for him. You asked him the same question when Liu told you to start sending checks to Leveraged Investigations, didn't you? Why do we need a P.I. agency in San Diego on retainer?"

"Liu told me that the corporation had business interests in San Diego that needed to be looked after and that Leveraged Investigations helped with those."

"Corporations put lawyers on retainer in a city four hundred miles away where you have business interests, not private investigative agencies." Moira. "Why a P.I. agency and not some high-powered attorney?"

"I asked David the same thing, but didn't get a very good answer. Just that Leveraged Investigations would be better than a lawyer." Chen tilted his head and lifted his eyebrows like we were all on the same team now.

"Better at intimidation." I looked at Moira, then back at Chen. "Are some of those business interests in the biotech and defense contractor fields?"

"Biotech, yes. I don't know about defense contractors. My uncle founded an organization called Bio-Ethic Strategies that educates companies about ways to adhere to ethical standards when dealing with biological systems and DNA. San Diego is one of the leading cities in the biotech industry."

I'd bumped up against biotech companies on a few cases over the years. A lot of money in it. And a lot of secrets.

"Your uncle is listed as the CEO of Bio-Ethic Strategies which has the same address as Obsidian Holdings. What exactly does it do?"

"It mostly funds third-party organizations that interact with biotech companies."

"Could some of those third parties be protesters?" Moira. More of a statement than a question. She caught me looking at her and went on. "I saw something on the news a few weeks ago about a group of protesters who called themselves Angels of Earth protesting outside of a San Diego biotech company. That would be one way to educate a company about adhering to ethical standards. Or pressure them to change practices that might benefit their competition."

I needed to get more tuned into the local news. Never know what piece of information might come in handy.

"It's possible. He was an activist when he was a student at university decades ago."

"What kind of an activist?" I asked.

"He was a member of the Democratic Progressive Party in Taiwan that helped reform the government and make it more democratic. He also protested against the over-industrialization of once rural areas."

"This is the same guy who now is the man behind the curtain of an international holding company? A former anti-industrialist?"

"Yes. He and my father used to argue about politics all the time. Uncle Albert was kind of a black sheep for a while. He mellowed as he got older, but he and my father never saw eye to eye on the family business."

"How did he go from anti-industrialist to captain of industry?" Moira.

"I wouldn't really call him a captain of industry. Obsidian Holdings has interests in a diverse field of enterprises."

He sounded like a brochure.

"You don't get more industrial than a defense contractor." I sat back down next to Moira on the small sofa. "We had a president once who said to beware of the military industrial complex on his last day in office. Fulcrum Security makes radar, sonar, and LIDAR for the Defense Department. Why did Leveraged Investigations all of a sudden start running background checks on prospective employees for Fulcrum Security?"

"I didn't know that they did. Like I keep telling you over and over, I don't know very much about them."

Something popped into my head that should have been there sooner.

"When I told you about the murdered woman in San Diego, you said you hadn't been to San Diego in months." I gave Moira a quick side glance. "How many months?"

"I was there in February." Chen's eyes went up to his left like he was trying to remember. "The first week."

"What did you do there?"

"I had to go to Leveraged Investigations." His eyes moved to the right. Now he was hiding something.

"Why?" I asked.

"David Liu asked me to." He didn't look at me.

Moira bolted up and threw her sarong at Chen. Again. It hit him in the face and fell onto the table. "Quit playing games and tell us why you went to Leveraged Investigations."

"I delivered a package to them."

"What was in the package?" Moira.

"It was wrapped up in shipping paper." Avoiding both Moira's and my eyes.

"Liu wrapped up something in shipping paper and then had you deliver it." I waited until he looked at me. "Let me guess, he had you drive the package down to San Diego instead of flying there, right?"

"Yes." He nodded his head.

"How much money was in the package?" I asked.

"How do I know? It was all wrapped up."

"Because you're not as stupid as you pretend to be and you wanted to know what was in the package Liu made you deliver to San Diego via car in case it was something illegal." I leaned forward on the sofa and rested my hand on my knees. "So you opened it. How much cash did you deliver to Leveraged Investigations?"

Chen stared down at the table some more.

"I'm coming up with new ideas on how to embellish my story when I talk to the police, Sam." Moira.

"Two hundred and fifty thousand dollars."

"Wow. That's a lot of money." Moira. "What was it for?"

"I don't know. I just delivered the package. I taped it back up after I looked at it, then drove it to San Diego. If I asked what the money was for, Liu, and then my uncle, would know that I opened the package."

"Who did you give the money to at Leveraged Investigations?" I opened the photo library on my phone and pulled up the picture of Mark Fields' driver's license, the onetime cop and now P. I. for Leveraged Investigations. I leaned across the narrow salon and held the photo up to Chen's face. "This guy?"

"No. It was somebody else. His name is Jeff Grant."

Moira and I looked at each other. Jeff Grant was the name on the first set of background check reports for the three late hires at

Fulcrum Security that disappeared, then reappeared with Mark Fields' name on them.

I yanked back my phone and pulled up the photo Moira snapped last year of the Leveraged guy who pushed her off the domestic case and the man in the Padres cap who I tailed from SDPD's press conference on Saturday. I showed the photo to Chen. "Is this Jeff Grant?"

"Yeah, that's him. That's the guy I gave the money to that day. And I saw him one other time. He was with Liu up here about two weeks ago. Liu used my office to talk to him but didn't include me in the meeting."

Moira and I exchanged glances again.

"Two weeks ago, when? Give me the exact date." My heart pistoned in my chest. Today was Monday, May 22. I met with Sara Bhandari on Thursday, the 11th. She was murdered sometime on Saturday night, the 13th. Sometime roughly two weeks ago could be a coincidence. Any time specifically between the 11th and the 13th wouldn't be.

"Let me see." Chen pulled out his phone and tapped the screen a couple times, probably pulling up his calendar. "It was actually Friday the 12th."

The day after I met with Sara Bhandari for the secret lunch. And the day before she was murdered.

CHAPTER THIRTY-NINE

MOIRA AND I sat in my room at the Best Western a few blocks from Obsidian Holdings. Moira on the bed, me on the wooden desk chair.

"The police are convinced that Sara Bhandari was murdered by the Coastal Rapist, Rick." Adamant. "I saw clips on the news of their press conference on TV that you saw in person. There's probably a lot more to the rapist's MO and signature than your reporter friend knows about."

"Jeff Grant shows up at Obsidian Holdings for a closed-door meeting with David Liu the day after Sara Bhandari had a secret lunch with me to tell me about the odd things going on at Fulcrum Security. Particularly the odd things about the background reports done by Leveraged Investigations. And the next day she's murdered? That's not a coincidence."

"What about the rapist's M.O. and signature?" Moira raised her hands.

"I told you, Mark Fields used to be Detective Skupin's partner. He gets together for a beer and a little shop talk with his old buddy and learns enough about the Coastal Rapist to duplicate the M.O. and the signature when he or Jeff Grant or both murder Sara. It's not a perfect match, but it's close enough. The serial rapist makes the next progression that most of these sick bastards eventually do. Murder."

"So, you and Sara Bhandari meet for lunch and the next day Jeff Grant meets with David Liu to get the go-ahead on the murder and Fields sets up a get-together with his ex-partner who is elbows deep in a murder investigation but has time to chat about the serial rapist's methods and then the next night there's another rape, which ends in murder?" Moira looked at me like I had brain damage. Which I did. "First of all, would Skupin even have time to meet with Fields and would he give up that much information? Secondly, wouldn't Fields be worried that Skupin might think it's odd that there's another rape the day after he downloaded the Coastal Rapist's methods to his old buddy?"

"Skupin could have told Fields about the rapist a month or two ago. Maybe they meet every couple weeks for beers and shop talk. Fields gets the okay from Liu through Grant and one or both of them kill Sara. Fields has the info on the Coastal Rapist in his head from his weekly chats with Skupin and they stage the murder accordingly."

"That would be tough to prove in court."

"I don't have to prove it in court."

"What is that supposed to mean?" She folded her arms in front of her.

"I just need to gather enough evidence to make the police take a second look at the evidence they already have."

"That's easier said than done. Particularly now that SDPD has made its theory about the Coastal Rapist public."

"That's where Max Andrus and the power of the press come in. Some outside pressure from the media and Sara's family."

"I thought you were on the outs with Sara's sister because of the dick pick."

"I am. But you're not."

"What do you mean?" She tilted her head to the right.

"When we get back, please put a report together to give to Shreya Gargano. She may think I'm a creep, but she wasn't sold on the police's theory a hundred percent when I talked to her. Of course, this was before their press conference. If she's still not convinced, she can get in front of the cameras any time she wants. She's not only family, she's a former fourteen-time Emmy Award–winning news reporter."

"Fine, but we hardly have everything all buttoned up. And we only have a pervert's word for most of what we've learned up here. Plus, we don't have anything strong enough to be close to a motive for Leveraged Investigations to murder Sara Bhandari."

"We're close." I bounced an index finger in front of myself. "Chen delivers the two hundred fifty grand to Grant the first week of February and roughly two to three weeks later Leveraged Investigations starts doing background checks for Fulcrum."

"But why all the extra money on top of their retainer just to run background checks for a new client? It doesn't make any sense."

"The money was used to pay off someone at Fulcrum to start using Leveraged for background checks." I stuck my thumbnail against my teeth, then yanked my thumb out of my mouth. "Buddy Gatsen, the production manager responsible for hiring people that work on the radar, sonar, and LIDAR systems, would be the logical choice."

"That's a possibility, but back to the background checks themselves. Mark Fields' name is on all the reports Leveraged does except for the ones that end up missing, which were signed by Jeff Grant until they were found and had Fields' name on them, right?"

"Right. Why didn't they want Grant's name on the reports?" We looked at each other, then let our eyes drift in thought.

Moira spoke first.

"You didn't find any records for a Jeff Grant that matched the photo you showed Chen, right?"

"Right?" I wasn't sure where she was going.

"What if Jeff Grant is just an alias that this guy uses? Something not connected to a social security number or a driver's license that he only uses for things that won't be scrutinized—"

"And he used it on the background reports he did for Fulcrum without thinking." I sat up straight in the chair. "Then he realized what he'd done after he sent them in and was worried that if someone examined the reports, they might find out there was no Jeff Grant, so he had to change the name."

"Right. Or maybe Fields was out of town or couldn't do the reports for some reason and when he sees Grant's mess-up, he resends the reports."

"Yeah, but none of this can be done without someone on the inside at Fulcrum. Someone who is deft at working with computer data who can make data disappear and not be easily found. Someone who could add a dick pic and lewd comments to an existing email and alter the date and time and make it look like it was on the original."

"The thing we're missing is why would Leveraged go to all this trouble for a few background reports on new employees?" Moira bit her lower lip before she spoke again. "It would make some kind of sense if the employees they did the background checks on worked for the Fulcrum Security division that makes products for the Department of Defense, but that's impossible, right? A governmental agency does all the background checks on employees that work for that side."

"DCSA."

"And there's a firewall between the two divisions at Fulcrum Security, right?"

"That's it!" I stood up from my chair and started pacing.

"That's what?" Moira got off the bed, caught up in my energy.

"Andrew Burke, the systems analyst Leveraged Investigations did the background check on who Fulcrum hired. What if Obsidian wanted him working for Fulcrum because he could get through the firewall? He applies for a position and Leveraged polishes up an immaculate background report so Buddy Gatsen has his ass covered when he hires the guy."

"Why does Obsidian want this guy hired? Intellectual property theft?" Moira stood in front of me. I stopped pacing and shook my head. She squinted at me. "Are you going where I think you're going?"

"Albert Chen is the key to this whole thing. Everything about Leveraged Investigations and Sara's murder."

"Because you think he's a Chinese spy?" Moira put her hands on her hips and tilted her head to the side. A mother questioning her fabulist child.

I didn't answer right away and started pacing again. Finally, "He's a former anti-industrialist who saw the light and is the genius behind a global holding company from his position as a college professor? A company that has no visible means of income but funds a crooked P.I. agency and activist groups that protest biotech companies? Where does all the money come from to fund all of these activities?"

"And you think it's the Chinese government?" Moira, still not believing.

"It may sound crazy, but if all the other information we've uncovered is true, then it's the only thing that makes sense. Defense contractors, biotech companies. You don't think the Chinese government would be interested in these kinds of businesses?"

"Of course they would be, but that doesn't mean they have an international spy ring run out of Monterey, California, through Obsidian Holding Company."

"Why not? Do I have to remind you that they had a spy chauffeuring around a U.S. senator for twenty years and another one sleeping with a U.S. congressman? Why wouldn't they operate out of some obscure holding company a hundred miles from Sacramento and San Francisco and two hundred miles from L.A.?"

Because you're not James Bond and I'm not Ethan Hunt." Moira put her hands on her hips.

"Who's Ethan Hunt?"

"Tom Cruise in the Mission Impossible movies."

"You're right, you're not Ethan Hunt. You're much taller."

"I'm not kidding." Moira stood up and two-handed shoved me in the chest. "If you go to Detective Skupin and tell him Sara Bhandari was killed by his former partner on the command of a Chinese spy ring, he'll laugh you out of his office."

"I'll tell him the facts we know and leave my conclusions to myself. For now." My phone buzzed in my pocket.

I took it out and checked the screen. Leah.

I looked at Moira and she read my face immediately.

"I'm going to my room. We'll finish this later."

I answered the phone.

"My Thursday client cancelled so we'll be in San Diego sometime Wednesday." Leah's voice, devoid of emotion. Almost worse than anger. Disconnected. Uninvolved. And she'd said she'd be in San Diego instead of be home. In her mind, she'd already made the permanent move up to Santa Barbara.

"Okay." I wasn't okay, but wasn't in a position to argue after what happened at the Landingham house. "I'm sorry about this morning."

"It's hardly the first time I've seen you enraged, but you were out of control today." Voice still flat. "I've been dealing with your anger for months. I've tried to be patient and not push you to seek help. I've tried to let you work through things on your own, like I know you prefer. After this morning, I see that was a mistake. You need to get some professional help or we're not going to be a family anymore. Not in Santa Barbara, San Diego, or anywhere else. We can talk more about this on Wednesday. I'm certainly not going to do it over the phone."

She hung up.

I dropped the phone like it was on fire. I thought of Krista's wails ricocheting down the halls of the Landingham house this morning. The fear in Leah's eyes as she saw my rage completely unmasked for the first time. Her choice of Santa Barbara and her work and family over me.

The absence from my family and the distance in Leah's voice and words hollowed me out. My world, the life I'd carefully constructed, was spinning out of control. My control. I sank down to the carpet. For once, the emptiness and frustration inside me was filled with sadness. Instead of rage.

CHAPTER FORTY

WE GOT ON the road a little after eight the next morning on the drive south. Moira didn't say a word or even look at me when I took the 46 East at Los Robles off the 101 to eventually catch the 5 South. There'd be no sightseeing on this drive. Or the potential for a Santa Barbara drop-in. We'd be forty miles east of Santa Barbara on the wrong freeway.

The route I wished I'd taken on the way up.

A couple hours into the drive, Moira started typing out a rough report on her laptop about what we'd learned in Monterey. She had a copy of my running report in her email. Going all the way back to my first notes from my lunch meeting with Sara Bhandari. Her concern about the missing, then found, background reports that I'd initially thought was just some run-of-the-mill office mess-up that was overblown. If not paranoid or delusional.

I could not have been more wrong.

The way I'd handled Sara's initial request still bothered me. Not the work I did, which was diligent from the start, but my attitude when I talked to her at lunch. I'd let my blowup with Leah and her running off with Krista up to Santa Barbara affect my disposition that day. Sara had come to me for help and I'd made it seem like an inconvenience. She was concerned about something at work that she could have easily ignored and gone on with her everyday life. Most people wouldn't have given it a second thought. If it didn't affect them or their income, let it go.

But Sara Bhandari didn't let it go. Something was wrong, against the norm, and she had to figure out, and fix, whatever it was. She'd gone out on a limb alone, risking her job to ask for my help. She'd done what I'd strived to do ever since my first wife died. Find the truth.

She'd been right about her concerns and I wasn't going to let her death be in vain.

Moira peppered me with questions about the case as she typed and I drove, forcing me to defend my conclusions. A good exercise and it enabled her to sharpen the report she planned to present to Shreya Gargano. If Shreya would agree to see her. An added benefit to Moira hearing my defense was that I was slowly winning her over to my conspiracy theory. I could hear it in her voice and in the adamance of her questions. The questions she asked me, she also silently asked herself. And agreed with my answers.

I read Moira better than I did my own wife. My strength as a partner versus my shortcomings as a husband.

Moira finally put away her laptop around noon.

"Did you also write a report for Angus?" I asked.

Angus Buttis was the lawyer she sometimes did work for and who was going to potentially sue Leveraged Investigations on her behalf. And, I guess, mine too.

"Just some notes to myself." Moira didn't sound enthused.

"Do you think anything we learned would help in a lawsuit against Leveraged?" I glanced over at her.

"Probably not something civil. I'll leave that to Angus." She looked straight ahead through her sunglasses. "That's not my main concern right now. Finding out what Leveraged Investigations was up to at

Fulcrum Security and if they had anything to do with Sara Bhandari's murder is. And if they did, making sure they get caught."

"Roger that."

* * *

I called Dylan Helmer's cell phone through the Bluetooth connection in my car as we started up the Grapevine, the pass through the Tehachapi Mountains from the San Joaquin Valley into Los Angeles County. I wanted to see if she'd learned anything more about the Leveraged background reports on the three hires.

Five rings then voicemail. I left her a message to call me. A minute later a text pinged through the entertainment system of my car, which was connected to my phone through Apple Play.

The female mechanical voice declared a text from Dylan. I hit *play. Can't talk right now. Police are here. Buddy Gatsen is dead.*

CHAPTER FORTY-ONE

"The production manager?" Moira snapped her head toward me.

"They're tying up loose ends," I said. "He's the one who did the hiring for production. The guy who Sara said made the decision to start using Leveraged Investigations for background checks."

"You're jumping to conclusions again. We don't even know how he died. He could have died in a car accident or had a heart attack."

"The police don't show up at someone's work for a car accident or a heart attack."

"Let's wait until we talk to Dylan Helmer before you get paranoid."

Dylan called me a half hour later, as Moira and I passed by Pyramid Lake in Lebec, north of Los Angeles. I put the call on the car speakers.

"I'm with my partner, Moira MacFarlane. You can trust her. Okay?"

"Okay." Dylan's voice had the hollow echo like she was in a stall in the employee bathroom again.

"Tell us what happened to Buddy Gatsen."

"All I'm sure of is that he's dead. Someone from the production floor told me that Buddy committed suicide."

"Committed suicide?" I looked at Moira, whose sunglasses were locked on mine.

"He sat in his truck in the garage with the door closed and turned on the ignition." Dylan's voice quivered.

"Did you talk to the police?"

"No, but they talked to Madolyn."

"Did you talk to her afterward?"

"Yes, I asked her what the police wanted after they talked to her, but she just told me to go back to work and then she took off."

"You mean she left work?" I asked.

"Yes. She got in her car and drove off. Bridget and I watched her from the window."

"She and Buddy were friends, right? She must have been pretty upset."

"I don't know how good of friends they were. Most of the time I saw Buddy, he was in Madolyn's office arguing with her. She wasn't crying or anything like that when she left. She almost seemed afraid."

I glanced at Moira. Her eyebrow were raised above the frames of her sunglasses.

"Who found his body?"

"The shop foreman." Dylan's voice, now steady in the hollow echo of the bathroom. "Buddy didn't come to work today and didn't call in sick. He never missed work. The foreman called and texted him all morning because there was an issue with a big order, but Buddy didn't answer, so the foreman drove over to his house a couple hours ago to check on him. When he got there, he smelled exhaust fumes coming out of the garage. My friend told me that the foreman opened the garage door and found Buddy in his truck. Dead."

"Do you know if the engine was still running?" Moira asked.

"I don't know. That's a good question. Are you thinking about time of death?" Dylan's cop father's DNA and experience running through her veins.

Moira tilted her head and pressed her lips together, surprised by the question.

"Yeah, but we'd have to know how much gas was in the tank and when the truck was started to get a time of death window that way," I answered and mouthed "father was a cop" to Moira. "Unless the ignition was turned off when the foreman found Gatsen. Then you've got a murder, not a suicide. The odd thing is that no neighbors smelled the exhaust if the truck ran for a long time. If they did, you'd think they would have called the police."

"I guess so." Dylan.

Moira took out her phone and started tapping away on it.

"Do you know where Gatsen lived?" I asked.

"No. Sorry."

Moira looked up from her phone. "Dylan, do you know what Buddy's given name is?"

"No. I'm guessing Bud."

I muted our side of the call. "What's up?"

"I looked up what name Buddy was a nickname for, and not only is it one for Bud, it can also be one for Robert, Donald, and William."

"That widens the field a bit. You trying to find his address?"

"Yes. I thought we could take a look at his house on the way home."

"I'd better go now." Dylan through the car phone.

"Okay, but be careful." It was possible that Buddy Gatsen committed suicide. But it seemed more likely to me that someone killed him. And I bet Madolyn Cummings felt the same way. That's why she fled from work.

"I will." Dylan Helmer hung up.

I looked at Moira after I hung up. "I shouldn't have gotten Dylan involved in this, should I?"

"You didn't know as much then as you do now, but, yeah, even then it was a dicey call."

I didn't say anything and Moira went back to work on her phone. The need to find the truth no matter what. Rebirthed after being dormant for the past year and a half. In my blood. My DNA. The pursuit of the truth was an admirable quality in most people. The "no matter what" was problematic when I got other people involved. It always had been. But now more innocents were involved. Not only the ones who were sucked into situations out of their control, but my family was in play now. They could be hurt as part of collateral damage from the evil I sought out and confronted.

My life no longer allowed me the selfishness of my heroic quests.

"I think I found him." Moira's voice pulled me out of my thoughts.

"Who?"

"William, probably also known as "Buddy," Gatsen. Luckily, there aren't that many Gatsens in San Diego County. I found a William Gatsen in Rancho Bernardo. Age, fifty-six. Does that sound about right?"

"Yeah. I put him in his late fifties, so that works. And Rancho Bernardo is just south of Escondido."

The traffic had turned to sludge in the northern part of L.A. It didn't matter what time of day it was, you were always going to hit stop-and-go traffic somewhere along the way on a journey though Los Angeles. Doing eighty in the free flow of traffic was a lot less hazardous than going five miles an hour in bumper-to-bumper.

I felt Moira staring at me and risked a quick look. Her sunglasses were pulled down on her nose, her eyes boring into me. "I know where Rancho Bernardo is. I've lived in San Diego my whole life. That's why I targeted this William Gatsen." She held up her phone to me. "Is this him?"

I grabbed the phone and held it in front of me so I would have the traffic in my background vision. I shot a look at the picture she'd pulled up on the phone, then handed it back to her.

"Yeah, that's Buddy Gatsen. What else did you find out about him?"

"Divorced. Two grown children. One of each. No police record. Your average middle-aged American male."

"Except he supposedly got into his truck, left the garage door closed, turned on the ignition, and left it in park."

"Yeah. That part's not average."

CHAPTER FORTY-TWO

WILLIAM GATSEN LIVED at the end of a cul-de-sac a couple streets north of Rancho Bernardo Road. Rancho Bernardo is a master-planned community in a hilly part of the county about thirty miles north of downtown San Diego. A lot of greenery and one of the nicer places to live in Southern California.

We knew we'd found Gatsen's house when we turned down his street. The house was police-taped off and there were still a couple of San Diego Police cruisers and a slick-top detective car parked out front.

I parked along the curb three houses back from Gatsen's.

The location of the house probably explained why no neighbors called the police about the smell of exhaust fumes. The lots on the street were large and Gatsen's house was set back a ways from the street at the end of a long driveway. Someone out walking their dog on the sidewalk would probably be too far from the closed garage door to smell anything.

A Channel 6 News van was parked just outside the police tape. Cathy Cade walked toward the van, followed by a cameraman who held his camera to the side. Packing up and heading back to the station or to the next story for the five o'clock news.

"Shit."

"What?" Moira asked.

"I have to go talk to Cathy Cade."

"The reporter? Why?"

"To find out what she knows about Gatsen's death." I opened the car door and slid out. "Be right back."

I leaned against the car and stretched out my hamstrings. We only stopped once for gas in Buttonwillow four hours earlier. My body took longer to loosen up than it did only a couple years ago.

I made it to the van right after the cameraman put his camera away and closed the back door. Tall, thin, with a beard and a man bun. He'd been at Cade's side for years filming her as she dug into people's grief at the worst time of their lives. In some ways, Cade and I weren't that different. But I didn't have someone filming me while I rummaged around in the wreckage of people's lives.

Cade rolled down the window of the passenger door as I approached. Thick brown hair, coiffed perfectly, sparkly brown eyes behind oversized horn-rimmed glasses, resting above the up tip of her nose. She wore a red form-fitting dress.

"Rick Cahill, private eye." The confident voice that could turn from solemn to perky in a blink, for whatever news events necessitated. "It's good to see you out and about again. I like the new-look glasses."

The guy with the man bun got in the driver's side of the van, but didn't turn on the ignition.

"Thanks. They're for vision, not fashion." I smiled. I'd had a couple encounters on camera with Cade in the past. And a couple off camera. She was bold and relentless. That's what made her a good reporter. It was never personal to her. Just a story. It had always been personal to me. Just my life. I never held it against her, though. At least, not for more than a week or two. "Police tape and you're here to report. Who died?"

"What brings you to a crime scene this far from Bay Ho?" She knew where I lived. She'd hounded me all the way up to my front door once a few years ago. Live on camera. That one took more than a couple weeks for my steam to settle.

"Crime scene?" I raised my eyebrows. "Was someone murdered?"

"Yellow tape. You know what I mean. It's a suicide." Cade squinched her face at me. "Why are you here?"

"Happenstance."

"No such thing." She smiled. A dazzler that played well in front of the camera when a soldier was reunited with his family or a couple celebrated their seventy-fifth wedding anniversary. "Did you know the deceased? Are you investigating him for a case you're working on?"

"Didn't know him personally. Fulcrum Security is one of my background check accounts. Heard thirdhand what happened and was in the neighborhood, so I came by for a look."

"So, you never met Buddy Gatsen?" Thick brown eyebrows rose above her eyeglasses. "And you're not investigating him?"

"No." Mostly true. The usual amount I reserved for the press. If I talked to them at all. "Why are you all the way up here from your station in Clairemont? I didn't know that suicides of unknown factory production managers were newsworthy."

"Sleeping pill suicides in the privacy of your own bedroom aren't newsworthy. Closing your garage door and turning on the ignition of your truck isn't as spectacular as jumping off the Coronado Bridge, but it does have a certain compelling public interest to it."

"I love how you romanticize the news." I winked at her. "Did he leave a note? Anything suspicious?"

"Why would there be anything suspicious?"

"Just doing my due diligence."

"So, you are investigating this?"

"Trying to get answers for a friend of Gatsen's at Fulcrum Security." Mostly a lie. "A favor. Was there a note?"

"What's the friend's name?" Cade, still digging for a deeper story.

"It's just someone who wants to know what happened. No grand conspiracy, big-picture thing. But I'll ask the person if they want to talk to the press. If they do, I'll make sure you get first dibs. For now, it's confidential."

"Okay." She grabbed a purse from the floor of the car and pulled out a business card and handed it to me. "Tell the friend that they can be interviewed on camera or off. Whatever they're most comfortable with."

"Roger. Did Gatsen leave a note?"

"You'll just have to watch my report at 5:00, 6:00, and 11:00 p.m."

"Come on, Cathy. I gave a little, now it's your turn."

"Okay, but keep it to yourself until after the five o'clock broadcast. He left a handwritten note that simply said, 'I can't take it anymore.'"

CHAPTER FORTY-THREE

"I CAN'T TAKE it anymore?" Moira repeated the phrase I told her.

"Yeah. In his own hand." We sat in the car. "Or, supposedly in his own hand. I guess if the police are interested enough, they could talk to someone who knew his handwriting or have an expert compare it with something he'd written earlier."

"He could have been forced at gunpoint to write the note," Moira said. "But the killer couldn't sit in a truck with the engine running in a closed garage and hold a gun on Gatsen unless he was breathing through a scuba tank. If the coroner's toxicology report shows Gatsen was sedated, then maybe we have a murder. Otherwise, it's suicide."

"I guess so." I pulled away from the curb. "You want me to drop you home, or you up for making one more stop?"

"What do you have in mind?"

"See if you can find Madolyn Cummings' address." I spelled out Madolyn for her.

"Okay. I'm up for that." Moira went to work on her phone.

"I think I found her." Moira looked up from her laptop a few minutes later. "Not too many people in San Diego County spell Madolyn that way. I found a three-year-old California driver's license for Madolyn Cummings Wirshing. Married to Kenneth Alan Wirshing. Former residence Reno, Nevada." Moira handed me her phone. "Is that her?"

The woman in the photo on the phone had a Poway address. She had long blond hair and a lot of eye makeup. Cummings' hair was shorter and brown, but the eyes matched. Brown. The Madolyn Cummings at Fulcrum Security wore eye makeup that was much more restrained. However, there was a facial resemblance and a similar curl to the lips. I'd only met Cummings the one time and couldn't be certain without more information. The age of the woman on the driver's license was listed at forty-two, three years ago. I'd put Cummings in her early to mid-forties, so the age range was close enough.

"I think so, but can't swear to it. If it's her, she'd changed her look a little. Dark hair now. Less makeup."

"The woman on the CDL was married three years ago. Maybe she got divorced and reverted back to her maiden name, Cummings. Or maybe she dropped the Wirshing unofficially."

"Maybe. It happens all the time." I took one last look and handed Moira back her phone.

"I found something else kind of interesting on Madolyn Cummings Wirshing on Google. Six years ago, she won $103,000 playing video poker at Caesars Palace in Las Vegas." Moira scrolled though her phone, then stopped. "The *Reno Gazette Journal* reported that she won a progressive jackpot with a royal flush. Apparently, she was with a bunch of girlfriends for a bachelorette party weekend. 'Gambling wasn't even on our itinerary,' said bride-to-be Lissa Greene. "But Maddie gambled alone late into the morning the night before we left. She bought us all drinks on the plane home the next day.' The article concluded with, 'Wirshing declined to be interviewed for this story.' There wasn't a picture attached to the article."

"She gambled alone late into the night on a bachelorette weekend trip in Vegas," I said, as much to myself as Moira. "You have to sit at the video poker machine for hours to get a progressive pot to build like that."

"And she lived in Reno. Easy access to casinos twenty-four hours a day."

"So, you're thinking the same thing I am?" I asked.

"That Madolyn Cummings may have a gambling problem? Maybe." Moira looked back down at her phone. "Let's drop by her house. I have her address."

"Poway?" The city listed on the copy of the California Driver's License.

"No. She now lives in Escondido in a house she bought under the Cummings Wirshing name. Maybe the Poway residence was when she was married."

"She's got a handful of casinos with video poker machines within an hour of Escondido. The closest being Harrah's and Valley View in Valley Center." I took my phone out of my pocket, looked up a contact, and tapped it. The call was picked up on the second ring. I put it on the car speakers. "Bao?" Rick Cahill."

"Rick, how goes it?" Still a noticeable Mandarin accent after living twenty-five years in the States.

"Good, and you?"

"Very perfect. No more inside cheats after the work you did for me. What favor do you need?"

To the point. The way I liked it.

"I need to know if you or Valley View, Harrah's, Pala, or Casino Pauma have a Madolyn Cummings or Madolyn Cummings Wirshing on your VIP list." I spelled out her name. "And if you do, if she's ever gotten out of line."

The sound of keystrokes on a keyboard came though the speakers.

"We never have. Give me a half hour, and I'll find out about the others." He hung up without a goodbye. Business over all else.

"Who was that?" Moira.

"Bao Zhao." I started the car and exited the late Buddy Gatsen's street. "He's the casino manager at Barona Casino. They got hit by a cheating ring a few years ago and I confirmed for him that it was an inside job. Three dealers and a pit boss were in on it with an offshoot of the Tran ring. Took Barona for about a hundred grand, but some other casinos for a lot more. The FBI got involved in the end and made some arrests."

"I remember hearing about that. You never told me you were involved in that investigation."

"You never asked."

"Asshole."

I got onto I-15 and headed north. Moira tapped away on her phone the whole time. By the time I got off the freeway at West Via Rancho Parkway, she'd already sent emails back and forth with her realtor friend and found out that Cummings still owed $780,000 on the home she bought for $999,000 two years ago. And she'd been three months in arrears on her mortgage back in January of this year, but was now current.

"She's three months behind on her mortgage in January." I shot a glance at Moira. "Samuel Chen drives to San Diego and drops off two hundred and fifty grand to Leveraged Investigations the first week of February, and they're suddenly doing background checks for Fulcrum Security where Madolyn Cummings is the VP of HR who hires P.I. agencies to run checks and all of a sudden, she's current on her mortgage."

"But you said that Buddy Gatsen was the person who made the change to Leveraged to run the background reports."

"That's what Sara told me, but Dylan wasn't sure. Maybe he and Cummings were in on it together and something went wrong. Thus, all the angry meetings between Gatsen and Cummings in her office."

"Maybe, but let's follow the facts first, not your assumptions." Moira, the regulator as usual.

"Yes, Mother."

"Shut up."

Two minutes later, I turned down Cummings' street. Moira gave me the address. Two houses down on the left. A late model silver Audi TTS sat in Madolyn Cummings' driveway.

"Nice car," I said.

"Yeah. I wonder if she bought it sometime after the first week of February."

"The week when Samuel Chen dropped off $250,000 at Leveraged Investigations."

"Me, too."

I drove past her house, did a Y turn, and parked a few houses down on the opposite side of the street. We'd wait and see if Madolyn Cummings stayed holed up at home or went on the run. With Buddy Gatsen gone, she had to wonder if she'd be next.

Moira and I watched for a solid thirty minutes. The only action being a car leaving a house on the block and another one turning onto the street and passing by us. Each time we slid down below the dashboard.

My phone rang twenty minutes in. Bao Zhao. I took the call through the phone's speaker function since the car was turned off.

"Madolyn Cummings is a VIP at both Pala and Casino Pauma. Degenerate gambler. Video poker and roulette. Been as deep as thirty-five with Pala and twenty-five with Pauma. Been all square for a few months. Still hits one or the other two or three times a week."

"All square as in she paid off her tab in February of this year?"

"I didn't ask for that much detail. Both managers just told me that she's been all paid up for a few months."

"Thanks, Bao. I owe you."

"No problem. A small favor." He hung up.

"A degenerate gambler." Moira kept her eyes on Madolyn Cummings' house.

"Yup. Who got right with all her delinquent bills around February when our pal Samuel Chen hand-delivered two hundred and fifty grand to Leveraged Investigations."

"The last loose end?"

"That's my bet."

Forty-five minutes after we parked across from her home, Madolyn Cummings hurried outside rolling two suitcases. She put the suitcases in her trunk, scanned the street, then got into her car and drove off.

CHAPTER FORTY-FOUR

I WAITED UNTIL Cummings turned left onto the cross street, then started the engine.

"Grab the binos out of the trunk," I said to Moira and tapped the trunk release button under the dashboard."

Moira dashed out of the car. Two seconds later, the trunk lid slammed shut and she jumped back into the car.

"Don't lose her." Moira held the binoculars up to her eyes as we turned left on Quiet Hills. "She just turned right on Avenida Magoria."

"Roger."

With Moira on the binoculars, I could stay a half a mile behind Cummings and still keep track of her on a freeway. Surface streets were more difficult. More curves, turns, and elevation so you had to stay closer. Usually within rearview mirror range of your target. The problem for the person manning, or womaning, the binoculars was that for most of the drive it looked like you were about to rear-end cars that were a hundred yards ahead of you. It took some getting used to. And I drove fast.

Cummings made her way onto Interstate 15 North. She drove fast, weaving in and out of lanes. I tried to stay mostly in a lane to her right, a quarter to a half mile back. It was close to 6:00 p.m. and traffic was thick. She passed the Highway 76 exit and continued north.

My guess was that she was headed to Ontario Airport or LAX. San Diego's Lindbergh Field was thirty miles in the other direction. She had two suitcases and had left her home in a hurry.

She was running. But traffic had slowed her to a walk fifteen minutes into her escape.

The congestion eased up around Fallbrook, but slammed to bumper-to-bumper south of Temecula.

"She moved over to the right-hand lane." Moira, binoculars still up to her eyes. I edged over into the slow lane. "I think she'll be getting off on Temecula Parkway. You need to make up some ground if she gets off there. She could go anywhere once she's off the freeway."

I scanned the road and all my mirrors. No CHP in sight. I yanked the steering wheel to the right and drove on the shoulder.

"She took the Temecula Parkway off-ramp, but she's stopped in traffic."

I sped along the shoulder for a quarter mile, then whipped back into an opening in the slow lane just before the exit.

"She turned onto the Parkway." Moira dropped the binoculars into her lap and blew out an angry breath.

I jagged over into the next lane and cut off an SUV and did the same in the next lane under a cacophony of car horns. The third lane had fewer cars in it and turned right onto Temecula Parkway. But traffic was still sludge. The light turned green, but we barely moved.

Moira put the binoculars back up to her eyes when we slow-motioned conga-lined into the turn. "I don't see her. We lost her."

"I know where she's going."

"What?" Moira dropped the binos again. "Where?"

"Pechanga."

"Oh." Moira pinched her lips and nodded her head. "Pechanga."

Pechanga Resort Casino was owned by the Pechanga Band of Lu-iseño Indians and the largest casino on the West Coast. Snuggled in Temecula in the valley of the Temescal Mountains.

Temecula was a bedroom community at the southwestern corner of Riverside County just north of San Diego County. It had a piece of both counties in its DNA. A little bit of the suburban beauty of San Diego and the inland ranginess of Riverside. It sat among rolling hills that produced a thriving wine industry.

I stayed in the outside lane on the Temecula Parkway, then swerved across two lanes to make the turn onto Pechanga Parkway. Even if I knew where Madolyn Cummings was headed, we still needed to get a visual on her to find out what room she was staying in. I sped down the street, blowing through a yellow to red light at Loma Linda Road. Moira again had the binoculars to her eyes.

"Got her! She's approaching Via Eduardo."

I pinned the gas to the floor and made the light at Wolf Creek Drive.

"She had to stop at the light." Moira took down the binos. Cummings' Audi now visible to the naked eye.

The light turned green. Cummings started up and I got the tail end of the yellow and sped to the entrance of Pechanga. I gained ground on Cummings as she turned onto the resort property.

The casino had a massive Vegas-like footprint and even a golf course, but the outside of the casino itself had a rustic vibe. Cummings pulled up to the entrance of the casino and the valet parking. I pulled over to the side, thirty yards behind.

"Find out her room number and get a room on the same floor."

"Do we really need a room?"

"No, but we need room keys to be able to operate the elevators."

"Oh." She popped out of the car and hurried along the walkway toward the entrance.

Cummings got out of her car and opened the trunk of the Audi to let the bellhop grab her suitcases. I laid back and waited for her to enter the hotel. Moira followed her inside. I parked on the second floor of the parking structure fifty yards away.

My phone pinged a text as I walked to the casino.

Moira: *I couldn't get her room number, but she's staying on the eleventh floor.*

Me: *Where are you?*

Moira: *In the lobby.*

Me: *Be there in five.*

I walked into the marbled lobby and saw Moira standing next to the thirty-foot-high chandeliered water feature. Vegasy, but tasteful.

"What do you want to do? Stake out the elevators?" Moira.

"I might have an easier way." I pulled out my phone and tapped the most recent call.

"Two favors in one day, bro?" Bao Zhao's gruff voice. "After not hearing from you for over a year? What's the ask this time?"

"Harder than the first one." I looked at Moira and mentally crossed my fingers. "I'm in the lobby of Pechanga and I'd like to know if you can find out which room the woman I asked you about earlier just checked into. Do you have a contact here?"

"I do have a contact there, but I can't ask her a favor like that." Dismissive. "Too much potential liability if something were to happen to this woman in her room. Hell, bro, I wouldn't give you that information for my casino."

"I understand. It was a big ask." And a creepy one on its surface. This Hail Mary was going unanswered. "Thanks, anyway."

Moira frowned.

"I said I couldn't get you her room number." Bao sounded offended. "I didn't say I couldn't do anything. Give me a little time. Same name as earlier, right?"

"Same both names. Madolyn Cummings and Madolyn Cummings Wirshing. Thanks, Bao."

"Wait until I see what I can do before you thank me. Stick by your phone." He hung up.

CHAPTER FORTY-FIVE

"WHAT'S YOUR PLAN if your friend doesn't come through?"

Moira and I sat on a bench in the lobby of Pechanga Resort Casino.

"Have you stand in front of the elevators on the eleventh floor until she comes out of her room and we see where she goes and who she meets, if anyone. If she spends the next couple days just gambling then we wasted our time, and she packed her suitcases and rushed out here because she had a gambling Jones that had to be fed."

"If that's the case, she would have driven twenty-five minutes to Valley View Casino instead of coming up here."

"Probably."

My phone vibrated in my pocket. I took it out. Bao Zhao.

"This is the best I could do for you, bro." Straight to the issue. "Madolyn Cummings is a VIP member at Pechanga. VIPs get loyalty points almost any time they spend money in the hotel or casino. They gamble, they get points. They get dinner in the restaurant, they get points. They just have to punch in their loyalty number or give it the casino cashier, waitress, blah, blah, blah. It all goes into a computer. The casino manager can get real-time updates on what a VIP has spent their money on and in what area of the casino. We track it all to know what enticement works best and where."

"Enticement," I echoed.

"Supply and demand, my friend. Anyway, Regina, the casino manager at Pechanga, is going to monitor this Cummings woman and contact me when her loyalty number goes into the system. She'll know if she's on the casino floor, in the restaurant, or playing video poker at the bar. Then Regina will contact me and I'll call you. Got it?"

"Roger. Thanks."

"One last thing." His normal flat voice livened a heartbeat. "Don't make a scene with the woman. That would reflect badly on me. I used up some chits for this, bro."

"Got it. Thanks, Bao."

I relayed what Zhao told me to Moira. We were both hungry after only eating a couple energy bars on the drive down from Monterey, so we went to dinner. We each ordered New York strips at the Great Oak Steakhouse.

My phone vibrated three bites in. Bao.

"She's playing video poker on the casino floor."

"Roger. Thanks."

"What?" Moira.

"Video poker on the casino floor." I quickly sawed off another bite of steak and shoved it in my mouth. The few bites of food had only reignited my hunger instead of partially sating it. "Why don't you go looking on the floor and I'll get these boxed up and pay the bill?"

"Me? Now?" Moira quickly took another bite of her own steak and talked with her mouth full. Like me. "She just started playing and we know she likes to gamble. We probably have time to finish dinner."

Another quick bite for each of us.

"Can't risk it. One of us has to go and I'm paying the bill."

"Damn it." Moira stood up, finishing chewing, leaned over and sliced off another piece of meat, forked it into her mouth, and hurried away from the table to the restaurant exit onto the casino floor.

I held up my hand for the waitress. A gesture I always thought was rude when I managed a restaurant. Maybe everyone I saw do it over the years were private investigators who had to run to catch a tail. At least I didn't snap my fingers.

Moira texted me as I shoved meat into my mouth while I waited for the waitress to return with the check and my credit card.

Moira: *Shes seated at video poker machine in middle of casino next to a bunch of slot machines. Im at slot machine diagonally across from her.*

Me: *Roger. Five minutes.*

A busboy boxed our steaks and put them in a plastic bag. The waitress returned with my card and the check.

"Could you do me a big favor?" I asked the waitress and I wrote in a fifty-dollar tip and handed her back the check. "Could you have someone put the bag in a refrigerator for us while we take care of some business?"

"Sure." She glanced at the check. "I'll write your last name on the bag, Mr. Cahill."

I hustled out to my car, changed into a white T-shirt from my suitcase. It was wrinkled, but that would enhance the look of a low-profile gambler. I put on the Padres cap I wore when I drove on long trips and went back into the casino.

I spotted Moira first, then Madolyn Cummings on the floor of the casino. Early evening on a Tuesday night in May isn't peak time for casino action, but twenty-five percent of the slot machines and video poker machine chairs were full. Enough bells and chimes and dongs sounded to remind you where you were. In eternal night with neon lights where the occasional wins are accented with manufactured joyful sounds and the cascading losses are endured in grim silence.

I texted Moira.

Here.

Moira: *I know. I spotted you walking up.*

So much for my stealthy capabilities. Or she could have been lying to mess with me.

Most of the gamblers were dressed similar to me. Casual, not so chic. Moira fit right in with the weekday evening gambling community in her white T shirt and blue jeans. She looked totally engrossed in the slot machine in front of her, but she had the angle on Cummings. From behind and to her right.

I sat down at a row of slots to Moira's right, farther away from Madolyn Cummings. The middle-aged woman next to me smelled of cigarettes, whiskey, and desperation. I bought in twenty bucks' worth and pushed the button every minute or so while I kept my eyes on Cummings.

She wore faded jeans and a threadbare black AC/DC T-shirt that she either wore every day or was twenty years old. My guess, the T-shirt was a good luck charm. In the years I'd known degenerate gamblers, good luck charms were more imagination than sure things. Or any things.

I saw Cummings glance around the casino a few times, even looking behind herself. The glances didn't correspond with any of the jackpot sounds occasionally going off. They weren't "let's see what's going on looks." She was searching, studying faces. Concern in her eyes. Looking for someone in particular. Her glances moved past Moira quickly. I never let her catch my eyes hidden below the bill of my Padres ball cap. After each circumnavigation of the casino, her eyes went right back to the video poker machine and so did her fingers.

Neither AC nor DC appeared to be working because I didn't hear a lot of mechanical bells and whistles coming from her direction. I was about fifteen bucks down, which was fine. The less bells and whistles going off around me attracting attention, the better. I heard one whirling jackpot from Moira's machine. She played it low key like an experienced gambler.

Forty-five minutes in, Cummings reached quickly into her back pocket and pulled out her phone. She looked at the screen instead of putting the phone to her ear. A text. Her head snapped up from the screen and she looked directly to her left. I was blocked by slot machines and couldn't see who or what she was looking at. She stuffed her phone back in her pocket, punched a button on the video poker machine to collect whatever credits she had left inside it, picked up a purse at her feet, slung it over her shoulder, and hurried off in the direction she'd been looking.

Moira gave me a quick glance, then slowly rose from her seat and pulled her own phone out of her purse and walked in the same direction Cummings had. I sprang up from my seat and angled diagonally toward the lobby at a forty-five-degree angle from the path Cummings had taken. Banks of slot machines still blocked my view of her.

An incoming text.

Moira: *She's with Mark Fields.*

CHAPTER FORTY-SIX

MARK FIELDS.

The ex-cop, and ex-partner of Detective Skupin, who worked for Leveraged Investigations and signed all the background reports they did for Fulcrum Security except for one, which he ended up signing stealthily later. Cummings must have been Leveraged's in to Fulcrum and thus, Obsidian Holdings' in. I wondered if she knew who she'd let see the inner workings of her company. I wondered if Fields even knew who he ultimately was working for. More than likely the Chinese Communist Party.

Me: *Where are they going?*

Moira: *Looks like the lobby.*

Shit. The lobby. The elevators were right behind it. I had to get to the elevators first and beat them to the eleventh floor if they were headed that way. I needed to find out what Madolyn Cummings' room number was. Unless Fields also had a room or they were leaving the hotel. I had to gamble.

Me: *Make a commotion. Now!*

I picked up the pace, just short of an Olympic speed walker. Five seconds later a crashing sound came from Moira's direction. I shifted gear and hit a full jog clear of the casino floor, into the lobby. I shot a quick glance to my left before I disappeared into the elevator bay. Mark

Fields and Madoyln Cummings were walking this way. But their heads were turned back and to their right where the noise had come from. Whatever Moira had crashed into or knocked over had done the trick. Now I just needed to get into an elevator and head up to the eleventh floor before Fields and Cummings made it into the bay.

I punched eleven on the keypad outside the elevator. And waited. And waited. Male and female voices right outside the bay. The woman's voice sounded like Cummings'. The triangle above the elevator to my right ponged. The door opened. I jumped inside the elevator, jammed my key into the security slot, and punched number eleven. The voices grew louder.

The door started to close.

"Hey, hold the elevator." Male voice.

If they got into the elevator, the game was up. Cummings would recognize me, even without a dick pic, and Fields probably knew who I was after I'd spent a couple hours following his partner around on Saturday. I stayed in the back of the elevator and willed the door to close.

"Let's take this one." Cummings' voice.

They got into another elevator. Now I had to beat them to the top. My elevator climbed without stopping. The door opened and I dashed out into the foyer and then the hall, looking for a door to the ice machine room. A ping behind me. My gamble had paid off. Their elevator stopped on Cummings' floor.

Ice machine room on the right. Ice machine next to the door and two vending machines opposite it. I tossed my hat out of view of the doorway and went to the vending machine and stood in front of it with my back to the door like I was deciding what candy bar to spend two bucks on.

"Did you ask him about it?" Madolyn Cummings' concerned voice wafted into the room as she and Fields strode by behind me.

"Wait until we get to your room." Fields. His tone not as com-manding as his words. My guess was that they were more than acquaintances.

Neither of them said anything else. I peeked one eye around the corner of the doorjamb and saw the two of them stop eight doors down. Cummings pressed a keycard against the door and they both entered the hotel room.

I stayed where I was and called Moira.

"Did you follow them?"

"They're in her room. Number 1115. What was the crash I heard?"

"I bumped into a cocktail waitress. She had half a try of drinks. I need to change into clothes that don't smell like whiskey sours. Where are you? I need the car keys to get my bag and change clothes."

"Eleventh floor. Ice machine room. First door to the right out of the elevator foyer."

Moira arrived at the ice machine room three minutes later. Her white T-shirt had yellow splotches on it and she smelled like a fifth of whiskey drowned in a gallon of lemon juice.

No movement from room 1115, yet.

"Wash the stink off, change into whatever else you have in your suitcase, put on your Padres cap, and come back up here." I handed her my keys. "We can trade places and I'll wait down in the lobby. I don't want them to see the back of the same person in here that they did passing by."

"Yes, boss." Moira snatched the keys out of my hand and left the room.

*   *   *

An hour later, after Moira and I had changed places, she called me while I milled around the elevator bay.

"Fields just left Cummings' room alone and got into the elevator. Are we going to follow him or sit on her or do both?"

"Hold tight. I'll see if he shows up down here and leaves or meets someone else, then decide."

"I think we should stick with Cummings." Moira's machine gun voice at full rattle. "She's the weak link. Her colleague either just committed suicide or was murdered. I think we should brace her and get her to talk."

"Let's see what Fields does first." I hung up and continued to watch the elevators.

Ten seconds later an elevator door opened and Mark Fields emerged. I kept my head pointed toward the casino floor, but side-glanced him as he headed toward the lobby. I slid off my seat and followed him from fifty feet behind. He walked through the lobby and out to valet parking.

I hurried to the front entrance and watched though the glass as he got behind the wheel of a black late model Mercedes-Benz S class. The kind of car a bent private eye in the pocket of a criminal organization could afford. The Mercedes' windows were tinted, but I saw just enough to see that he was alone. I caught a glimpse of the license as Fields drove away and registered the last three numbers, 044.

Decision time: follow or stay on Cummings? A bird in the hand or one driving away in a $100,000 car?

I walked outside into the warm evening and texted Moira.

Fields took off in a Mercedes S Class. Going to my car for a costume change then the gift shop then up to you.

CHAPTER FORTY-SEVEN

I KNOCKED ON the door of room 1115 with a $150 vase of red roses held up to obscure my face from the peephole. I wore the blazer I'd worn when I met with Samuel Chen and David Liu at Obsidian Holdings yesterday. My glasses were in my pocket and my short hair was now gelled to its maximum height.

"Ms. Cummings?" I spoke loudly, but put a friendly lilt on the end of her last name. I did my best to slip in a Midwestern accent. "I have a delivery from the casino manager for you."

I waited. Nothing. I knocked again and repeated the message.

Cummings' voice from the other side of the door, no doubt her eye was to the peephole.

"What is this about?" Cautious.

"Regina." I remembered the name Bao Zhao had given me over the phone. "Our casino manager asked me to deliver these roses to you. You're our VIP member of the day."

"Who are you?"

"Jack Renee. I'm in charge of hospitality here at Pechanga Resort Casino." My eyes were visible just over the roses. As was my spiky hair.

"How does this Regina person even know I'm here?"

"Your VIP points, ma'am. We like to make sure our VIP guests know they're appreciated."

The door opened halfway before I was done with my spiel. Cummings was in a white cotton bathrobe with a Pechanga logo. Her hair was disheveled, like she and Fields had done more than talk during the hour he was in her room. I had to squint my eyes down to get a good look at her.

I handed her the roses and she got a better view of my face. Her eyes and mouth opened wide. "Wha—"

Moira stepped into the doorway from her secreted spot to the side.

"Madolyn, we have to talk to you." She was calm, but firm. "You're in danger, but you already know that. That's why you fled here. But if we can find you, so can the people who killed Sara Bhandari and Buddy Gatsen. We can keep you safe."

"Leave me alone." Cummings looked stunned, but she didn't question Moira's declaration about Sara and Gatsen. Still holding the heavy glass vase full of roses with two hands, she stepped back from the door to allow it to shut. Moira put her hand against the door to keep it open.

I stepped around Moira into Cummings' room. Another trespass. Moira continued to hold the door open, but stayed outside the room.

"Get out!" Loud. Panicked. Cummings held the vase in front of her like a barrier between the two of us. If she continued to shout, we'd have company very soon. The scene Bao Zhao explicitly asked me to avoid. Potentially another bridge burning behind me.

"Madolyn, you can talk to us or you can talk to the police or the FBI."

"The FBI?" Her face squished up into a question mark. Panic in her eyes. Gone was the icicle cool customer who ignored me last week when I was at Fulcrum Security with Shreya Gargano.

"We know about the payoff from Leveraged Investigations in February." I pulled my glasses out of my coat pocket and put them on. "But what you probably don't know is where that money really came from. A front for the CCP. The Chinese Communist Party."

The vase slipped from Cummings' hand and hit the floor with a thud. Ejecting water and roses as it tumbled along the carpet, but didn't break. She took a step back, further into the room.

"What?" Her face wide open in disbelief. "What are you talking about?"

I heard the door close and felt Moira's presence behind me.

"Leveraged Investigations has one client. Obsidian Holdings, a shell company out of Monterey. Obsidian is financed by a man with CCP connections who lives in Taiwan." I filled in the gaps of what I knew about Albert Chen with supposition that I believed to be true. No correction from Moira. "They wanted to infiltrate Fulcrum to get at your new LIDAR system. They used Leveraged Investigations to get a hacker hired—"

"Every new hire for the defense contractor division is vetted by the Defense Counterintelligence and Security Agency. You know that. The new hires that Leveraged Investigations vetted are all on the retail side. Just like the ones you vetted."

Moira stepped around me, bent down, and picked up the empty vase and refilled it with the red roses.

"They needed to get someone inside your building. Inside your closed system." I kept my voice calm. Reasonable. Just relaying information. "Someone who could attach a dick pic to an email I sent to Sara Bhandari after the fact and add lewd comments to others. Someone who is capable of hacking on a much grander scale. We think that's Andrew Burke, the systems analyst your friend Mark Fields ran a background check on and had you hire. Inside your closed system, Burke has probably already found a way to hack the data on your LIDAR system."

"This is ridiculous. None of this is believable." But the concerned expression on her face belied her words. She had to be starting to put the pieces together or, at least, questioning the things that had happened at Fulcrum Security over the last few weeks. She backed out of the entry and went over and sat on the edge of the California king bed.

Cummings' reaction to the information I'd given her told me that, while she was dirty or, at the least, unethical, she didn't know about Leveraged Investigations' connection to Obsidian Holdings and what Leveraged was really up to.

"Why did you change the background reports on Charles Parme, Milton Aksne and Burke that Leveraged Investigations did for you?"

Cummings just stared at me, her mouth open.

"I know this is all confusing and kind of scary." Moira set the vase of roses down on the dresser next to the television. Her voice, a warm blanket. "You must be reeling. You got caught up in something that's out of your control. The truth is going to come out at some point. We can help you get through this."

"Sara Bhandari was a friend of mine. I didn't send her that dick pic or whatever you found in her emails and showed her sister to poison the well. Our guess is that Andrew Burke added whatever you saw in Sara's emails before you went through them after she died." I walked over and stood in front of her. "Sara was a good person who cared about your company and she saw something that she knew was wrong. She tried to do the right thing and was raped and murdered and posed naked with her ass up in the air and a metal rod rammed into her rectum because of it. I'm here to find out who did that and bring them to justice."

The blood drained from Cumming's face. She drifted backward then snapped forward, hunched over dry heaving. I grabbed the vase, flung the roses out, and held it under her face. Cummings grasped the vase and started retching up lunch or dinner into it. Vomit splattered out of the vase against her face.

CHAPTER FORTY-EIGHT

MADOLYN CUMMINGS SET the vase full of vomit down onto the carpet and took husking breaths, still bent over. Moira grabbed the vase and dashed into the bathroom. The sound of running water competed with Cummings' breathing. Moira rushed back into the bedroom with a damp towel. She sat down next to Cummings and wiped her face with the towel then folded it over and pressed it against the back of her neck.

"Take some nice deep breaths," Moira cooed and pulled Cummings' hair back away from her face.

I grabbed one of the uncomplimentary bottled waters off the dresser, opened it, and handed it to Cummings. She took a sip of water and then a longer swallow, then straightened her posture on the bed.

"The police said that Sara was a victim of that serial rapist." Cummings was back under control. "The Coastal Rapist. I watched their news conference on Saturday. I even called Detective Skupin to confirm that Sara had been raped by the same man who raped all those women."

"Why did you do that?" I watched her face. She held steady. Back in survivor mode. "The police already announced it at the press conference."

"I care about my employees, Mr. Cahill. Sara was a good worker. Of course, I needed to know the details about her death."

"There's more to it than that." I spread my legs and put my hands on my hips. An old cop reflex that sometimes came in handy when I was questioning a reluctant witness. "You were concerned that Sara's death might have something to do with her investigating the irregularities going on at Fulcrum Security. Your instincts were good. You had it right the first time. And the police will finally figure out that Sara's murder was staged to look like the Coastal Rapist had committed it. He didn't. Someone you know did."

"What do you mean?" She stood up, her face flashing from ashen to pink. "I don't know anyone who would do that."

"Your boyfriend, Mark Fields, used to be partners with Detective Skupin on the San Diego Police Department. He could have gotten enough inside information on the Coastal Rapist to stage a rape murder of Sara Bhandari. Either he or his partner at Leveraged Investigations, Jeff Grant. Or both of them."

"I don't believe any of this." Cummings walked over to the window and looked out at the Temescal Mountains. She leaned her palms and forehead against the glass.

I walked over to her.

"You came up here because you're scared. You know that Buddy Gatsen didn't commit suicide. Once you found out he was dead, you bolted." I put a hand against the window. "Maybe I'm wrong about Sara, but you know somebody got to Buddy Gatsen. Why was he killed, Madolyn? Did he want a bigger cut? Did he threaten to blow the whole thing up?"

"What?" Cummings turned toward me. Her dark eyebrows knitted downward.

She was truly baffled.

"Gatsen wasn't in on it?" I glanced over at Moira.

Cummings turned back to the window. She stared out at the mountains and said nothing.

"Why was Buddy killed, Madolyn?" Moira's soothing voice again. "Was he going to go to the police?"

"There was nothing to go to the police about." Cummings spoke without looking up. "We didn't do anything illegal."

"What *did* you do?" I asked.

"Nothing. We just hired someone new who Buddy didn't like. He wanted to fire him and I told him he didn't have just cause."

"Andrew Burke?" I asked, but I was sure I already knew the answer.

"Yes." Cummings walked over to the minibar and twisted the tiny cap of a two-and-a-half-ounce bottle of vodka and took a sip. Seemed like a risky move after what she just spewed into the flower vase, but everyone handles stress differently.

"Why did Buddy want to fire him?"

"He was hired to implement our new inventory control system and Buddy didn't think he was making progress quickly enough."

"That's it?" I asked.

"Buddy thought he was secretive, too."

Slow and secretive because he was probably spending all his time trying to burn a hole through the firewall between the system for the luxury retail line and the defense contractor projects.

"What happened after you told Gatsen he couldn't fire Burke?" I followed Cummings to the minibar.

Another sip. This one longer. Finally, "He said he was going to talk to Trent about it."

"Boswell?" The founder and CEO of Fulcrum Security.

"Yes."

"When was this?" Moira.

"Yesterday." She drank the rest of the mini vodka bottle and opened another one.

The last day Gatsen was at work. They found his body this morning. Tuesday. Nobody said anything for a solid ten seconds.

"Do you know if he told Boswell?" If he did, then whoever killed Sara Bhandari and Buddy Gatsen would have at least one more person to kill.

"Trent is on vacation in Barbados until next Monday." Cummings. Two-thirds of the way through with her second mini vodka bottle. "He doesn't like to be disturbed on vacation unless it's an emergency. Wanting to fire someone wouldn't qualify."

"But Gatsen was going to tell him when Boswell came back to the office next week, right?"

"I tried to talk him out of it." Cummings' voice cracked high with emotion. "I asked him to give Burke a little more time."

"We know the whole just cause thing was bullshit." I shot a look at Moira then back at Cummings. "You told Fields that Gatsen wanted to fire his handpicked employee and Fields' employer couldn't let that happen. When did you tell Fields and what did he say when you told him that Gatsen wanted Burke gone?"

Cummings downed the last of mini vodka bottle number two.

"I think it's time for you to leave." She put the empty bottle down on the dresser, then turned toward me and crossed her arms. A power move, maybe buoyed by the vodka.

"You think they're going to let you live?" The truth. Blunt and hard. My power move. "They killed Sara Bhandari just for asking questions. Gatsen was only trying to get a bad employee fired. According to you, he didn't even know that Leveraged Investigations had funneled Burke into Fulcrum Security. They were just secondary players, unaware of what was really going on. You're a main player in this. Without you, Andrew Burke would have never infiltrated Fulcrum. Sara and Gatsen didn't know anything and they had to go. You know everything. How long do you think the people behind Leveraged Investigations are going to let the one person who can expose them and what they're up to keep breathing? You're a liability and you're dangerous. Surely, after Buddy Gatsen's death, you're starting to put the pieces together."

Madolyn Cummings walked to the end of the dresser, hesitated, and walked back the other way. She continued to pace in silence. I glanced at Moira. She micro-frowned and slowly shook her head. Her sign that I'd overstepped. I didn't care. Cummings was the linchpin holding the criminal enterprise together. She may not have understood the magnitude of what she'd done in the beginning, but she did now. And all the wreckage that had come from her decision to accept a package full of money to cut corners and step beyond the company's boundaries in hiring people. And then report on a couple of Fulcrum Security workers who tried to look out for the company's best interests.

"What happened with the background reports of the three employees, including Andrew Burke, that Jeff Grant signed off on?" I asked.

"I don't know what you're talking about." There was a reason Cummings played video poker instead of the real thing. Her entire face was a tell. It was red and angled away from mine.

"Mark Fields asked you to pull them, didn't he? He didn't want Grant's name on anything because it was an alias. And you forgot to replace them with the new ones Fields signed until Sara found that they were missing. Right?"

"It was a simple clerical mistake." Cummings stared at the carpet.

"Why did Fields meet you out here today, Madolyn?" Moira asked.

Cummings let go a long breath. Air out of a balloon. The truth would come out next.

"I called him today after Ernesto, our shop foreman, found Buddy ... found his body at his house." She stopped pacing, but her voice was tight. "I'm not stupid. The day after I told Mark that Buddy was going to talk to Trent about Andrew Burke, Buddy supposedly committed suicide. I asked Mark if Thomas killed him."

Moira and I looked at each other. *Thomas*. A new person we knew nothing about.

"Thomas?" I asked.

"Thomas Wendall. He also goes by Jeff Grant."

I took out my phone, pulled up the photo I had for the man who worked at Leveraged Investigations who I believed to be Jeff Grant, and showed it to Cummings. "Is this Wendall?"

"Yes."

"What did Fields say when you asked him if he thought Grant/Thomas killed Buddy Gatsen?"

"He said he didn't think Thomas killed Buddy. That it sounded like a suicide."

"Why did he think that?" I side-glanced Moira.

"Because I told him that Ernesto found Buddy in his car in the garage."

"That's it? Did you tell him about the smell of exhaust fumes?"

"Not right away."

Buddy Gatsen was in his mid-fifties, overweight, and had a stressful job. I'd seen him in Cummings' office, last Friday. Tense, red face, gesticulating. It looked like he didn't handle stress well. If I'd heard he'd been found dead in his car in his garage, my first thought probably would have been heart attack. Not suicide by carbon monoxide.

"Did you believe him?"

"At first." She looked at the carpet.

"But not anymore."

Cummings started pacing again and didn't say anything.

"Madolyn, why did you immediately think that Thomas Wendall killed Buddy?" Moira.

"I didn't say I thought he killed Buddy. I just wanted to make sure he didn't."

"But why would the thought even come to mind?" Moira, softly pressing forward.

"He . . . he scares me."

"In what way?" I asked.

"I can't explain it." She stopped pacing and looked at me. Fear in her round eyes. "He's just creepy. And when you look in his eyes, there's nothing there."

Moira looked at me. The same reaction she'd had to Jeff Grant/ Thomas Wendall. Or whatever his real name was when she came across him last year. I hadn't gotten close enough to him to get a vibe, good or bad. But I trusted Moira's instincts. As much as my own.

"Did Fields tell you to meet him out here?" I asked.

"No. He called me while I was on my way here and wanted to know where I was."

"Why did you tell him where you were going?"

"He's . . . he's my boyfriend." She sounded like she was trying to convince herself.

"You met in a casino, didn't you?" Moira, ahead of me.

Cummings stopped pacing and dropped her shoulders. Her mouth fell open. "How did you know that?"

"That's where I'd look for you if I was trying to befriend you."

"What?" Now shoulders high, hands on hips. "What do you mean by befriend me?"

"Someone looking to get close to you." I jumped in. "You like to gamble. You even made the *Reno Gazette* newspaper because of it a few years ago. Won a big jackpot in Vegas playing video poker while attending a bachelorette party. You played through the night while all your friends were sleeping off a night of partying."

"Gambling is your recreation and your vice." Moira piggybacked on her own theory. The silkiness rubbed out of her voice. Replaced with declarative certainty. "Casinos are where you spend most of your free time. You're a VIP here and at other casinos. A good-looking distinguished gentleman sits down at a video poker machine near you and starts to chat while splashing some money around. And you two hit it off."

"Fuck you! Both of you." Cummings stomped over to the window again. But she didn't ask us to leave.

"When did you meet him?" I asked. "Sometime in February? A few weeks after Fulcrum Security put out a press release about their breakthrough LIDAR system?"

"It wasn't like that." Cummings sounded like she couldn't even convince herself.

"What was it like?" I asked.

Cummings hugged herself and didn't say anything.

"Look, Madolyn." Moira, comforting again. "I know this is all very shocking. But you have to be careful. You're not safe here. Maybe we're wrong about Mark Fields, but if he knows you're here, so does Thomas Wendall. He can't let you live."

"You ran because you were scared," I said. "Your survival instincts kicked in. But, because you asked Fields if Wendall killed Buddy Gatsen and then ran, Wendall knows that you know too much. Moira's right—he can't let you live."

"Oh no." Fear and panic raced across Madolyn Cummings' face. "Dylan."

"What about Dylan?" I fired the words out.

"I told Jeff that Dylan talked to you alone in the breakroom last Friday. We were supposed to have dinner together tonight, but he left here a couple minutes after I told him."

CHAPTER FORTY-NINE

I WHIPPED MY phone out of my pocket and stabbed Dylan Helmer's phone number. One ring, then another. Three more, then her voicemail message came on the speaker function of my phone.

Madolyn Cummings' eyes widened in fear.

"Dylan, it's Rick Cahill. Go to your boyfriend's house right now." Firm, but steady. "Don't pack anything. Just go. And don't go home if you're out. Call me as soon as you can."

I hung up.

"Do you think . . ." Cummings' looked at me, the fear rounding her eyes.

"Do you know where Dylan lives?" I asked Cummings. I had her address in my work files on my computer at home from when I ran a background report on her before Fulcrum Security hired her. I couldn't access the files remotely. For the first time in my life, I wished I'd used Google Docs.

"Not her address, but I know she lives in Valley Center, but kind of in the middle of nowhere. Her uncle's old house on a big piece of land at the end of a dirt road. It's too late for anyone to be at the office who could look it up."

"I'll head to Valley Center." I turned to Moira. "Look up Dylan's address and call me, then call the SD Sheriff's Office and try to get a welfare check on her. I'm pretty sure Valley Center is in their jurisdiction."

"Roger." Moira took out her phone and tapped on the screen. I turned to Madolyn and grabbed both her forearms. The disdain she'd shown me ever since I saw her at Fulcrum Security blurred out of her eyes into tears.

"You have to go with Moira down to San Diego and talk to Detective Skupin. Tell him everything you know about Mark Fields and Thomas Wendall. Everything they asked you to do." My voice calm, but as forceful as a sledgehammer. "You're right, you didn't break the law so you don't have to worry about the police arresting you. But you do have to worry about Fields and Wendall and what they've already done. And what they might do."

She nodded her head. Mascara tears ran down her cheeks.

I hurried to the door and heard Madolyn's voice over my shoulder.

"I didn't think Mark would ever . . ."

I did. And I should have known that what Dylan Helmer knew would put her in danger.

*   *   *

Moira called before I'd even left the Pechanga parking garage and gave me Dylan Helmer's Valley Center address that she found online.

"SDSO said they'd try to get someone to Dylan's sometime in the next hour. I couldn't convince them that she might be in imminent danger."

"Let's hope she isn't."

"Call me when you get to Dylan's." Anxiety in Moira's voice. She feared the same thing that I did. That I might be too late.

"Roger." I prayed that we were both wrong. "I'll call Skupin and tell him that you're on your way to SDPD headquarters."

I fed Dylan's address into my car's GPS. Valley Center was a half hour south of Pechanga. The quickest way was via two-laned twisting mountain backroads and eventually Highway 76. I told Siri to call Detective Skupin and kept both hands on the steering wheel.

I got his voicemail.

"Detective, it's Cahill. I have information on Sara Bhandari's murder that will crack the case. Call me ASAP." I hung up.

I checked the clock on the dash. 8:53 p.m. Over fifteen minutes since I left Dylan Helmer a voicemail. No return call. I decided against calling her again. If Fields or Wendall had her, a second call so soon would alert them that I was worried and might be on my way or had contacted the police. It they had Dylan at her house, and she was still alive, I needed them to stay put.

Pala Temecula Road snaked through the pitch-black foothills of the Temescal Mountains. No other cars on the lonely road. The moon, the only source of light, drifted in and out of the clouds. I sped along the unfamiliar winding road. Turns strobed suddenly in the headlights. I pressed the gas pedal deeper and pushed the limits of safety and sanity.

Dylan Helmer was in danger. Because of me. She'd asked Madolyn Cummings about the missing background reports because I'd asked her to investigate. The echoes from my earlier life reverberated into the present. Find the truth no matter what. The no matter what had pushed Dylan beyond safe limits.

Now, Dylan was my responsibility. Nothing else mattered. I'd failed other people who'd become my responsibility. Fatally. I couldn't let that happen again.

A sharp turn flashed in front of me. I tapped the brakes and the car jerked and slid across the opposite lane. A black drop-off loomed below me. I snapped the wheel into the slide, then the other way, fishtailing the back end, as the rear tires grabbed at the dirt just above the drop. They caught purchase and I steered the car back across the road and let it decelerate on its own.

Flop sweat broke across my forehead and under my arms. My breath staccatoed in and out. My hands trembled on the steering wheel. I was out of practice. A desk jockey thrust back into a dangerous game.

I edged the speed up. Fast, but not reckless.

My phone rang through the sound system of my car. Detective Skupin.

"What's this bullshit about you cracking the Bhandari murder, Cahill?" He snapped the words off hard and fast.

"You still at Headquarters?"

"Why?"

"My partner, Moira MacFarlane, is bringing in a witness in the Sara Bhandari murder." No triumph or I told you so in my tone. Just the facts. "She's on her way from Temecula, so it will take her an hour or so. You going to stick around at Headquarters?"

"Are you telling me that she has a witness to the Coastal Rapist?" Nonbelief in his voice.

"Sara Bhandari wasn't murdered by the Coastal Rapist. After you listen to Moira and the witness, you'll come over to our side."

"You're still going with your crazy theory about who murdered your girlfriend? Why are you wasting my time? We know who killed Sara Bhandari. We just haven't identified him yet."

"Does that mean you won't be there when Moira brings in the witness?" I wasn't ready to download my Chinese spy theory on him yet. That would snap his mind shut against anything else that came out of my mouth.

"I'll be here, Cahill. You better not be wasting my time."

"Two other things, Detective. There's a woman in Valley Center who may be in danger." I gave him Dylan Helmer's name and address. "Please contact someone at the Sheriff's Department to do a welfare check on her. And while you're talking to SDSO, tell them our witness can help them on Buddy Gatsen's murder. His body was found in his garage in Rancho Bernardo this morning. They may have him as a possible suicide, but our witness will make them dig deeper."

"I never heard of Buddy Gatsen." Dismissive. "And you need to give me more on this Dylan Helmer woman. Why do think she's in danger?"

"Because your old partner Mark Fields, or someone named Thomas Wendall, may try to kill her."

CHAPTER FIFTY

DYLAN HELMER'S ADDRESS led to a rusty-gated dirt road. The gate was open. No SD sheriff's cruisers on the long entry. Maybe they were on their way. Maybe not. I didn't have time to wait.

I turned off my lights and pulled slowly down the road. A couple dark trees loomed above on the right. Probably oaks. Forty yards down, I spotted a ramshackle shed on the same side. Twenty yards beyond it sat an old small clapboard house with a porch light on. I passed the shed and sensed something next to it. A car. Blocked from view of the road by the shed.

A Mercedes-Benz. Looked like an S class. Last three digits of the license plate were 044. I backed up and parked on the other side of the shed, so if Fields looked out the window of the house, he wouldn't see my car.

I opened the door and slowly got out of my car. The inside dome light didn't go on because I'd disabled it soon after I bought the car. Years of surveillance. The same with the trunk light when I opened the lid. I peeked over at the house again, before I ducked my head into the trunk and removed the covering to the spare tire compartment. I grabbed the small gray duffle bag and unzipped it.

My black bag. No one but me had ever seen its contents. A burglary kit used against bad guys, not civilians. It held a pen flashlight, lockpick set, plastic flex cuffs, duct tape, black ski mask, black nitrile gloves, wire cutters, wireless signal jammer to disrupt wireless security alarms. And a loaded Ruger SR40c. A compact handgun that hit heavy. It had a nine-round magazine loaded with Smith & Wesson .40 caliber projectiles. Small. Powerful. Deadly.

The lockpick set and transporting a loaded gun were the only things that were illegal. Misdemeanor. But everything found all together could pose more of a problem.

Tonight, I needed it.

I removed the flashlight, lockpick set, and the Ruger from the duffle bag and ducked out from under the hood of the trunk. The lockpick set and flashlight went into the pocket of my bomber jacket. The gun, into a two-handed grip. I peeked around the corner of the shed. The house stood silent twenty yards away. A light illuminated ten or so feet off the washed-out gray entry and rust-colored wooden porch. No movement.

I slipped around the shed over to Fields' Mercedes and touched the hood near the radiator. Still warm. He probably had to have his partner find Dylan's address online like Moira did for me. But I knew she lived in Valley Center and took the most direct route to the rural town. Fields may have already been on Interstate 15 when he got her address.

Those extra minutes might give me enough time to save Dylan.

I crept along the edge of the Mercedes, then over against an oak tree. The tree cast a shadow darker than the night, and I used it for cover approaching the house. My arms and the Ruger formed a triangular shooting platform out in front of me.

My senses redlined. My body tingled at full alert. An echo from my past, now putting me square in the moment. An ancestral adrenal blast. Fight or flight. I moved forward. Always forward. Toward danger.

My eyes and ears strained for data. Movement in a window. Mur-
mured voices. Anything. But there was nothing.

I edged up against the side of the house. Then I heard it. A woman's
voice coming from an open window ten feet in front of me.

"Please. Let me go." Dylan Helmer. Pleading, but not hysterical.
Fighting to maintain her composure. To stay calm so she could act
when given the slightest chance. "I don't know anything. I don't know
who you are and I don't care."

"Keep your head down." I didn't recognize the voice, but I did the
tone. A finality I'd heard before. From killers. "For the last time, what
did you tell Rick Cahill? I know you talked to him alone last Friday
at your work. Madolyn told me all about it today. Tell me what you
told Cahill and we can work something out. Otherwise . . ."

I slid along the side of the house and peeked through the window.
The curtains were drawn so I kept moving to the back of the house a
few feet away. I prayed there was a door that led outside.

There was. Glass-paneled double doors.

Mark Fields stood over Dylan Helmer who lay on a bed on her
stomach, clothed only in a bra and panties. Her wrists and ankles were
bound by rope. Her head was turned to the side. She couldn't see the
handgun with a suppressor attached to the barrel in Fields' hand
pointed at her head.

I aimed the Ruger at Fields, but the glass in the door was old and
thick. It might deflect the bullet from its target. It could go
anywhere.

"Last chance." His voice a rasp, pressed through his teeth.

I kicked the doors open. Glass and wood shards exploded into the
room. Dylan screamed. Fields swung his gun toward me. I fired.
Twice. Two, center mass. Fields' gun hissed a thud into the wall to my
left. His body hit the floor before the gun did.

"Ahhh!" Fields grabbed at the two holes in his left upper chest seeping blood through his blue oxford shirt.

I kicked his gun away from his body, but kept mine pointed at him. Fields continued to moan through gritted teeth.

"Are you okay?" I asked Dylan. She'd struggled up to a sitting position, her eyes wide with fear.

"Yes." Her body slumped like all the air suddenly came out of her. Tears collected at the bottom of her eyes. She'd held it together long enough to stay alive and emotion spilled out of her now that she was safe.

I untied her and handed her my phone.

"You're okay now. Everything's going to be all right. Call 911 and get the police and an ambulance over here. Can you do that?"

She nodded her head, tears now running freely, and took the phone.

CHAPTER FIFTY-ONE

I GOT OUT of the Valley Center Sheriff Substation a little after midnight. After two hours of interrogation. I told them everything I knew. First about what happened tonight, then everything I knew about Sara Bhandari, Fulcrum Security, Leveraged Investigations, and Obsidian Holdings. At first, they were about as receptive as Detective Skupin at SDPD. But, after the detectives interviewing me left the room for about a half hour and returned, their attitude changed. They must have talked to Dylan who would have corroborated much of what I told them.

They confiscated my gun, but never got a look at my lockpick set. Or anything else in the duffle bag. I hid it in Dylan's shed while she called the police.

Mark Fields was in the hospital. I didn't care whether he lived or died.

Finally alone for the first time in over twenty hours, I wanted to call Leah as I made the forty-five-minute drive home. But it was too late and I'd see her and Krista in just twelve or so hours. Back on my home turf without the negative influence of Leah's father coloring Leah and my relationship. But my blowup Monday did its own damage. My rage had been clear in black and white. Yet, Leah was willing to talk about it. About us. Willing to give me a second chance.

Too late tonight, but there would be a tomorrow. Too late even to pick up Midnight from my neighbor. The adrenaline that had carried me through the night, into danger, leaked from my pores on the drive home. By the time I turned down my street, I was exhausted. Spent. A weariness I hadn't felt in almost two years.

A weariness I oddly welcomed. Well-earned. This time, only the bad guys got hurt on my watch.

I drove down the street and saw Leah's SUV parked in the driveway of our home. My breath caught in my chest. My girls home early. Another twelve whole hours to be with them, or just have them in the same house. As the disease stole more hours, days, and years from me, every second mattered.

A surprise homecoming from Leah as an entreaty to working things out? To save our family? I made a silent prayer that it was as I pulled into the driveway.

No lights were on in the house. I got out of the car and quietly entered my home. I didn't want to wake my family. *My family*. Back in San Diego. Back in my house. Our home.

The house was dark inside. Then I heard it. A whimper from upstairs. Not Krista or Leah. Midnight. A weak cry. A sound I'd never heard from my protector, my savior. He was in pain. I took a quick step toward the staircase and a light in the living room flipped on.

I stopped. Leah sat on the couch holding Krista who was asleep with her head on her mother's shoulder. Leah's eyes were bloodshot and tears ran down her cheeks.

A man sat across from her in my recliner holding a gun. Pointed at Krista's tiny head from three feet away.

My Colt Python.

"Rick, you're finally home." The voice from the man I knew as Jeff Grant was high pitched, yet hollow. Like his eyes. The dead eyes that had frightened Moira a year ago and Madolyn Cummings more recently. I saw it now. Soulless. Evil. "I found the Python in the hall closet. Nice weapon. Nice home. Nice family. Had some time to rummage around. Found your computer, too. Thanks."

I glanced at Leah. She held Krista gently, but securely, against her body. Krista, mercifully, was still asleep.

"Are you okay?" I kept my voice calm as I looked at Leah. She nodded her head, but the tears poured harder out of her eyes.

Midnight's whimpers grew louder from upstairs after I spoke. He heard my voice. A sickening slumping sound came before each whimper. Like he was trying to propel himself along the floor upstairs.

To get to me.

"Sorry about your dog." Not an iota of remorse in his voice. "I've been waiting for you for hours. I finally hear a car in the driveway, peeked outside, and saw your wife and kid. Your wife's one thing, but I didn't want to deal with a damn kid. I hid upstairs and a couple minutes later your wife comes in with the damn dog and he flew right upstairs and found me." A cracked smile on a face that would blend into almost any crowd. "Figured he would have bled out by now."

Fire burned along my nerve synapses like a lit fuse. The heat reached my face and blowtorched sweat along my forehead. The room turned red. My breathing jackhammered.

The rage. I couldn't let it loose. Not yet. Krista and Leah would die.

"Look. My wife and child are no threat to you, so you can put down the gun. They don't know anything about you." Voice still calm as the rage boiled up inside me. "In fact, I don't know much about you. I don't even know your real name."

"It's Robey." The devil's smile. "Nice to meet you, Rick."

"Robey, let's you and I go outside and take a drive. We can discuss whatever you need to in the car."

"No, I'm comfortable here, Rick. Sitting with your family." He looked over at Leah and Krista and I snuck a half step forward. "But we do have something to talk about. Why don't you tell me where Madolyn Cummings is and I'll be on my way."

A lie of course. Leah and Krista were still alive only as pawns that he could leverage to get the information he wanted. Once I answered, he'd kill us all. The killer was about fifteen feet away from me. I could cover that ground in about a second from a dead start. I might be able to get to him before he spun the gun from Krista toward me and fired. But not quickly enough to keep him from pulling the trigger with the gun aimed at Krista now.

No good options, but if I didn't act, my family would die.

I needed time. The right moment. But for what? No cavalry was coming. It was just me and a sadistic killer. But I didn't have anything else. Another second, another minute, another breath might give me a chance to get between the gun and my family and give Leah a chance to flee to safety with Krista in her arms.

"You going to kill Cummings like you did Sara Bhandari?" I watched the gun, not his face. It remained trained on Krista.

"I don't know what you're talking about." Feigned ignorance with a sick chuckle at the end. "The police said the Coastal Rapist killed her. Remember? We were both at the press conference when they said it."

"You made mistakes. Detective Skupin is already figuring it out. Whether you kill us or not, you're going to have to go on the run." I glanced at Leah. Resolve fighting the tears. "My wife can't help them find you. I can. Let's go for a ride together and figure out a way for you to get out of the country. I have connections that can make it happen. Tonight."

Another drag and whimper from Midnight upstairs. He was still trying to get to me. To protect me and my family with his life's last remaining energy. My skin boiled atop my bones. My whole body a clenched muscle. The rage strained to break loose from the shredded reins holding it back. I fought for control.

"Enough." A jagged edge to his voice. "Where's Madolyn Cummings?"

"I don't know where she is. Maybe you should ask Mark Fields."

"He seems to be missing, too. Know anything about that?"

Leah looked at me.

"I don't know where either of them are."

"Wrong answer." The devil cocked the hammer of my gun pointed at my daughter's head.

"No!"

A growl above me. Midnight tumbled down the stairs.

The devil swung the gun at the staircase. I bolted at him.

Leah spun off the couch clutching Krista. Her body between our daughter and the killer.

I dove the last five feet. The gun boomed. Hot shard in my chest. My shoulder hit the killer's face. We tumbled over the back of the chair. My full body weight slammed down on top of him. The gun bounced along the hardwood floor. Krista wailed to my left. The devil clawed at my eyes underneath me. I punched him in the face with my right hand. The snap of cartilage. Another punch. My hand a piston. Again. And again. My body burned red at a thousand degrees. My face pulling away from my bulging eyes. Machine gun breaths. The piston kept firing. Blood splattered with each blow. The body underneath me stopped moving. Only shuddering with each punch from my fist.

"Rick!" Leah.

The piston kept firing.

Krista wailed.

The room, red.

The thing below my hand, formless.

The piston kept firing.

"Rick! Stop! He's dead!"

I kept punching. Blood and bone casting off my fist with each blow. "Rick!"

I kept punching.

"Dada!" A shriek from my child I'd never heard before broke through the sound of crunching viscera with my final blow. I looked at Krista, red-faced and wailing. My baby girl who I'd watched over in her crib every night. Double-checked the doors and windows and alarm. Yet somehow, I'd brought violence into her life. Me. Her father. Her protector.

Midnight whimpered at the bottom of the stairs and I shot up from the thing that had once been human and alive under me and ran to Midnight.

"Rick! You're bleeding!" Leah.

Midnight's black coat darkened and moist. A hole in his left shoulder oozing blood. His breaths shallow.

"Rick!"

Krista shrieking now.

I ran to into the bathroom and ripped a hand towel off the rack, then sped to the hall closet and yanked open my tool chest and grabbed a roll of duct tape.

"I need an ambulance." Leah shouted our address into our phone. "My husband's been shot!"

I ran back to Midnight and pressed the towel against his seeping wound. Not even a whimper this time. He looked up at me. Fear in his eyes. I tightly wrapped duct tape around the towel and his chest.

"Ambulance is on the way!" Leah, still holding shrieking Krista.

"They'll try to help me, not Midnight." I picked him up. A yelp that went straight to my heart, but meant that he could still feel pain. Good.

I rushed outside to my car, Leah's screams and Krista's wails echoing behind me.

*   *   *

I burst through the door of the twenty-four-hour emergency veterinary clinic with Midnight in my arms. The same clinic that had saved his life ten years ago when a killer poisoned him. After I tried to help someone else and, again, brought violence to my home.

I prayed for another miracle. A startled woman in a green surgeon's smock ran out from behind the counter.

"My dog's been shot! He's lost a lot of blood."

A second later a man burst through the doors to the back room pushing a gurney. I set Midnight down on it.

"Oh my God." The woman. "You're bleeding. Did someone shoot you, too?"

The walls of the clinic pushed in on me until I was staring down a narrow tube. Then darkness.

CHAPTER FIFTY-TWO

Beeping. Tubes. In my face and my arms.

Leah.

Darkness.

When I woke up again sometime later, Leah was gone. A nurse looked down at me.

"You're going to be just fine, Mr. Cahill."

My gut turned over and breath caught in my chest. Midnight.

"Midnight?"

"No, it's closer to noon."

"My dog. Is he alive?"

"Your dog? I don't know."

"Where's my wife?"

"She went out to get something to eat a little while ago."

"Rick?" Leah walked into the hospital room. The nurse left us alone. "How do you feel?"

Leah didn't smile. She didn't touch me when she stood next to my bed, either.

"How's Midnight?"

"He's still at the clinic, but he's going to live." A micro smile on her lips, but not in her blue eyes. Eyes that used to warm my soul and flutter my heart every time I looked in them. Now, just cold beauty. "The vet said you saved his life by driving him to the clinic when you did. He'd lost a lot of blood and probably wouldn't have lived another twenty minutes without a transfusion."

A gust of air blew out of me and tears burst down my cheeks. My best friend. My protector. My family, before Leah and Krista, was alive.

"How's Krista?" I wiped the tears off my cheeks. "How are you?"

"Krista's been traumatized, but she asks about you every day." Not even a micro smile. "She saw her daddy beat someone to death with his bare hands and then saw her daddy with blood streaming out of his chest pick up her dog who was also bleeding and run away."

"What else could I have done? You just told me that if I waited any longer Midnight would have died."

"You could have stopped punching a dead man's face into ground meat in front of your child. You could have not taken a case that got you involved with a psychopathic killer. You could have let the police handle things when you realized the case was dangerous." Leah put her hands on her hips. "That's what you could have done."

"The police wouldn't have gotten involved unless I followed through with the case and brought it up to a level that got their attention."

"So what?" A shriek. Her hands flew up into the air. "Would that have been the end of the world if you didn't get a chance to save the day and didn't endanger your family?"

"I couldn't predict what was going to happen." But I could have been more careful. Could have thought farther out than just the task at hand. Cast a wider safety net. Put my family first.

"That's right, but you chose your perverted sense of justice over your family anyway." Tears bubbled out of her eyes.

"Leah." I fought my own emotion. "It wasn't like that. Sara Bhandari deserved justice. I had to make sure the police found her killer."

"And our family deserves a father and a husband who puts us first and keeps us safe instead of putting us in danger,"

She stormed out of the room. The hospital room. Where I was recovering from the fourth gunshot wound suffered while I tried to help people. Trying to do the right thing. At least my version of it.

Not my wife's.

EPILOGUE

MARK FIELDS SURVIVED and sang to get a plea bargain. He pinned Sara Bhandari's murder on Robey Knight, aka Thomas Wendall, aka Jeff Grant, but admitted to giving Knight the information he'd learned about the Coastal Rapist to make it look like Sara was another one of his victims.

Fields also pinned Buddy Gatsen's murder on Knight. He said Knight forced Gatsen to down his few remaining prescription sleeping pills, then maneuvered Gatsen into his truck while he was still mobile and turned on the engine. Gatsen went to sleep from the pills and stayed that way forever from the exhaust.

Samuel Chen's yacht was found a mile off the coast of Monterey, but he wasn't on it. His body was never found.

David Liu fled to Hong Kong.

As far as anyone knows, Albert Chen is still in Taiwan. What the Chinese CCP refers to as China.

The systems analyst known as Andrew Burke disappeared into the ether.

The cleanup was complete.

The FBI got involved and carried the ball for a few months then disbanded the case. No one wanted to admit that Chinese spies could infiltrate private American companies so easily. Pandora's box was best kept closed, even though its evil had already slipped out.

The Coastal Rapist was still on the loose and struck again in Point Loma and La Jolla in the next three months.

No charges were brought against me. I was again portrayed as a hero in the press. But not by my wife or her family.

My hand took longer to heal than the bullet wound in my upper chest. I broke four bones in it when I beat Robey Knight to death. Beyond death. I had to wear a cast for six weeks.

Moira moved into my house for a couple weeks during my home recovery. Leah and Krista are living with her parents in Santa Barbara for now. Leah told me she was looking for a new house. But at least we're talking. I see Krista for a couple weeks a month here in San Diego.

My neurologist prescribed marijuana as a more holistic approach to deal with my rage, since the harder drugs weren't working. It's had mixed results. And I haven't gotten used to the numbness that comes with it. That numbness is a buffer from real life, which is meant to be lived. And felt.

I'm in therapy, too. Telling a stranger my secrets and fears every week. He's become less and less a stranger with each session.

The red rage still takes over me sometimes, but not as often, and it's slowly fading to pink.

I still have a few background-check accounts, but most of my work takes me out of the office. Back on the street. Where I was meant to be.

Midnight now walks with a limp, moves a little slower, and is grayer around the jowls. He lights up when Krista visits and moves even slower after she leaves. Just like me. It's mostly just the two of us now. My protector at my side. My family's savior.

My truest friend.

BOOK CLUB DISCUSSION GUIDE

1. Rick has received a life-altering medical diagnosis. Why does he keep his worsening condition a secret from the woman he loves? How does his evolving medical state affect him emotionally, and how does knowing his life span may be shortened impact his decisions and actions?

2. Rick has settled into a routine working "desk cases" from his home office in order to ease Leah's concerns about his physical safety, but he finds himself at loose ends. What is the root source of Rick's dissatisfaction, and would a man like Rick ever be able to be content with working cases from behind a keyboard?

3. Rick has developed a close, almost sibling-like, relationship with fellow P.I. Moira MacFarlane. What role does this relationship play in Rick's life?

4. Rick lives by a personal code he inherited from his father: sometimes you have to do what's right, even when the law says it's wrong. How has following this code gotten Rick into trouble, and are the consequences worth it to him?

5. Rick has been alone for many years after his first wife's death. Now, married to Leah and with a new child, he is finally creating the family he never thought he'd have. What challenges do the realities of marriage and fatherhood pose to Rick? Why do you think Rick would endanger his family for the sake of a case?

6. Rick personally encounters horrifying violence when he discovers Sara Bhandari's body, though unfortunately he has seen death up close many times before. How has witnessing violence over the years impacted Rick? Has it changed him, and is he now inured to it?

7. Midnight has been the only constant in Rick's turbulent life, and he is much more than a mere household pet. What does Midnight mean to Rick? How do their roles as protected and protector shift throughout the book?

8. How would each of the characters in *Doomed Legacy* describe Rick? How do you think Krista will describe her father when she's a grown woman?

9. Rick often meets violence with violence in return. Would you describe Rick as a good person?

PUBLISHER'S NOTE

We hope that you enjoyed ***Doomed Legacy***, the ninth novel in Matt Coyle's Rick Cahill PI Crime Series.

While the other eight novels stand on their own and can be read in any order, the publication sequence is as follows:

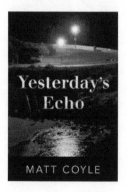

Yesterday's Echo

A dishonored ex-cop's desperate chance for redemption

"Coyle knows the secret: digging into a crime means digging into the past. Sometimes it's messy, sometimes it's dangerous—always it's entertaining."
—Michael Connelly,
New York Times best-selling author

Night Tremors

Powerful forces on each side of the law have Rick Cahill in the crosshairs

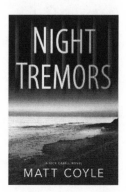

"Following an Anthony Award-winning debut isn't easy, but Matt Coyle slammed a homer. Hard, tough, humane—*Night Tremors* is outstanding" —Robert Crais,
New York Times best-selling and Anthony, Macavity, and Shamus Award-winning author

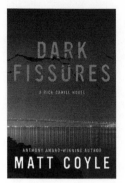

Dark Fissures
Hard-edged suspense with a heart for fans of
Robert Crais and Michael Connelly

"*Dark Fissures* is a roller coaster ride through the streets of
San Diego. Tightly plotted with memorable characters.
An outstanding read!"   —C. J. Box,
New York Times best-selling author

Blood Truth
Rick Cahill can't escape his past—or his father's

"Matt Coyle's protagonist, Rick Cahill, is haunted both by
the sins of his father and by his own mistakes—but he's
driven to find the truth, no matter where it takes him, and
that's what makes this story so compelling. Coyle is the real
deal, and [*Blood Truth*] is the best PI novel I've read in years,
period."   —Steve Hamilton,
New York Times best-selling author

Wrong Light
Rick Cahill defies all limits in his quest for
truth

"An equation involving everyone from the Russian mob
to Irish Travelers to ex-cops, this is a fascinating,
fast-paced, spidery-webbed novel."
—Reed Farrel Coleman,
New York Times best-selling author

Lost Tomorrows
Perfect for hard-boiled PI fans who like a tainted hero living by his own code

"Sharp, suspenseful, and poignant, *Lost Tomorrows* hits like a breaking wave and pulls readers into its relentless undertow. Matt Coyle is at the top of his game."

—Meg Gardiner,
Edgar Award–winning author

Blind Vigil
Rick Cahill defies all limits in his quest for truth

"Southern California has turned out its fair share of thriller and *noir* superstars—some of them transplants, of course, before making their names on the west coast—such as Michael Connelly, Robert Crais, T. Jefferson Parker, James Ellroy, Raymond Chandler, and Ross MacDonald. Matt Coyle is quickly writing himself onto that list." —*New York Journal of Books*

Last Redemption
Rick Cahill battles powerful forces— and an insidious disease—as he tries to help his best friend find her son and survive long enough to see his first child born

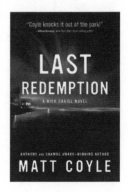

"PI Rick Cahill is on another thrill ride of a twisty mystery, but this time it's far more personal—he's looking for his best friend's son amid a backdrop of murder and high-stakes medical research. Just when you think Coyle has reached the top of his game—he does one better."

—Allison Brennan,
New York Times best-selling author

We hope that you will read the entire Rick Cahill PI Crime Series and will look forward to more to come.

If you liked *Doomed Legacy*, we would be very appreciative if you would consider leaving a review. As you probably already know, book reviews are very important to authors and they are very grateful.

For more information, please visit the author's website: mattcoylebooks.com

Happy Reading,
Oceanview Publishing